FLASHES

FLASHES

TIM O'ROURKE

SCHOLASTIC INC. / NEW YORK

Library of Congress Cataloging-in-Publication Data

O'Rourke, Tim, author.
Flashes / Tim O'Rourke.—First [American] edition.
pages cm
"First published in the United Kingdom in 2014 by Chicken House."
Summary: Charley Sheppard is a seventeen-year-old girl who has flashes of visions,
which lately seem to all be of girls who have died down by the railroad tracks, and
Tom Henson is a nineteen-year-old police constable who comes to believe in her—
and together they must find the killer before he strikes again.

ISBN 978-0-545-82959-5

1. Serial murderers—England—Cornwall (County)—Juvenile fiction.
2. Murder—England—Cornwall (County)—Juvenile fiction.   3. Criminal
investigation—England—Cornwall (County)—Juvenile fiction.   4. Visions—
Juvenile fiction.   5. Cornwall (England : County)—Juvenile fiction.
[1. Mystery and detective stories.   2. Murder—Fiction.   3. Criminal
investigation—Fiction.   4. Visions—Fiction.   5. Cornwall
(England : County)—Fiction.   6. England—Fiction.]   I. Title.

PZ7.1.O76Fl 2015
823.92—dc23
[Fic]

2015001444

10 9 8 7 6 5 4 3 2 1   15 16 17 18 19

Printed in the U.S.A.   23
First edition, November 2015
Book design by Carol Ly

In loving memory of my friends Patrick Taylor and Richard Bevan, who flashed so brightly. I just wish you had done so for longer. I miss you both with all my heart.

CHAPTER 1

I turned my back on my best friend's grave as her black-suited family gathered about it. A cold wind whipped around the eaves of the nearby church. Crows, their feathers as black as the mourners' clothes, sprang from the tops of gravestones, the beat of their wings sounding like gunfire in the bleak December morning.

Suddenly, the fear that my friend might just reach out and wrap her cold, white fingers around my ankle froze my heart. My skin prickled like goose bumps and I thought I was going to vomit. I heard a thump as a loose clump of earth broke free from the grave wall and dropped onto the coffin lid. The sound made me snap to attention as if I'd just been yelled at. Stuffing a bony fist into my mouth, I bit down and stifled the urge to scream. Then I placed one foot in front of the other and staggered away. I leaned against a nearby tree and crumpled.

Grief took me, its soulless fingers squeezing at my heart. The tears that had been standing in the corners of my eyes since Natalie's coffin was carried into the church now spilled down my cheeks in hot streaks. Behind me, I heard the priest's soft voice, only just above a whisper.

"Heavenly Father, we thank you for giving us Natalie to love and care for. Now that Natalie's life among us is over, we give her back to you . . ."

"No!" I sobbed into my hands. "You can't have her back."

Just as I felt my knees buckle, I heard a rustle behind me. My father. He'd followed me away from the grave. Wrapping his arm about my waist, he pulled me toward him.

"Charley—" he began.

"Get off me!" I whispered, pushing him away.

"But, Charley," he said, looking back over his shoulder at the mourners. "This is not the time nor—"

"Please . . . Dad!" My lower lip trembled as I wiped away the silver stream of snot leaking from my nose.

I just wanted to be alone. Why couldn't he get that? He wasn't Natalie. He didn't understand me—not like she had. Natalie had been the only one. And now she was dead, cut to pieces beneath the wheels of a train. I squeezed my eyes shut, wringing terrifying images from my mind. I didn't want to see them. Not now, not ever.

Stop it!

"Charley . . . I'm so sorry."

"Leave me alone, *please.*" I lurched away from the tree, glancing back in the direction of the hole. Natalie's parents were still standing beside it, red eyed and gaunt. I looked once more at my father, and then started off back across the graveyard.

"Charl—" I heard my father start, but he stopped short as if thinking better of it.

Rain began to fall and the wind rushed through the branches of the nearby trees. The sound did little to smother the noise of the grave diggers shoveling earth.

I ran. My auburn hair plastered flat against my cheeks and forehead. Plumes of breath jetted from my mouth and floated upward into the overcast sky. Not knowing—or caring—what direction I was heading in, I raced toward a dark smudge of trees in the distance. As I drew closer, I could see that there was a small building nestling among their trunks.

I sped up, my long black skirt whispering against my legs.

Eventually, I came to rest just beyond the tree line. Gray chinks of light slanted through the branches and glinted off the broken window-panes of the dilapidated building. There was a rustling sound from nearby.

"Hello?" I called out. "Is anybody there?"

Silence.

Pulling the collar of my coat tight about my throat, I moved closer. The structure looked like some kind of derelict outbuilding. The outside walls had once been white but were now weather-beaten gray and covered in a mosaic of graffiti and moss. I could just make out a faded British Rail logo beneath the grime and dirt.

The door had been pulled from its top hinge, though it still hung in its frame. I continued toward it, wanting to hide—never to be found again. It was quiet out here, peaceful, apart from the thrumming of the rain bouncing off the leaves above my head. I just wanted to be alone, to grieve.

Then I heard the distant roar of a passing train. I didn't want to hear that sound. It reminded me of what had happened to Natalie. Closing my eyes, I pretended it was the faint rumble of thunder.

I opened the door to the rickety outbuilding and stepped inside. There were holes in the roof. The floor was covered in dead leaves, old tires, and a rain-soaked mattress. I shivered, pulling my coat tighter about me. I suddenly felt lonely. It was a feeling I hadn't felt since Natalie and I had become friends. But now it was back. I squeezed my eyes shut, desperate to stop the flood of tears. When everyone else had taunted me, when those who I thought I could most trust had posted crap about me on Facebook and Twitter, Natalie had been there.

My iPhone vibrated in my pocket, buzzing against my thigh like an angry wasp. I remembered setting it to vibrate as I'd left the house for Natalie's funer—I couldn't think of *that word*. To say it . . . even merely to hear it in my head would somehow make this all real. And to me it wasn't real. Natalie wasn't dead . . . it was only a bad . . .

BRRRR! BRRRR! BRRRR!

The iPhone continued to buzz against my hip.

"Why can't Dad just leave me alone?" I hissed. He would want to know where I was. He would want to tell me it was time to go home and put all this behind me. I could picture him searching the graveyard for me, a look of despair on his thin face.

BRRRR! BRRRR! BRRRR!

"Leave me alone!" I shouted.

I pulled the iPhone from my pocket and looked at the screen flashing blue, then white. On seeing the caller's name blinking on and off like a heartbeat, I dropped it as if it had stung me.

NATALIE CALLING!

My heart began to beat in time with Natalie's name flashing on and off.

NATALIE CALLING! NATALIE CALLING! NATALIE CALLING!

My throat felt dry and I swallowed hard.

NATALIE CALLING!

The iPhone screen flashed as it lay among the leaves covering the ground. With a trembling hand, I reached down and picked it up. Was this some sick joke? I remembered the last time I had received a call from Natalie. I knew exactly when we had last spoken. It had been ten days ago, just before she died beneath the train. It had been raining that day, too. She had been on the way to my house. Her cab had failed to arrive, so she was going to walk. Natalie never arrived. She took a short-cut across the tracks and . . .

I hadn't seen the words *NATALIE CALLING* on my phone since she had been found dead.

So how could she be calling me now? Someone must have found her phone. Perhaps a railway worker had discovered it on the tracks and was now calling everyone on her contact list? Perhaps whoever was calling was trying to return the phone to its owner.

I shook my head, my brain feeling as if it were slamming against the sides of my skull.

Trembling, I pressed ANSWER and put the iPhone to my ear.

"Hello?" I said, my voice just a whisper.

Silence.

"Who is this?" I asked, beginning to feel angry. "If you're playing some sick joke . . ."

I could hear short, shallow breaths on the other end of the line.

"Look, whoever this is . . . I'm gonna report you to the—"

"Who are you talking to?" a voice asked.

With a gasp, I looked up to find my father standing in the doorway of the outbuilding.

"No one," I mumbled, hitting the END CALL button and sliding the iPhone back into my coat pocket.

"You sounded upset," he said, wiping away the rain that dripped from his chin.

"Of course I'm upset," I breathed, brushing past him and making my way back toward the church.

"How long is this going to go on?" my father called after me. "Charley, you can't ignore me forever."

"Can't I?" I said under my breath.

With head forward, chin against my chest, and shoulders rounded, I made my way out of the crop of trees and across the grass. I didn't slow down until I could see the church ahead of me. The graveyard was empty now, apart from the two lone grave diggers in the distance. From the tree line they looked like ghosts, barely visible in the gloom of the dying afternoon light.

I turned away and headed out of the graveyard. Without the slightest idea where to go or what to do next, I just walked. From over my shoulder, I could hear the sound of feet. My father was trotting to catch up.

"Charley, wait a minute. This is stupid. Can't we just talk?" he called.

I quickened my step.

"Charley, please!" he called again.

Quicker still.

I reached the gates to the graveyard and dashed into the parking lot, my shoes sending up splashes of black rain from the puddles that had formed in the cracked tarmac. From behind, a hand gripped my arm and spun me around.

"Charley!" my father wheezed. "Please, Charley, I know you're hurting—"

"You don't know anything!" I said, refusing to look at him.

7

Gently taking me by the shoulders, he said, "I do know, Charley . . . I know . . ."

"Get off me!" I cried, pulling away from him. "Leave me alone!"

Keeping a grip on my sleeve, my father pulled me closer. I fought him, thrashing my arms about as if drowning.

"Listen to me! Just listen to me!" he pleaded. "You were just a little girl when your mum died . . . but I experienced the same feelings you're having . . ."

"Stop!" was all I could say. I didn't want to hear this now.

"I know what it feels like to lose the person you loved . . . the one person that means everything to you. I can help you through this, Charley . . ."

"You're glad Natalie's dead!" I spat, fresh tears spilling down my cheeks. "You never liked her. You wanted her out of my life from the moment you first met her!" Looking straight into his eyes, I added, "Now you've got just what you always wanted."

Releasing his grip, my father flinched backward, stunned, as if he had been punched. "Is that what you really believe, Charley?" he asked. "Do you really think so little of me?"

" 'You should keep away from that girl. She is as mad as you if she really believes you have flashes. You have exams to study for! The girl is a know-it-all. I don't like the way she stares at me. I'm your father!' Isn't that what you used to say?" I reminded him, choking on my tears. " 'Why doesn't that girl Natalie stop poking her nose into other people's business? Why doesn't she just leave you alone?'"

I watched my father's face turn ashen. "I only had your best interests at heart, Charley. I never wanted anything bad to happen to the girl . . ."

"Her name is . . . was . . . Natalie." To hear those words from my own mouth sounded odd—like the crunching sound of breaking bones.

"Okay. I never wanted anything bad to happen to Natalie," my father said.

"Well, it did," I sniffed. "And you can't take back all of the nasty things you said about her."

"I know I can't," he said. "I'm sorry, Charley." Again, he stepped toward me, his arms open wide. This time I fell into them.

CHAPTER 2

*F*lashes! That's what I call them. I'm Charley Sheppard, the girl who can see things, the seventeen-year-old with an overactive imagination, the *freak* who can see lights like a thousand photographers crammed inside her head, snapping away all at once!

With one hand clasped to the side of my head, I staggered into the bathroom. If anyone had been looking, I wouldn't have blamed them for thinking I was trying to hold my head together—as if it might just explode at any moment.

It was agony, like my brain was being rubbed against a cheese grater. I leaned over the sink. Bile burned the back of my throat. Then, as if slapped, my head rocked backward and my neck made a cracking sound.

Let go of me! I heard the voice say. *Please, I just want to go home!*

I opened my eyes long enough to find the tap and turn it on. Water sloshed into the sink. I splashed some against my face. The flashes of light came again, jerking my head violently to the right. My knees buckled beneath me and I crashed to the bathroom floor.

Please just take me home, the voice whimpered in my ear. It seemed so real, and for just the briefest of moments, I was sure I could feel the girl's breath against my cheek. I shuddered.

I promise I won't tell anyone about you, the girl whispered, her voice trembling inside me.

"Please stop," I groaned, gripping the side of the bathtub. I tried and failed to pull myself up. I lay sandwiched between the side of the tub and the toilet. It always happened like this. For as long as I could remember, it had always been the same. The voices first, then the pictures.

It was the pictures I hated the most. They came in sudden flashes of light, bright and unrelenting, searing their hideous images into my brain. They came so fast, jittering past my mind's eye, like a series of ancient black-and-white photographs. But somehow, today's flashes were different. Brighter and faster than ever before. And the pain—I felt as if I were dying.

The girl was being dragged. I could see her white sneakers splattered with mud. It was raining and there were puddles—God, so many puddles—and they rippled, sending out distorted reflections of the girl. Horror and fear masked her prettiness. Seventeen years old, maybe eighteen, but no older. Blue eyes, red lipstick, tear-smeared eyeliner.

Kerry.

Yes, her name was Kerry. The *flash* of the necklace showed me that. Jeans, jacket, raining . . . Her hair was wet and clinging to her face, blond even though the rain had darkened it.

Help me! the girl cried out, but what I couldn't figure out was whether she was calling to me or someone else.

Flash! A hill set against the night sky. There was a car nearby, the engine still running. I could hear its purr and smell its exhaust. Another sudden burst of bright light. A muddy field, the smell of earth, the smell of alcohol.

"Where are you?" I mumbled, my skull feeling as if it were being crushed in a vice. I twitched and it was as if I was no longer aware of the real world. All I was aware of was the girl, the dirty sneakers, and the puddles. There was something else, though. I could hear music. It was faint at first, drowned out by the sound of the rain and the girl's hysterical sobs.

That's my mum calling, the girl pleaded with him. *Please let me speak to her—she'll be wondering where I am.*

Shut up! Another voice. Male.

As I twitched on the bathroom floor, my eyes half-open, pupils rolled back into my skull, I knew the voice belonged to the man who had dragged the girl through those puddles.

Turn that thing off, he hissed at her.

The music was a ringtone. My head jerked to the right, hitting the side of the tub as I tried to listen to it. Those lightbulbs popped again in time with the music coming from the girl's mobile phone.

"'Burn,'" I whispered, recognizing the song. "You like Ellie Goulding—don't you?"

The girl was being dragged like an animal down a . . . dirt road? It was too dark to see clearly. The road was very narrow, there were trees on either side, and I could hear the rain and the wind as it tore through the branches.

The music ended abruptly.

He'd made a mistake. He cursed himself and it was as if I could hear his thoughts: *Stupid! Stupid! Stupid! I should have taken her phone!* The flashes shone light into his soul and it was black. No amount of light could illuminate such a place. I felt his fear as his mind scrambled through the consequences.

They'll triangulate the signal, he cursed inside, pulling the girl through the mud. *They'll trace it—find it.*

I felt his fear, and my body locked in a violent spasm. In some small way, I took pleasure in it. He was human after all.

Switch it off! he hissed at the girl, bringing his face close to hers.

"Let me see your face, you bastard," I called out from the bathroom floor, my voice muffled and distorted. But I knew I wouldn't see it. I only ever saw the faces of those about to die. Wide-eyed and full of fear.

Flash! One after another in rapid succession. Blinding me again before I'd had a chance to see him. Then, somewhere close by, the sound of a train passing and a snapshot image of a broken chimney pot. What did those flashes mean?

Give me the phone, you silly bitch. He seethed, and my stomach knotted at the hatred in his voice.

I could see the girl's fingers curled around her mobile. She held it as if it was her last connection to the life she feared would soon end. The flashbulbs popped again, this time showing a close-up view of the girl's fingernails. They had been recently painted, and four of them were broken, but there was something white and flaky beneath them.

"Paint!" I cried out.

The fragmented images blinded me again. I saw the mobile phone cartwheeling through the air.

Mum! the girl screeched, knowing that any connection to the world she had once known had now gone.

Keep quiet, he hissed, and the girl flinched at the sound of his voice.

But you're going to hurt me, she whispered.

You know that, he whispered back.

CHAPTER 3

TOM—MONDAY: 02:19 HOURS

Who are you?" Detective Constable Jackson asked, pulling the collar of his jacket up against the rain.

Strobes of blue light from the nearby police vehicles lit up the night. The air crackled with the sound of radios sending messages back and forth between the control room and the officers who were searching the dirt road that led down to the railway tracks. The beams of their flashlights lit up the undergrowth.

"PC Tom Henson," I replied, trying to find my ID card in the dark.

Before I'd had the chance to show my ID, Jackson was talking at me again. "So you're the new proby? The guv mentioned you might be joining us for an attachment."

God, I hated that word—*proby*. I wasn't a probationer anymore, I was a police constable. I fished my ID card from my back trouser pocket and held it up, but Jackson had already turned away, no longer interested.

"I'm not a probationer anymore," I told him, despite his apparent lack of interest.

"Whatever," Jackson said, flicking away a cigarette he had been shielding from the rain with his hand. "You're the kid who has a hotshot lawyer for a dad, ain't-cha?"

I'd heard this all before. There was resentment from some of my colleagues because I was only nineteen and had been singled out by my senior officers for an attachment to the Criminal Investigation Department. It had nothing to do with my father. He hadn't even wanted me to be a copper. I'd been sent to CID because I'd worked hard for it. Nothing else.

But old sweats like Jackson always had this look of dislike and distrust whenever someone young and ambitious joined their team. I had seen it more than I cared to remember over the last two years. It shouldn't have bothered me, but it did. Officers like Jackson were guarded, reluctant to share their knowledge, preferring to see officers like me make mistakes, when all I wanted was to learn.

"I didn't ask to be posted to CID," I said, hoping I might win the trust of Jackson if I explained how I'd ended up working alongside him.

"So what are you doing here, then?" Jackson asked, acting as if he wasn't bothered either way.

"Superintendent Cooper suggested . . ."

"Jeez," Jackson scoffed, running a hand through his rain-soaked hair. "You've been in the job five minutes and you've already got that old wanker Cooper eating out of your hand. Are Cooper and your old man in the same lodge?"

"My father isn't a Freemason, if that's what you mean," I said. Jackson wasn't much older than thirty, yet he was acting as if he knew every freaking rule in the book. "Superintendent Cooper is my mentor."

"Mentor?" Jackson laughed out loud. "What is this job coming to? Mentor, my arse. When I was a proby, it was sink or swim, mate. I didn't have anyone wiping my bum."

"He's not wiping my arse," I said, putting away my ID card.

"I ain't really interested," Jackson said, walking to the shelter of a nearby tree and lighting another cigarette. Jackson was tall, about six foot three, and had one of those builds that said he spent way too much time in the station gym, probably getting off on watching himself lift weights in the mirrors. His hair had gone prematurely gray and was cut short like a marine's. I watched the end of his cigarette wink on and off in the darkness as he smoked.

"Where's the guv, anyway?" he asked.

"Gone to collect Taylor. She was—" I started.

"Here they come now," Jackson cut across me, stepping out from beneath the tree.

I shot a glance back over my shoulder and shielded my eyes against the glare of the approaching headlights. They lit up the narrow dirt road, casting eerie shadows among the trees. Leaving the lights on, Detective Sergeant Taylor and Detective Inspector Harker climbed from the car.

"Oh, for crying out loud," Harker groaned as he plunged his foot straight into a puddle.

Jackson stifled a grin. He hid it quickly by chewing on the cigarette that dangled from the corner of his mouth.

"Don't just stand there gawking, son," Harker barked at me. "Fetch my wellies from the trunk."

"Okay, sure. Sorry, sir," I said, making my way to the rear of the vehicle.

"And while you're there, fetch a couple of Hi-Vis jackets. If we're going trackside, we'll need 'em," Harker yelled.

"Yes, sir," I said again, rummaging through boxes of exhibit labels, statement forms, interview tapes, and evidence bags that had been crammed into the trunk of the car. I eventually spied the Wellington boots and a couple of fluorescent jackets, pulled them out, and with the items balanced in my arms, struggled to close the trunk with my elbow. The rain came down harder, bouncing up off the roof of the car and drumming into the puddles.

I could see Harker sitting half out of the passenger seat, and he looked back just in time to see me slip on the mud and go flying through the air and onto my back.

"Oh, for the love of God," Harker groaned. "We've been sent a right one here."

To make matters worse, as I hit the ground, the air exploded from my lungs, causing me to make a hideous belching sound.

"What a clown," Jackson laughed, and I could feel my cheeks burning red with embarrassment.

"That's enough, Jackson," someone else said.

I looked up to see Taylor holding out her hand toward me. Rain ran through her black hair and down her pale face.

"Get up," she said.

Gratefully, I gripped her hand and she yanked me to my feet.

"Thanks," I muttered, trying to rub the mud from my jacket and trousers but succeeding only in smearing it further into my clothes. "I feel like an arse." Then, noticing Taylor's look of disapproval, I quickly added, "Sorry, Sarge, but you know what I mean."

"We can all get a little overexcited on our first day." She half smiled as she stooped to pick up one of the fluorescent jackets from the mud. "You're among friends."

"Am I?" I breathed, looking over the roof of the car at Jackson, who stood in the rain, smirking at me.

"Take no notice of him," she said, slipping on the bright yellow coat. "Jackson can be full of shit at times, but his heart's in the right place. You'll get used to him. He just feels a bit threatened by you."

"Threatened?" I asked.

"Beats the hell out of me," she said, and half smiled again. Then, turning away, she said over her shoulder, "It must be a guy thing."

"What's wrong with this picture?" Harker roared, one rain-soaked foot sticking up in the air.

I looked at him. "Sorry, sir?"

"Boots!"

———

I had met Detective Inspector Harker only once before. It was two days ago when I'd first arrived at Marsh Bay Police Station, before the start of my first night shift. I'd wanted to go and introduce myself, but he had been busy and just as pissed off as he seemed now. Perhaps that was just the way he was.

He was a tall man with a shock of white hair, and so thin, his body looked emaciated beneath his gunmetal-colored suit. Harker's face was long, and nets of wrinkles circled his gray eyes. He pulled on the second Wellington boot and stood before me in the driving rain.

"So what have we got?" he said.

"Um," I started, realizing that he was hoping for some kind of update from me. But since arriving on the scene, I'd only succeeded in making a donkey of myself and didn't know any more about what was happening other than the fact that someone had been struck by a train on the nearby railway tracks.

"So?" Harker asked me, raising one of his jet-black eyebrows.

"Um," I mumbled again, glancing at Jackson for help.

Jackson shot a glance back at me, with a smug look on his face. He stepped forward and said, "Guv, it's a one-under. Looks like a young girl."

"Looks like?" Harker asked, doing that thing with his eyebrow again.

"Well, there ain't too much of her left. Poor little cow," Jackson told him.

"What I want to know is, why has uniform called us out on a night like this?" Harker asked.

"Is it suspicious?" DS Taylor asked.

"Not really," Jackson said.

"Not really?" Harker snapped. "What's that supposed to mean? It's either a suicide or it's not."

"What does uniform think?" Taylor asked, looking at Jackson, then at me.

"Suspicious, I guess," I said, just wanting to add something to the conversation. "Or they wouldn't have called CID."

"No shit, Sherlock," Jackson said. "I'm so glad that we've got you around to tell us this stuff."

"Knock it off, Jackson," Taylor said, yanking the cigarette from his mouth and throwing it away. "And stop smoking. This could be a crime scene, for crying out loud."

"A crime scene?" Jackson scoffed. "You're having a laugh, ain't-cha? For the last half hour, I've stood and watched uniforms trample all over the frigging place in their size-twelve boots."

"Well, perhaps you should have put a cordon in place. You know, protect the scene," Taylor said. "After all, you're meant to be a detective." Then, turning her back on him, she winked at me. I felt much better.

Harker looked at the both of us, and I cringed at the disappointment in his eyes. I regretted wasting my time justifying my existence to Jackson, when really I should have spent my time trying to find out what had taken place down on the railway tracks.

"C'mon," Harker sighed. "I guess we'd better go and take a look."

CHAPTER 4

CHARLEY—MONDAY: 01:57 HOURS

I could feel myself being swept up off the floor. The bathroom ceiling swam from side to side as if the house were caught in an earthquake. A set of strong arms held me and I could smell soap. Dad. The soap smell was familiar; he had been with someone—a woman.

My head beat from the inside out, but the flashes had stopped. Now came the feeling of wanting to be sick, the taste of hot bile in my throat as if I had swallowed a pint of battery acid. He picked me up and carried me out of the bathroom. I could see my bedroom walls, and the pink lampshade hanging from the ceiling.

I really need to get rid of that, I thought as it sailed past above me. *Pink*—I wasn't a little girl anymore. Then the feeling of something soft as I was lowered onto my bed. Those strong arms slipped from beneath me, and Dad's face came into view.

"Charley?" he whispered. "Are you okay?"

With my eyelids fluttering, I tried to focus on the face hovering over me.

"The flashes," I murmured.

"It's okay, I'm here now," he said.

My father brushed the hair from my brow. For such a big man, his touch was really gentle.

I felt him move away from the bed. I stretched out my hand. "Don't go," I said. My anger and frustration had lessened a little over the last few days since Natalie's funeral.

"I'm just going to fetch a cold cloth; your face is burning up," he said. "I'll be back in just a second."

"Don't go," I said again, that sense of loneliness I so often felt creeping over me.

Taking my hand in his, I felt the bed dip as he sat beside me. "I'm not going anywhere. I'm right here, Charley."

I held his hand against the side of my face and it felt warm. "I had more flashes," I whispered as he stroked my hair.

"You had another fit," he said softly.

"Flashes," I whispered, and closed my eyes. "I don't have fits. The doctors have all said they can't find anything wrong with me."

"I'm going to get a second opinion," he said.

"We've had six already," I said, willing the thudding sensation in my head to go away.

"It's not normal," he said. I flinched and he quickly added, "You know what I mean."

He meant the fits weren't normal. He didn't believe in the flashes.

Then, to my surprise, he said, "What did you see this time, Charley? That's if you want to talk about it."

My father rarely asked what I saw in the flashes. But since Natalie's death and our argument at her funeral, he too had seemed to mellow just a little. I guessed he felt guilty about everything he had said about Natalie when she was alive. Was asking me about my flashes his way of trying to make amends?

I took a deep breath. "A girl," I whispered, and although those flashes had long since faded, I could still see her petrified face. I opened my eyes so I didn't have to see it anymore. "But it was different this time."

"How?" he asked, resting himself against the headboard so we lay next to each other on my bed. I liked the way he did that. It meant he was going to stay awhile and listen to me instead of running for the hills like he usually did.

"The pictures—*the flashes*—were more vivid," I told him. "More real somehow."

"But you know they're not real, right?" he asked. And although this was his standard answer, this time he didn't sound angry or frustrated. He sounded like he was kinda interested in what I had to say for once.

"They are," I whispered, closing my eyes again. I saw the girl's name. Kerry, the name on her necklace had read, and I could see it swinging before me. "Burn" by Ellie Goulding played in the background like some hideous sound track. I opened my eyes. "Her name was Kerry."

"Whose was?" he asked.

"The girl I saw tonight. She was being dragged by someone, a man, up a narrow dirt road. She was about my age and she was calling out for her mum. I could hear the girl's phone ringing and trains thundering past in the distance—"

"But don't you see?" my father interrupted.

"See what?" I asked him.

"Your friend Natalie was recently killed by a train," he said. "You've been through a very traumatic experience, Charley, and your mind is playing tricks on you."

"The girl I saw wasn't Natalie," I said, wondering if it was him or me I was trying to convince. "Natalie's death was an accident, but the girl I saw in my flashes was murdered."

"So what did her killer look like?" he asked, cocking his eyebrow at me.

"You know I only ever see the victims," I said. "I couldn't see his face."

"So how did you know it was a *he*?"

"I heard his voice," I said, closing my eyes and trying to hear it again. But it was gone.

"So what did his voice sound like?"

"I dunno," I said, opening my eyes and looking at him. "It was muffled, like it was coming from behind a wall or something."

My father looked at me. Was it despair I could see in his eyes?

"They're just dreams," he said.

Was he trying to comfort me or persuade me?

"Nightmares," I muttered.

"Them, too," he added, as if trying to convince me that's all they were.

"But I'm awake when I have them."

"You were unconscious when I found you."

I tilted my head slightly so I could look up into his face. His green eyes had lost their sparkle and were now gray. I saw the concern etched in the wrinkles that covered his brow. His once jet-black hair was now flecked with white, and he looked tired.

"You have headaches, right?" he continued, looking down into my face. "You've had them for as long as I can remember. I think that has something to do with these dreams you have."

"I know what you're going to say," I said. We had been here before—me lying on my bed, my head thumping, while he tried to convince me the flashes were nothing more than my mind conjuring up images to block out the fear that I might have a brain tumor of some kind.

"I could be right," he said.

"Dad, the flashes come first—not the headaches," I said. "And besides, I rarely black out. Tonight, the flashes were bad—strong. They came at me all at once, and it was like my brain couldn't cope with them."

"I still don't believe they're visions," he said softly. His voice had a tone that said he was never going to be convinced. I got that. After all, if the flashes were really visions of some kind, then what would that make me? A medium? Clairvoyant? Psychic? Or just someone who could see people's deaths? Because that's what I always saw in those flashes—I saw people dying. Tonight, I had seen a girl about to be murdered.

"I think you're wrong, Dad," I whispered beside him. I caught that faint waft of soap leaking from him again. "I think the flashes are visions."

"Of what, Charley?" And I sensed the first hint of frustration in his voice. "Are all these deaths you see real? Have they happened? Are they about to happen? What?"

"I don't know."

"You need to get some perspective on this," he said, and again I sensed his rising frustration. Or was it fear that his only daughter—his only child—was going mad?

"Perspective on what?" I shot back, trying to hide my own frustration.

"I've seen you," he said, "sitting in front of the laptop for hours on end, searching for the names of the people that you see in your vis . . . *flashes*. And have you found a single one?"

"No," I whispered.

"See, none of it is real. It's just your vivid imagination."

"I'm not six anymore."

"And that's my point, Charley. You're seventeen years old, for heaven's sake. When was the last time you went out with a group of friends? Had some fun? Instead, you're sitting in front of the laptop, searching for people who don't exist." Dad could sense I was getting angry. "Look, Charley, all I'm saying is that perhaps you should get out more. Make some new friends now that Natalie has gone."

"You just didn't like her because she believed me," I said.

"Now, you know that's not true," Dad said, looking hurt. "It wasn't that I didn't like Natalie. I just thought she encouraged you to dwell on those morbid dreams . . . nightmares . . . that you say you have. It just wasn't healthy, the amount of time you two spent discussing what you claimed to have seen. Other girls go out and have fun."

"We did have fun."

"Okay, look," he sighed. "I don't want to get into another argument. I just think it might help you if you got out more. You know, with some friends, instead of hanging around the house, looking for ghosts on the Internet. You're seventeen, Charley. You should be having a life."

"What, like you?" I asked, leaning away from him.

"What's that supposed to mean?" He stared at me.

"Nothing." I looked away, knowing that perhaps I had said too much.

"No, go on, Charley," he said, sounding a little pissed off with me now. "If you've got something on your mind, let's talk about it."

"I know you have women *friends*," I said, still unable to meet his stare. "Why don't you ever bring them back here?"

"This has nothing to do with you," he said firmly.

"At first I thought it was because you were ashamed of me," I said, ignoring him. "I wondered if you were worried that I might start talking about my flashes—my head might start aching, or worse, I might throw a fit. But then I realized why you never brought your lady friends home."

"I'm not ashamed of you—"

"It's because of Mum, isn't it?" I said, and now I did look at him. "It's been, like, eleven years since Mum died. I really don't think she would mind you sharing your bed with someone else."

"Charley, don't say something you might regret later," he said, and now it was his turn to look away.

"All I'm saying is that Mum wouldn't have expected you to spend the rest of your life on your own. You're only forty-five. She would understand."

"It has nothing to do with you, Charley," he said. "And nothing to do with your mum."

"No?" I said. "So why, then, do you sometimes come home without your wedding ring on? I mean, you always wear it, even after all this time. You take it off when you're with them. It's like you have to break the connection with Mum. You feel as if you're cheating on her when you're with those women. You always smell of soap, like you've had to wash them off you—destroy the smell of their perfume. I thought at first it was me that you were trying to hide their smell from. But I was wrong. It's Mum."

"You're wrong," he said, a grim look on his face.

"Am I?" I said, trying to keep my anger and confusion from boiling over. "Christ, Dad, I've even seen you out in the drive, scrubbing down the backseats of the car. What, have you had them in there, too?"

"I'm a taxi driver, for crying out loud!" he said. I'd never heard him sound so upset before. "You should see some of the people that I have to ferry around. I have to put up with people puking their guts up, smoking, ramming kebabs down their throats! Of course I keep the car clean and tidy. It's where I work—it's my job!"

I knew I'd said too much, but however much I wanted to take it all back, I couldn't. Those words were already out there. "I'm sorry," I said.

"Yeah, so am I," he whispered, and went to the bedroom door.

"You don't have to hide stuff from me. I'm not a little girl anymore."

"Then stop acting like one," he said, leaving my room and closing the door behind him.

His last comment made my stomach ache even more than it already did. I was feeling bad about what I'd said, and now I felt even worse. It had never been my intention to upset my father. Lying on my side, with my iPhone gripped in my hand, I got one last lingering flash of that girl, Kerry, gripping her phone.

Closing my eyes, I prayed I wouldn't see her. Vision or fantasy, I didn't want to see her being dragged down that narrow dirt road, to see the puddles, to hear Ellie Goulding mixed with the sound of trains thundering past in the distance. I just wanted some peace. I just wanted the dead to leave me alone.

CHAPTER 5

TOM—MONDAY: 02:47 HOURS

The rain had started to ease a little, but the walk down the embankment, although not particularly steep, was still treacherous. This time I held on to any branch, shrub, or piece of railway fixture that I could find to stop myself falling head over heels again. One screwup in front of my new boss was enough for one night. In the distance, I could see a stationary freight train and the flashlights of police officers.

The guv was the first to reach the tracks, and the sound of his feet crunching over the gravel echoed back at me. I hated going trackside, to be honest. The place was fraught with danger: slips, trips, and every other kind of hazard, and that didn't include the one hundred and forty tons of steel screaming past every few minutes. The only saving grace was that all trains in the area would be on "stop" or "caution" so we could get the job done on the tracks.

I'd been to a few one-unders during my short time in the police, and I wasn't ashamed to admit that I hated them. Some said they liked them, but that was just a bunch of crap. Bravado.

Given the choice, I wouldn't have attended any of them. But when I had to, I prayed that the victim under the train had been pulverized. It was easier to pick up a whole bunch of mush than something that still looked close to being human. Because they didn't look human, not really, not with their arms and legs tangled about them like a slipknot, their head twisted so badly that they looked as if God had placed it on their neck the wrong way around as some cruel joke. Even the bodies of the ones who looked human were usually so dismembered that it could take hours to find every piece of them, if they could be found at all.

The stench was usually unbearable, too, so I always kept a small jar of Vicks in my coat pocket. Just a dab of it on the top lip usually did the trick. As I stood in the track's access strip and fished the Vicks from my pocket, Jackson shone his flashlight on me.

"What you looking for?" he said.

"This," I said, holding it up to the light.

"Oh, for Christ's sake," he said, rolling his eyes. "Show some backbone, can't-cha? You're in CID now."

"It helps." I shrugged, smearing my top lip with the stuff. My eyes watered as the menthol vapor bombarded my nostrils.

"Hey, guv, have you seen this?" he called after Harker, who was making his way along the access strip in the direction of the freight train.

"Seen what?" Harker called back, not slowing down.

"The proby has got the Vicks," he laughed.

"Looks like he might need it," Harker said as he shone his flashlight in the direction of the train.

I saw pieces of flesh and entrails glistening back at me from between the two sets of tracks. I knew at once that the girl had been dragged along beneath the train before it had come to a full standstill.

Ignoring Jackson, I passed him in the access strip and caught up with DS Taylor, who was just behind Harker. Several officers were gathered at the rear of the train, shining brightly in their fluorescent coats. On hearing our feet treading over the ballast, they turned, one of them shining his flashlight through the dark.

"Get that light out of my bloody eyes," Harker barked.

"Sorry, boss," the officer said, and lowered the flashlight. "I thought you might be the ambulance crew."

"Bit late for that, son, don't you think?" Harker sighed.

I flinched as I caught sight of the upper torso of a female sticking out from beneath the train. As we gathered with the uniformed officers, I took in a deep breath and looked down. I had seen worse. The girl's upper body was still intact, although one of her arms was severed to the bone and lay at an odd angle to the rest of her body. Her hair and face were smeared black, not with blood but with grease and grime from beneath the train. Her eyes were open, as was her mouth, and her expression was one of fear. She couldn't have been any older than eighteen.

"Any ID?" Taylor asked, hunkering down to inspect the body.

"We haven't found any yet, but we found this just up the track," one of the officers said, holding out a gold neck chain. "It says *Kerry*."

"Okay, constable, I can read," Harker said. "Bag it for the time being."

"So what's the problem?" Jackson asked.

"Problem?" the uniformed officer asked.

"I think what my colleague is trying to say," Taylor said, "is why the need for CID? You know the score—we only get called out if there's any suggestion that the death might be suspicious. Is it?"

"Well—" the officer said.

"What does the driver say?" Harker said.

"That's the problem, sir," he replied. "The driver says the girl was just lying on the ground between the tracks—like she was asleep or something."

"Asleep?" Harker asked. "What made him think that?"

"I dunno, really," the officer said.

"You don't know or you didn't ask?" Jackson said, unable to keep his mouth shut for too long. It was as if he had to keep reminding everyone that he was still there.

"You two, go and speak with the driver," Harker said, looking at Jackson and me. Then, turning to the uniformed officers gathered around the body, he said, "Well, don't just stand their gawking; put something over her. Show her some respect, for Christ's sake. And I want these tracks searched for any ID. She must have had a purse, bag, mobile phone, something to say who she was. And when you've done that, I want the closed-circuit TV pulled from the nearest stations in both directions."

"CCTV?" one of the officers asked as I headed up the tracks toward the front of the train.

"Just do it," Harker ordered.

"I don't know why he's bothering," Jackson said as we made our way through the dark to the driver's cab. "I can already tell you what's gone on here."

To him, it was obviously an open-and-shut case. No need to go sniffing out witnesses or evidence.

"So what's your theory?" I asked him, pampering his ego.

"Well, if you hadn't stuffed half a jar of Vicks up your nose, you would've been able to smell the alcohol coming from the girl. She stank of the stuff," he said with some pride.

"So?" I asked him.

"So she probably staggered out of one of the pubs down in the town, missed the last bus home, spent the last of her cash on one too many vodkas, and in her drunken state, decided to walk home."

"In the pouring rain?"

"She was drunk, wasn't she?" Jackson glared at me.

"Still doesn't explain how she ended up under a freight train," I shot back.

"Like I said, she was drunk and decided to walk home. She got halfway there, it started to rain, and fearing that her new hairdo might get ruined, she decided to take a shortcut across the tracks. I've seen it a hundred times before. These kids think that just because the last train has gone for the night, it's safe to screw around on the tracks. But what they fail to realize, until it's way too late, is that freight trains run up and down these lines all night long. So what do you think to that, Sherlock?"

"Not bad, I guess." I shrugged.

"Not bad?" Jackson snapped. "Bull! I'd like to see you come up with something better."

"We'll see." I smiled to myself, enjoying winding him up.

"Okay, if you're so sure there's another way she ended up under this train," he sneered, "why don't you put your money where your mouth is? I bet you a twenty that I'm right and you're wrong."

"I'm not a betting man," I told him, reaching the front of the train.

"Then CID ain't the place for you." He grinned back at me, hoisting himself up into the cab.

The driver sat at the controls and stared vacantly out the cab window. At first, I wondered if he even knew we were there.

"Hello," I said.

"Huh?" he murmured, turning to look at us.

"Police," Jackson said.

I took my ID card from my pocket and offered it to the driver. "I'm Police Constable Tom Henson from Marsh Bay Police—"

"And I'm *Detective* Constable Rob Jackson." He glanced sideways at me, then back at the driver. "So what happened?"

"I've been through this already," the driver said softly. "I've already told that other police officer what I saw."

"I know," Jackson sighed. "But the guv can be a real pain in the arse at times. He doesn't like any loose ends."

"What loose ends?" the driver asked.

"Just tell us what you saw," I said gently, seeing that the man was in shock.

His narrow face was as white as paper, and his hands trembled in his lap. I couldn't even begin to imagine what it must be like to have someone lying in front of your moving train and be powerless to do anything about it. In a car, at least you can try and swerve out of the way.

Again he turned to stare out the window and onto the tracks, which disappeared into the darkness. I could see his eyes, large and round, and I knew that he was watching his train collide with the girl, Kerry, all over again.

"I was traveling at line speed," the driver whispered. "It was raining, but I could still see some way ahead. Then I saw her just lying on her back across the tracks. I blew the horn and applied the emergency brakes, but I was too close. There was no way I was going to stop in time. Then she was gone. Disappeared beneath me."

"You said earlier that you thought perhaps she was asleep?" I said.

"She was just laying there, her arms folded across her chest," he said, still looking ahead and into the darkness. "I blew the horn and she didn't even flinch."

"Did you see anyone else?" I asked. "Was anyone standing beside the tracks, perhaps?"

The driver shook his head.

"That's good enough for me," Jackson said as he climbed from the cab.

"Hang on," I called.

"I'm done," he shouted, crunching back up the tracks.

"Thank you for your time. I know that this must be very difficult," I said. "Is there anything I can do for you?"

He shook his head. "I'll be all right. A relief driver is being sent to take over."

"Okay," I said. I pulled out a business card from my wallet. "Take this."

"What for?"

"Just in case."

"In case of what?" he said, almost dreamily taking the card.

"You might remember something later." I watched him slip the card into his shirt pocket, then I left the cab.

I could see Jackson's silhouette in the distance as he headed back toward the rear of the train and Harker. Careful not to twist my ankle, or worse, I made my way as quickly as possible over the ballast. We both reached Harker and the others at the same time, to find DS Taylor rummaging through a small handbag. A young officer stood next to her, looking very pleased with himself. I guessed it had been he who had found the bag.

"The deceased was a Kerry Underhill," she said, holding up a temporary driver's license. "Eighteen years old and lived at 8 Hill Lane, Willow Shore."

"Which, if I'm not mistaken, is over in that direction." Jackson pointed to the other side of the tracks. Turning to me, he said, "See, I was right. The infamous shortcut home across the tracks."

"What?" Harker asked, eyeing both of us.

"I've been sharing my wealth of experience with the proby." Jackson smiled. "You know, telling him how these incidents usually pan out."

"And how is this incident panning out?" Harker asked. "What did the driver say?"

"Just that she was lying across the tracks. He blew the horn to give a warning, then—*wham*!"

"So he didn't see anyone else, then?" Taylor asked, placing the driver's license back into Kerry Underhill's bag.

"No," Jackson said flatly.

Harker was silent for a moment, then, cocking his eyebrow at me, he said, "What do you think?"

"I think the driver is in shock and perhaps it would be worth reinterviewing him in a few days' time," I said.

"Why?" Harker asked, not letting me off the hook now that I had chucked my opinion into the ring.

"Something doesn't quite add up," I said, feeling Jackson's eyes boring into me.

"What doesn't add up?" Jackson said.

"You said that she smelled of alcohol, right?" I said.

"So?"

"And that she probably staggered out of one of the pubs in town. Having spent the last of her money on booze and unable to afford a cab, she decided to walk home in the pouring rain, then take a shortcut across the railway tracks, where she met her death."

"Well, it looks pretty obvious to me," Jackson said, glancing at Harker and Taylor.

"Pass me her bag, will you, Sarge?" I said to Taylor. "It's just that I thought I saw something when you had it open a few minutes ago."

Taylor passed me the bag. I opened it, praying that I hadn't been mistaken. With some relief, I held up a twenty and a ten. "She had the money to get a cab—she didn't have to walk. She must have been drunk out of her mind to choose to walk in the dark and in this weather."

"Like I said, she was drunk," Jackson barked. "She didn't know what she was doing. She staggered out onto the tracks and collapsed unconscious because of all the booze sloshing around inside of her. She was hammered."

"Drunk?" I shot back. "She would've had to have been absolutely wasted to decide to walk home. Hill Lane has got to be at least five miles from town, four with the shortcut."

"That's what I'm telling you, numbskull. She was so drunk she collapsed onto the tracks. She was so drunk she didn't even hear the driver blowing the horn. I just don't get the point you're trying to make." Jackson looked at me as if I were something he had just scraped from his boot.

"My point is if she was so drunk that she decided to walk five miles home in the pouring rain, how did she get this far?" I asked him. "To be that far gone, she would have been all over the place, barely able to put one foot in front of the other. Also, the driver said she was lying on her back with her arms folded neatly across her chest. That doesn't sound like someone who has collapsed. If that's what had happened, wouldn't she have been sprawled across the tracks?"

"Oh, this is such a load of old crap," Jackson said, looking at Harker.

Harker stood silently for a moment, his eyes never moving from mine. Then, turning to the uniformed officer, he said, "Okay, get the circus rolling. I want Scenes of Crime Officers and a search team."

"SOCO?" Jackson said. "A search team?"

Ignoring him, Harker looked at Taylor. "You and Jackson speak with the coroner's office and tell them I want the toxicology reports ASAP. I want to see how drunk this Kerry Underhill really was. Then start knocking on a few doors. Get the CCTV from the pubs in town. And look for her phone."

"Phone?" Jackson asked, glaring at me.

"She was eighteen, for crying out loud, not eight," Harker said. "She'd have a phone. If you find it, get the tech guys to go over it. She might have made a call or sent a text to someone." He pointed his finger in my direction. "You're coming with me."

"Where?" I asked, following him up the tracks toward the dirt road.

"To tell the Underhills that their little girl is dead," he shouted over his shoulder.

"Good luck," Jackson sniped.

"I wish I'd taken that bet now," I said with a smile.

Jackson waved his middle finger at me. "You're wrong. This is just one big waste of time."

As I turned away, I wished in a strange way that he was right. Because to me, it sounded very much like Kerry Underhill had been deliberately placed on those tracks.

CHAPTER 6

The house was in darkness and situated in a nice part of town. I could see by the hanging baskets at the front door and the neatly cut privet hedge that the house was lovingly looked after. The Underhills were obviously the kind of people who took pride in their home.

"Whatever you do, for God's sake, don't tell them their daughter has been involved in an accident," Harker whispered at me as we waited on the doorstep.

"Why?" I whispered back.

"An accident means that there is someone to blame," he said, looking at me through the driving rain. "It means that it was someone's fault."

The hall light came on, and I saw a vague outline of someone approaching the front door. The lock was turned and the bleary-eyed face of a middle-aged woman peered around the edge of the door.

"Maybe you'll remember your key one of these days—" When she saw Harker and me sheltering on the step, she made a small gasping sound in the back of her throat.

"Mrs. Underhill?" Harker said, cocking his eyebrow.

"Yes," she said, pushing the door shut an inch. "Who are you?"

"I'm Detective Inspector Harker and this is Constable Henson from Marsh Bay Police Station." He held up his ID card.

"Yes?" she asked, her face turning pale. It was as though she somehow knew. It's never going to be good news if you're woken in the early hours of the morning by the police.

"Can we come in, please?"

Slowly, and without taking her eyes off us, she opened the front door and ushered us into the hallway.

"Who else is at home with you?" Harker said.

"My husband," she said. "Why? What is this all about?"

"It might be best if you woke your husband," I said softly.

With her hand on the banister for support, and a tremor in her voice, she shouted up the stairs, "David! David! It's the police."

There was a noise from above, then the sound of footsteps.

"What?" a man's voice called. "What did you say, love?"

"The police are here." This time her voice nearly broke altogether. With a trembling hand held against her face, she looked back at us. "It's Kerry, isn't it? What's happened to her? Please tell me."

Mr. Underhill appeared in the gloom at the top of the stairs, raking his hands through wiry hair. A loose-fitting robe flapped around his legs.

"What's this all about?" he asked, coming down the stairs. "What's happened?"

"Perhaps we should go and sit down?" I said.

"No," Mrs. Underhill croaked, both hands held to her face now. She peeked at me through her fingers, as though if she couldn't see me, then what I was about to tell her wouldn't be true. "Tell me what's happened to my baby! It is Kerry, isn't it? That's why you're here?"

"Kerry?" Mr. Underhill muttered, still looking half-asleep, his hair sticking out in clumps from the side of his head. "What's going on?"

Knowing that I couldn't keep the truth from them any longer, and feeling sick with nerves, I said, "I'm sorry to have to inform you that your daughter Kerry has been involved in an incident tonight . . ."

"No!" Mrs. Underhill almost seemed to screech, coming forward and gripping my rain-soaked coat. She pushed me back along the hallway toward the front door. "Get out," she screeched. "Whatever you're going to say isn't true. I don't want to hear it. Get out!"

"Please, Mrs. Underhill . . ." I knew breaking the news was never going to be easy, but this was horrendous. To see the look of fear in Mrs. Underhill's eyes was unbearable.

"Carol," Mr. Underhill whispered, coming forward and prying his wife's hands from me.

"No!" she wailed, slapping her husband over and over again. "No, David! No! Tell them to get out!"

Mr. Underhill gripped his wife's wrist and folded his arms around her. "Shhh," he whispered in her ear. After she had calmed down a bit, he looked at us over her shoulder. "What's happened to my daughter, officer?"

"She was struck by a train and I'm afraid she's . . ." I found it nearly impossible to look him in the eyes. I didn't want to see his pain, too.

"No!" Mrs. Underhill sobbed, and then seemed to crumple even further.

"A train?" Mr. Underhill asked, shaking his head in bewilderment. "How was she struck by a train?"

I took a deep breath. "She was lying on the tracks and the train . . ."

"Suicide?" Mr. Underhill asked, his face screwing up in disbelief. "Impossible! Kerry wouldn't have killed herself. She was a happy girl. She wouldn't have done this to us, not just before Christmas. No way."

"We believe that she was taking a shortcut home across the tracks," Harker said.

"A shortcut?" Mr. Underhill asked, drawing his wife tighter against him. "She wouldn't have walked home on a night like this. She would have got a cab or called me to pick her up."

"We don't have all the facts at this time," Harker said.

I was glad that Mr. Underhill wasn't the only one who believed that the chances of his daughter taking a five-mile hike in the middle of the night in the pouring rain was something close to zero.

"Do you have anyone you would like us to contact?" I asked. "Family or friends you would like to be with you . . ."

"I want to see her," Mrs. Underhill said, pulling herself from her husband's arms. "I won't believe it until I see her."

"That's not possible at the moment," Harker said.

"I want to see my baby!" Mrs. Underhill hissed, her eyes so red and sore, it looked as if she had rubbed mustard into them. "I won't believe it until I see my baby's beautiful face."

"That might not be possible," Harker said.

"Oh, dear God, no," Mrs. Underhill said. "Please, God, no. Not my baby's beautiful face. No. Please, God, no!"

Harker reached into his pocket and pulled out the see-through evidence bag containing Kerry's gold necklace. He offered it to Mr. Underhill. "Do you recognize this?" he asked.

Kerry's father took the bag and held it as if it were the most precious and delicate treasure in the world. Without looking up, he nodded his head. "Yes, that's our Kerry's. We got it for her for her eighteenth birthday—October just gone, it was."

Harker held out his hand to take back the bag, but Mr. Underhill pulled it away. "Please, Mr. Underhill. I know this is very difficult, but we need to keep hold of the necklace for the time being. You will get it back, I promise."

With tears running down his face, Kerry's father handed Harker the evidence bag.

"Did Kerry have any brothers or sisters?" Harker asked, placing the bag in his coat pocket.

"No, Kerry was our only child," he said.

"Friends?" I asked.

"Lots," he replied, without looking at me. "She was a very popular girl."

"Boyfriends?" I took a pen and notebook from my coat.

"Just the one," he replied. "They broke up recently."

"How did she take it?" Harker said.

"My daughter didn't kill herself because her boyfriend broke it off with her, if that's what you're trying to imply," Mr. Underhill snapped.

"I'm not trying to imply anything," Harker said flatly. "If we're going to find out what happened to your daughter tonight, we need to get some idea of what her life was like."

"I'm sorry," he replied, wiping away his tears with the back of his hand.

"What was her boyfriend's name?" I asked him, pen poised.

"Jason Lane," he replied, and I scribbled it down along with the address that he supplied.

"If that is everything, officer, my wife and I would like to be left alone now."

"Of course; I understand," I said.

"Do you have a number that we can call you on?" Harker asked, heading for the front door.

Mr. Underhill nodded and recited it.

I looked at him as I wrote it down. "Did Kerry have a mobile phone? It's just that we haven't been able to find it. It might help with our inquiries. Like, did she ring anyone or receive any texts before she . . . ?"

"Yes, Kerry had a mobile phone," Mr. Underhill replied.

"Do you know the number?"

"Yes," he said, and I wrote it down.

I knew I would never forget that look in Mrs. Underhill's eyes as she realized what we were going to tell her. But I also knew that she would never forget. She would always remember the night that I came knocking on her door to tell her that her baby was dead. I mean, how would anyone ever be able to forget that?

Harker drove me back to the police station. I was glad my first night shift was at an end. I climbed into my car and drove out of the small parking lot at the rear of the station. I couldn't rid my mind of Mrs. Underhill's distraught face.

I knew that sleep wouldn't come easily, even though I had another night shift ahead of me and I would need some rest. And if I were to be honest, I wasn't exactly looking forward to my next shift. I knew Jackson was still going to be pissed at me for suggesting my theory to the DI. I mean, how dare I? I was just the proby, after all. I knew diddly-squat!

But I did know Jackson was wrong about how Kerry Underhill had come to be on those tracks. Sure, he had made the facts fit, but that was because he was arrogant and lazy and desperate to prove the new guy wrong. But none of that mattered. What mattered was discovering the truth.

I stopped at a set of traffic lights. With my hands strumming against the steering wheel, I looked left and then right. Left took me home to my flat and a nice warm bed. Right took me back in the direction of the railway tracks where Kerry Underhill had died.

The lights turned to amber, then green. I accelerated, hit the turn signal, and went right.

CHAPTER 7

CHARLEY—MONDAY: 05:56 HOURS

I woke up, my phone still gripped in my hand. I looked at the screen: 5:56 a.m. Groaning, I rolled onto my back and closed my eyes again, hoping for another hour or two of sleep. There was no reason to get up. College had broken up for the Christmas holidays and I had yet to find myself a part-time job, despite my father's constant reminders. I had been too upset by Natalie's death to look for work. With thoughts of my best friend already creeping into my mind, memories of the previous night's flashes and the conversation I'd had with my father followed.

Was he still going to be pissed at me because of what I'd said about his lady friends? It was his private life after all. I didn't enjoy arguing with my father at every opportunity, but that's all we ever seemed to do lately. If only I could prove to him that what I saw in those flashes was true. It wasn't as if I got some kind of kick out of having them. Did he really think I enjoyed seeing the disbelief in his face? Or being ridiculed by my friends?

I had once made the mistake of confiding in a girl I went to school with about my flashes. Lucy had discovered me in the toilet in our last year at secondary school, leaning over the basin with my head in my hands, recovering from flashes about a small boy drowning.

It hadn't been a severe episode—I hadn't collapsed at least. But the flashes had been strong enough to make me feel sick from the blinding bolts of pain that I'd felt inside my head.

"What's wrong?" Lucy had asked, dropping her bag to the floor and rushing to my aid.

"Aw, it's nothing," I told her.

"That's crap, Charley, and you know it," she said. "I've known you since primary school and you've always suffered from headaches. My mum reckons you've got a tumor."

"Thanks," I said, rubbing my temples. "Cheer me up, why don't you?"

"She doesn't mean anything by it," Lucy said. "You know she's just kinda concerned, that's all."

"I know," I said. "But I don't have a brain tumor, Lucy. I've had more tests than a lab rat."

"So what is it, then?" she asked, tossing a piece of gum around the inside of her mouth with her tongue.

"You wouldn't believe me, even if I told you," I said, taking my bag and phone and heading for the door.

"Ooooh!" Lucy said, snatching up her own bag. "That sounds kinda spooky!"

"It's not spooky," I said as we walked together through the maze of corridors zigzagging across the school. "Well, at least I don't think it's spooky. I've kind of got used to it."

"Used to what?" Lucy asked, her eyes almost bulging from their sockets.

I knew that now I had grabbed her curiosity, I would never hear the end of it until I told her. I could see it all now, a constant stream of texts and Facebook messages until I told her my secret.

We left the school building, found a nice shaded spot beneath a tree, and sat down on the grass. With my legs crossed, I looked her straight in the eyes.

"If I tell you something, you will keep it a secret, won't you?"

"Oh my God, Charley, you're pregnant," she gasped, and clapped a hand over her mouth. "Your dad is going to go ape when he finds out."

"Pregnant?" I cried. "I'm not pregnant."

"I thought that's why you'd been having all those headaches and feeling sick," she said.

"What, since I was six years old?" I groaned.

"Oh yeah," she said, and I caught sight of the gum again. "It's just that I'm sure I read somewhere on the Internet that pregnant women feel sick sometimes."

"I'm not pregnant," I sighed.

"So why all the headaches?"

"You promise you won't tell anyone?"

"Cross my heart," Lucy said, and drew the sign of a cross over her chest.

I took a deep breath. "I *see* things."

"You see things?" she asked, her brow creasing. "Like what?"

"Dead people, I think," I whispered. "Or people who are dying. I'm not sure if I see them as they're dying, or if they're showing me how they died once they are dead, if that makes sense?"

"You've lost me," Lucy said. "What, so you're, like, physic or sump'n?"

"You mean *psychic*," I corrected her, and smiled.

"Whatever," she said, swishing the gum around again.

"No, I'm not psychic," I said. "Or at least I don't think I am."

"What, then?" she asked.

"I see these pictures inside my head. Flashes of them. They, like, come really fast—hundreds, sometimes thousands of them all at once. Like snapshots, I guess. They never really make any sense."

"But you said you see people in them," Lucy said, her interest growing. "People who are dying?"

"That's right," I said, looking back at the school, anywhere except at that agog look on her face; I already knew she didn't believe me. Would I believe me, if I were her?

"So, what, like murders, you mean?"

"Sometimes," I told her, now feeling dumb.

"Cool," she said, and I just caught the faintest of smirks on her lips.

"It isn't cool," I said. "It's a pain in the arse."

"You could be, like, in your own movie or summ'in'," she said. "Like *Paranormal Activity*. You could set up a camera in your bedroom and we could see what happens in the night while you're sleepin'."

"It's nothing like that," I said, wishing that I'd kept my mouth shut. Why had I said anything? But I knew why. I needed to talk to someone about it and I'd hoped that because I'd known Lucy since primary school, she might have believed me.

"You could make a fortune." She smiled. "Remember me when you're rich and famous."

"I don't want to be rich and famous," I said, gathering up my bag and standing.

"I was just messing about." Lucy smiled up at me. "Don't go, Charley. Stay and tell me more about some of these dead people."

"No, it's okay," I said. "I've got to get home."

I had been right. I did get a stream of text messages and Facebook comments, not just from Lucy but a whole bunch of other people. Lucy started it first, just the smallest of comments, on my Facebook page, but then it spread.

Tracy from tenth grade asked me if I could contact Heath Ledger as she wanted me to tell him that she hoped he rested in peace and she thought he played a mean Joker! That comment got over three hundred *likes*.

Some guy I'd never even heard of left a comment on my page saying that his dad wanted me to ask Lady Di who was driving the white Fiat in the tunnel the night she died. Another wanted me to give their love to Michael Jackson.

Then the comments got nasty, more sick and cruel. Some called me a witch, a freak. Someone wanted to know if I could ask Mary Ann Nichols what Jack the Ripper looked like. And all the while, Lucy melted away into the background.

But there was one person who hadn't melted away, and that had been Natalie. I hadn't known her that well before the bullying started, but that changed when she found me crying as I waited for the bus home from school.

"What's wrong?" she asked. "Are you hurt?"

"Kinda," I said, sniffing back my tears.

"You're Charley Sheppard, aren't you?" she said, coming to stand next to me. She clutched an armful of textbooks to her chest.

I nodded, waiting for the taunts to start.

"Okay," she said.

"Okay, what?" I said, glancing at her through my tears, waiting for the punch line to come.

"Okay so far," she said with a kind smile. "It's just that I've heard all this weird stuff about this girl called Charley Sheppard, and so far I haven't been melted by the laser beams that come out of your eyes and the lightning bolts you shoot from your arse."

"Is that what people are saying about me?" I gasped.

"Yep," she said with another smile. "And unless you have it stuffed up your sweater, I can't see your broomstick, either."

"They're saying I have a broomstick now?" I cried.

"And that you're followed around by dead people—I think someone said you talk to zombies or something," she added.

"Are they being serious?" I breathed. "They really believe that stuff?"

"They sure do," Natalie said. "And they say *you're* the one with issues. That's what's so funny, don't you think?"

"I guess," I said with a frown.

"So why look so sad?" Natalie said. "The next time any of the others give you any kind of crap, shoot 'em down with your exploding farts or set your dead friends on them."

I didn't feel like laughing, but Natalie's unusual view of the bullying I had been subjected to made me chuckle.

Then, giggling herself, she said, "What I don't understand is, if you really are a witch like the others say you are, why are you standing around in the cold waiting for a bus when you could be home already by using your broomstick?"

"Beats the hell out of me," I said with a shrug and a wide smile.

And that's how Natalie and I became friends. She just believed me. She believed *in* me.

But if I ever wanted my father to have such faith in me, I would have to prove my flashes were real. I would have to try to locate the place I had seen and find the man who had killed the girl named Kerry.

I swung my legs over the side of the bed, deciding now was as good a time as any. I'd go in search of the tiny building I had seen on the hill and the narrow dirt road Kerry had been dragged along. As I pulled on a sweater and a pair of jeans, I wondered where I should start my search.

I remembered hearing the sound of trains. So, wrapping up warm in my coat, I crept out of the house and headed in the direction of the nearby railway tracks.

***

With my hands thrust into my coat pockets, I headed across Marsh Bay and toward the railway line that cut across the fields on the outskirts of town. It was cold, and the faintest glimmer of winter sunlight was making the early morning sky look turquoise in the distance.

Reaching the edge of town, I followed the winding country roads in the direction of the track. I didn't have an exact location to fix on. Everything I had seen in my flashes had just been a snapshot of information, but I could remember seeing a tumbledown building with a broken chimney pot on top. Could it be the same outbuilding I had hidden in at Natalie's funeral? No, that hadn't had a chimney. It had barely had a roof and it hadn't been on a hill. But there had been trains running close by. I had heard them.

It's just a coincidence, I heard my father breathe in my ear. *You're putting two and two together and coming up with five. You only saw an old building in your flashes because of the outbuilding you discovered at the edge of the graveyard. Charley, your mind is just trying to make sense of the traumatic experience you've been through.*

I pushed my father's words from my mind. They were his doubts, not mine. I had to believe in myself.

Bent against the nagging wind, I pushed on, following the winding roads that snaked across the countryside. As the last of the stars winked out in the early morning sky, I stopped in the quiet country road to get my bearings. It was then I saw it. In the distance and on the crest of a small hill was a chimney pot sticking up from behind some trees. Could that be the run-down building I had seen in my flashes?

I couldn't be sure without taking a closer look. It could have been any old farmhouse or outbuilding, but my knees felt as if they had turned to rubber. I lurched forward, the ends of my long auburn hair whipping about in the cold wind. If it was the building I had seen, then my flashes were real and so were Kerry and her murderer.

Taking a deep lungful of freezing air, I headed along the road. I hadn't gone very far when I came across a dirt road leading off toward the hill. I heard the sound of thunder and glanced up at the sky. It was dank and overcast, but there were no signs of a storm. I realized it wasn't thunder but the distant roar of a train. I closed my eyes, the sound of my heart now beating in my ears.

Had I found the dirt road where the man in my flashes had left his car? Was I standing near to where the girl named Kerry had been dragged, kicking and screaming, through the undergrowth? Fighting the urge to drop to my knees, I swayed from left to right as if being blown by the wind. I was about to topple face-first into the puddle-ridden road when I felt a hand grip my elbow and steady me.

"Are you all right?" I heard someone ask.

With a gasp, I opened my eyes. A guy dressed in a dark suit and tie had appeared from nowhere and was now holding me firmly by the arm.

"Are you okay?" he asked again, his light blue eyes fixed on mine.

"Sure," I said, pulling my arm away. I took a step backward, nearly losing my footing in the mud.

The young guy shot his hand out and took hold of my arm again. "Take it easy," he said. "What are you doing out here so early?"

"Who are you?" I asked, ignoring his question. How could I answer it without lying?

"I'm a police officer," he said.

His eyes were the color of the sky on a bright summer's afternoon. His hair was black, and the lower half of his tired-looking face had grown dark where whiskers had started to show through. He looked like he had been awake all night.

Suspecting I was in the very same place I believed a girl called Kerry had been murdered, and not knowing who this man was, I pulled my arm free from his grip again. The guy was way past just good-looking, but that didn't mean he wasn't a killer.

"How do I know you're a cop?" I asked, taking another step backward in the mud.

With his eyes still searching mine, he fished what looked like a silver badge from his trouser pocket and showed it to me. There was a picture of him fixed next to the badge in the little black leather wallet. "I'm Police Constable Tom Henson," he said.

"Am I in some kind of trouble?" I asked him.

"Not unless you've got something to confess." He half smiled, placing his badge back in his pocket.

I couldn't help but notice how his smile made his face look kind of mischievous, like he was trouble somehow. I liked that. Even so, I broke his stare and looked away.

"So do you have something to confess?" he asked softly.

"No," I told him.

"You never answered my question," he said.

"And what question was that?" I said, glancing sideways at him. "You've asked so many already."

"What are you doing all the way out here so early?" Again, his eyes fixed on mine, and even though his hair was a mess and the stubble gave him the good looks of a rock star, I had to remind myself that he was a police officer.

"Taking a walk," I said.

He glanced at his wristwatch. "What, at just before seven a.m.?"

"I couldn't sleep," I said, and it wasn't a lie. "That isn't against the law, is it?"

"No," he said with that smile again. "It's just that there was an incident out here last night."

My heart started to beat faster again, and not just because he was hot. "What kind of incident?" I asked as casually as I could.

He was watching me closely.

"A young woman got struck by a train," he said.

It felt like I had been slapped, and I couldn't be sure if I physically flinched or not. It wasn't the girl's death that surprised me as much as the manner of it—exactly the same way as Natalie.

"Do you know anything about that?" he asked.

"No," I said with a shake of my head, trying to recover from my shock. "Why would I know anything?"

"It's just that you look upset by what I told you," Tom said.

"I'm cold," I lied.

"So am I," he said, with that half smile tugging at the corners of his lips again. "In fact, I'm cold, tired, and very, very hungry. I've been awake all night and could do with some breakfast. What do you say?"

"About what?" I said.

"Would you like to join me for breakfast?" he asked, taking me by the arm and guiding me away from the entrance to the dirt road.

"I haven't got any money . . ." I started, searching for an excuse. I didn't want to be asked any more awkward questions.

"I'm buying," he said, leading me toward a car parked around the bend in the lane and hidden from view.

I looked at the car. "Isn't it meant to have lots of blue flashing lights?" I asked as he opened the door for me.

"I don't drive around in a marked police car," he said.

"How come?" I asked.

"I'm a detective." He smiled and swung the door closed.

So a detective was investigating the death of the girl I had seen in my flashes . . . Perhaps having breakfast with him wasn't such a bad idea after all. He might mention something about the girl's death I could link to what I'd seen.

CHAPTER 8

I stood in line and looked up at the breakfast menu. The girl stood beside me. I couldn't think of anywhere else to take her other than McDonald's. I was new in town and didn't know of any other cafés.

"What do you fancy?" I asked her.

She blushed and looked back at the menu. I was yet to ask her name, but she was really pretty. Fiery auburn hair hung over her shoulders and down her back, her skin was creamy pale, and she had sharp green eyes. I could only guess her age, but she didn't look more than eighteen. That was okay. I could ask her questions about the death of the girl up at the tracks; I wasn't planning on interviewing her, but should I need to, she wouldn't need an appropriate adult present.

I suspected that her being at the scene of a death was more than mere coincidence. She had gone up there for a reason. There was a nervousness about her that told me as much. I could've driven her straight to the station, but she would've clammed up, especially if she had come across top detective Jackson and his collection of thumbscrews.

"I don't know about you, but I think I'm going to have a Big Breakfast and some hash browns."

"I'll just have tea, please," she said.

"Are you sure?"

"I'm sure."

"Okay," I said, and placed the order.

"You know you're not going to stay in shape if you keep eating fast food," she said.

I turned to her and smiled. "You think I'm in shape? Thanks for saying so."

"It's not what I meant," she said, her cheeks flushing.

"No?" I teased. "So what did you mean?"

"You're not going to be chasing too many criminals if you stodge up on junk food," she said. "I thought cops had to be fit."

"So you don't think I'm fit, then?" I winked at her.

"Oh, please," she sighed, rolling her eyes. "I'm going to find us a table." She headed off across the restaurant.

I paid and carried the food over to the table. Sliding into my seat, I said, "So, you never told me your name."

"Why do you need to know my name?" she asked, taking her tea and warming her hands against the paper cup. "Is this some kind of interview?"

"Are you always so hostile with every guy who buys you breakfast?" I shot back, taking the lid off my food.

"You're not just any guy, you're a cop." She smiled over the rim of her cup.

"Is that a problem?" I asked, forking scrambled eggs into my mouth.

"No problem," she said. "It's just that cops are meant to always be on duty, aren't they?"

Putting my fork to one side, I reached into my coat pocket and removed my radio. It hissed with static. I switched it off and placed it on the table. "Okay, so now I'm officially off duty."

"My name's Charley Sheppard."

"Good to meet you, Charley," I said, reaching out across the table.

Slowly, she took my hand. Her skin felt soft but cold. I let her hand go so she could warm it again around her cup.

"So how old are you?" I asked her.

"Are you sure you're off duty? It's just that this is beginning to sound like some kind of interrogation," Charley said. "Why do you need to know my age?"

"Just being friendly," I said with a shrug, returning to my food.

There was a pause. "I'm seventeen. Seventeen and a half, in fact. Actually, I'll be eighteen in just a few months. Well, six months . . ."

"So you're seventeen and a half." I smiled.

"Is that a problem?"

"No problem," I said with a casual shake of my head.

"So what about you?"

"Nineteen years, two months, three days, five hours, and four seconds . . ." I said.

"Ha-ha, very funny," Charley said, looking through the window and out onto the cobbled high street. A few people passed by, bent forward against the rising wind.

"I was just messing with you," I said, fearing my teasing might have hurt her feelings. "Honest, I'm sorry."

"It's okay." She shrugged.

I didn't need to be a cop to know she was worried about something.

"You look tired," I said, not knowing what else to say but not wanting the conversation to dry up. I needed to keep Charley talking.

"So do you," she said.

"Is that a polite way of telling me I look like a sack of shit?" I said. She just looked at me. Now I felt like I was on the spot. "I've been up all night," I told her.

"Investigating the death of that girl?" Charley said.

Why was she so keen to know that?

"Yeah," I said. "So why were you really up on that deserted road this morning?"

Charley looked out the window again. She did know something. I could see her whole body tensing up. Picking up one of the hash browns, I tore it in two and offered her half. "Go on, it's good," I said.

Looking down at the food and not at me, she took it from between my fingers. She pulled a piece off and popped it into her mouth. I watched her chew it slowly, thoughtfully.

"My best friend was killed by a train on the railway tracks a few weeks back," she said. She must have seen my look of surprise, because she quickly added, "Didn't you know? I thought it would be your business to know something like that. Her name was Natalie Dean."

Charley was right; I didn't know. I had made the move from force headquarters in Truro to the coastal town of Marsh Bay a few days ago, so I wouldn't have known about her friend's death. But why hadn't Harker, Taylor, or Jackson mentioned it? Why had they kept that from me? I didn't like the fact that I was being kept out of the loop.

I tried to mask my surprise. "I'm sorry to hear about your friend, but that still doesn't account for you being up on that remote dirt road this morning."

"I just wanted to go up to where she died, to pay my respects . . ."

"So she died in the exact same place as the girl last night?" I asked.

"I don't know," she said, sounding confused, as if I'd put her under some kind of pressure.

"So what are the chances of you stumbling across the very same place where a girl died?" Charley was right; breakfast was turning into some kind of interrogation.

"Look, I didn't have anything to do with Kerry's death—" Realizing her mistake, she stopped mid-sentence and looked at me.

"Okay. So how come you know her name was Kerry?"

"I don't," Charley said, looking as shocked as me.

"Yes, you do. You just said her name was Kerry."

"What I meant to say was I couldn't be certain her name was Kerry," she said.

I placed my knife and fork down on the table. "Look, what's going on here, Charley?"

"Nothing's going on," she said, white-faced.

I wasn't convinced she was involved in Kerry Underhill's death, but she knew something about it.

"Charley, we can either talk about this now over a nice relaxing breakfast or we can discuss it down at the station. I would much prefer to stay here. What do you reckon?" I tried to keep my voice calm so as not to upset her. I feared she might not talk to me, and I liked her.

She wrung her hands together. "You've got to believe me, Tom. I wasn't involved in that girl's death last night."

"So how do you know her name?"

"I see things. I have flashes," Charley whispered, as if she were sharing some sacred secret with me.

"You see things? What kind of things? What did you see?" To ask so many questions all at once definitely wasn't a great interview technique, but I was confused.

"I know her name because I saw it on her necklace," Charley said.

She knows about the necklace? I really should take her down the road to the station, but if I did, would she clam up?

"How do you know about the necklace?" I asked, my breakfast now forgotten.

"So she did wear a necklace?" Charley said with a tinge of excitement in her voice.

"You tell me," I said. "What else do you know?"

Charley leaned forward and rubbed her temples. She groaned as if in pain.

"Are you okay?" I asked, wondering if this wasn't all some kind of act to divert my attention from what she had been telling me.

"It's just a headache." She winced, screwing her eyes shut. "I get them from time to time."

"You look awful," I said as what little color she had left in her face drained away. This was no act. I picked up the cup of tea and closed her fingers around it. "Here, drink some of this." I helped her guide the cup to her lips. "Better?" I asked.

"Kerry didn't walk up to that dirt road last night," she said, her voice hollow and breathless. "She was taken in a car. She was dragged onto the tracks. I could hear the trains . . ."

"Charley, what are you talking about?" I said, reaching for her hands twitching uncontrollably on the table.

She brushed me away. Although Charley looked scared, her eyes

71

sparkled with excitement. It was as though she had been proved right about something.

"A part of me is so scared, Tom," she said, looking at me, her eyes wide.

"Why?" I asked her, not knowing or truly understanding what was happening.

"I'm scared because I saw that girl being dragged to her death, but there is another part of me that's happy, too," she whispered.

"How can you be happy about a young girl losing her life?" I mumbled, fearing that perhaps Charley had mental health issues I had failed to pick up on.

"It means I'm not losing my mind," she breathed. "It proves I haven't been making this stuff up. The stuff I saw in those flashes wasn't the work of my overactive imagination. They weren't dreams, nightmares, or hallucinations. They were real!"

"Flashes?" I gasped, realizing this was the second time she had used this word.

"I saw her, Tom. I saw Kerry," she said, rubbing her trembling fingers against her temples. "I saw her last night in my flashes."

"Right, slow down. What exactly are flashes?"

"Tom, listen! I saw that girl last night. I saw images of what was happening to her in my mind as I lay on the bathroom floor."

"Do you know how crazy that sounds?" I said. "It's impossible!"

"Why is it impossible?" Charley said.

"Because . . ."

"Because the stuff I see in my flashes is just the product of my overactive imagination?" she said with tears in her eyes. "I've been told that my whole life, but now I know that what I see in my flashes is true."

"I can't believe that, Charley," I said. "But what you're telling me implicates you in her death. Can you see that?"

"You're right. I am implicated, in a way." She sounded scared again. "I saw Kerry last night, yet I wasn't there. It was like she was showing me what happened to her."

"But why would she do that?" I asked.

"I think she wants me to help her . . . catch her killer," Charley said. "Perhaps that's what they've all been showing me . . ."

"They've?" I cut in. "You've seen more than one person?"

"Yes." Charley nodded. "But this is the first time I've found a physical connection between those in my flashes and the real world."

"And that's the problem," I sighed, not wanting to belittle her. "Stuff like this just doesn't happen in the real world."

Staring at me, a grim look of determination on her pretty face, Charley clenched her fists. "Kerry had blond hair, blue eyes. She was about eighteen. She wore blue jeans and white sneakers. There was a dirt road close to where she died and it was swimming with puddles. A man dragged her up that road and all the time he was calling her a bitch. Her mobile was ringing and the killer snatched it out of her hands and tossed it away. The ringtone was that song "Burn" by Ellie Goulding. The killer drove a white car. He parked it in the lane. I could see what looked like some kind of outbuilding with a broken chimney pot on top."

I stared at her. "You would know all of that if you had been there last night."

"But I wasn't; I was home," she said.

"So you say." There was an uncomfortable silence.

"So arrest me, then!" she finally snapped, shooting to her feet and thrusting her wrists across the table at me.

I glanced sideways and could see some of the other customers staring. "Sit down," I hissed.

Charley took her seat again.

"What did this guy—the one you say dragged Kerry down onto the tracks—look like?" I asked. I really did want to believe her. I had learned to believe in my instincts, just as I had last night when dealing with Jackson. I knew he had been wrong, and if what Charley was telling me was half-true, then my instincts had been right.

"I don't see the faces of the living in the flashes, only those who've died," she told me.

"Convenient," I sighed, sounding more flippant than I intended.

"I don't make up the rules," Charley said. She drew a deep breath. "For years I've been ridiculed and laughed at because of my flashes. Even my own father doesn't believe I see things. Do you think it was easy to sit here and tell you this stuff? I know what you're thinking—you think I'm some kind of crazy. But why would I risk that? Wouldn't it have been easier for me to stuff my face with hash browns and head off home again? I told you what I saw in my flashes because I got the feeling that perhaps you were different. You had a kind smile and you got me to trust you. You told me you were off duty and we were just here for breakfast. But you're just like everyone else. I just needed to talk to someone—a friend. But you're not a friend. You can never really be anyone's friend because you're a copper first. You'd probably arrest your own grandmother if you had to, so you wouldn't think twice about arresting someone like me."

"Have you finished?" I asked. "You seem to be forgetting that I haven't arrested you."

And how could I? What would I be arresting her for? I didn't even know if a crime had been committed yet. I didn't believe that Kerry Underhill staggered blindly onto the tracks and collapsed, like Jackson wanted everyone to believe, but I needed more evidence first.

Regardless of whether Charley was telling the truth, she knew something about Kerry Underhill's death. Whether that came from a series of supernatural flashes or she had some kind of deeper involvement but was just too scared to tell me yet, I knew I had to keep her close. Regain her trust.

In my heart I knew I really should take her to the police station and do a proper interview, but what would Harker and Jackson make of her? Walking into the police station with someone who claimed they had been having psychic visions about the death of Kerry Underhill wouldn't do any wonders for my credibility.

No, I would keep it all to myself for now. I would wait until I had more proof before I risked telling my colleagues about Charley. Besides, I couldn't deny that I liked her—there was something different about her, and not just the fact she claimed to have visions.

"So are you going to arrest me?" Charley asked.

"No," I said.

"You believe me, then?" she said, her voice sounding hopeful.

"I didn't say that," I said, taking a business card from my pocket and sliding it across the table.

She picked it up and inspected it. "What's this for?" she said, turning it over in her hands.

"My number's on it," I told her. "Call me."

"And why would I want to do that?"

"So you can tell me what you see in those flashes." I smiled, fishing my notebook out. "What's your number?"

She gave it to me without any further questions. Deep down, some part of me hoped Charley would call, flashes or not.

CHAPTER 9

Tom parked the car outside my house. My father was in the drive, working on his car. He looked up. He looked surprised. Did he believe that I had been in bed? It was light now, but still early for me. My father held a cloth in his hand and I could see that he had been waxing the back of his cab, where there seemed to be some kind of dent. I hadn't been aware that he'd had an accident. It didn't look very bad. My father placed the cloth on the roof of the car and stood looking at Tom and me. The wind swept his graying hair back from his brow. There was a bucket of soapy water at his feet, and his fingers looked red and raw from where they had been in the water.

"Is that your dad?" Tom asked.

"Yep," I said, opening the door.

"I'll say hello," Tom said.

"No, it's okay . . ." But it was too late. Tom was already out and standing on the pavement.

"Hey, Dad." I smiled.

"I didn't know you were up," my father said, shooting Tom a sideways glance. "Where have you been so early?"

"Just out walking," I said, closing the car door with my hip.

He eyed Tom again. Why did he always have to be so freaking hostile to my friends? I was nearly eighteen; couldn't I choose the people I wanted to hang out with? He was always telling me to get some friends and get out of the house. But Tom was a guy—and that's what he didn't like. I was his little girl.

Tom walked toward my father with his hand out. "Hello, Mr. Sheppard," he said, smiling. "I'm Tom Henson."

My father wiped his hands against his jeans, then gripped Tom's hand. He pumped it briskly up and down. "Hello," he said, without a smile.

There was an uncomfortable silence, filled only by the sound of the nagging wind. I felt the urge to say something, but didn't know what.

"So you're a friend of my daughter's?" my father finally said.

"Kind of, I suppose," Tom said, looking at me.

I smiled back and shrugged. Were we friends?

"It's just that I've never heard my daughter mention you," my father said.

"We've only just met," I started to explain, and then wished I hadn't.

"And you're letting him give you a lift already?" my father said, raising his eyebrows.

"It's okay," Tom said, unhooking his badge from his pocket. "Charley's quite safe with me. I'm a police officer."

"A police officer?" My dad's brows furrowed. "Is my daughter in some kind of trouble?"

"No, don't be silly," I said. "Tom just gave me a lift home, that's all."

"I see," he said.

But I knew Dad didn't see at all. He only saw what he wanted to and that was a young, good-looking cop giving his daughter a ride home first thing in the morning. Did he think I had snuck out in the night to see Tom and had been caught sneaking home? I could see my father's eyes narrowing. Those were the thoughts I guessed all dads had when their daughter first brought home a guy. But I wasn't bringing home a guy. Tom wasn't my guy. He was a cop.

"Well, it was good meeting you, Mr. Sheppard," Tom said with a wave of his hand. "But I've been up all night and I could do with some sleep."

My father scowled and I couldn't help but wonder if Tom hadn't made that last comment to tease him. I'd already got the impression Tom liked to tease people. He was kind of cocky, but in a mischievous, not an arrogant, kind of way. I hid my smile, looking down at my boots. Tom climbed into his car and fired up the engine.

"Come on, Dad, I'll make you some tea," I said, taking his arm and leading him up the drive toward the front door.

I heard Tom's car pull away from the curb and glanced back over my shoulder. He smiled at me, then was gone, his taillights glowing red in the overcast light of the morning. I pushed open the front door and stepped inside. Dad followed me into the kitchen.

"So where have you really been?" he asked.

I switched on the kettle. He took a seat at the kitchen table. His hands still looked pink with cold. I took my coat off and hung it over the back of a chair. "I couldn't sleep, so I took a walk up to the railway tracks."

"Why?" he asked.

I took two tea bags from a box on the work counter, refusing to look at him. "I wanted to see if I could find the place where that girl died."

"What girl?" he asked, his voice sounding stiff.

"The girl I saw in my flashes last night. The girl called Kerry," I said, splashing milk into the cups. "I wanted to see if I could find the place where she was killed."

"Enough already," my father said. I heard the sound of his chair scraping as he stood up. "This madness has got to stop, Charley."

"It's not madness," I said, wheeling around to face him. "I'm not mad, Dad. I found the place where that girl died. I saw the tumbled-down house on the hill. It was the same house I saw in my flashes."

"It was the place you came across the other day at Natalie's funeral," he said. "Your mind is playing tricks with you. It's understandable, Charley; you're grieving . . ."

"My mind isn't playing tricks on me, Dad, and it wasn't the same place. I was nowhere near the graveyard where Natalie was buried. And besides . . ."

"Besides what?" His boots made a clacking sound on the tile floor as he took a step toward me. The boiling kettle seemed so loud. I wanted to cover my ears.

"There was a girl who died on the tracks last night and her name was Kerry," I whispered.

"And how do you know this?" my father asked, his voice dropping, too.

"That police officer . . . Tom . . . told me," I said. "He told me a girl named Kerry Underhill was hit and killed by a train last night. So my flashes are real, Dad." I hoped this was the proof he needed. All I wanted was for him to believe me. That's all I'd ever wanted. But it was as though he hadn't heard what I'd said.

"What did you tell that police officer?" he asked, coming closer still.

"What do you mean?" Why was he so worried about Tom?

"Did you tell him about your flashes?" he said.

I turned away to pour water into the cups. Steam coiled up all around me, and I just wanted to sink into it. I wanted it to hide me from my father so I didn't have to answer his questions.

"You told him, didn't you?" he asked.

"Yes," I said, picking up the cups of tea. I had nothing to hide. I had done nothing wrong. "Have you got a problem with that?"

"Yeah, I've got a problem with that," my father said, nodding his head and looking at me.

"I can't see the harm in telling Tom if it helps the police catch the person who killed that girl," I said.

"But you don't know the girl was murdered," he said, exasperated. "You can't go around telling the police stuff that you don't know is true—that you don't know is *real*! You could be leading them away from what really happened."

"I know what really happened," I said. I felt the anger and frustration I always felt around my father growing inside me.

"Charley, you don't know! You can't know!" he shouted.

"But Tom said—" I started.

"I couldn't give a crap what that cop said," my father barked. "Can't you see, Charley? That cop will just use you for information."

"I think he believes me," I shot back.

"He probably believes you were involved somehow. You're probably his prime suspect."

"That's just ridiculous," I said, putting my cup down. I didn't want it anymore.

"No, you're ridiculous, Charley," he said.

It felt as though he'd slapped me. Hard. My father must have seen the look of hurt in my eyes, because he came toward me again, arms open.

"Don't," I said, raising the flat of my hand at him. "Don't touch me."

"I'm sorry, Charley, I didn't mean that."

"Yeah, you did," I said, biting my lower lip in an attempt to stop it trembling. I refused to cry. I wouldn't allow myself to shed one more tear in front of him. I was never going to fall apart in front of anyone ever again. Looking straight back at him, I took a deep breath. "I only went looking for that place because of you."

"What are you talking about?"

"I was so desperate to prove to you that my flashes were true, I crept from my bed and out into the dark and cold," I told him, my heart racing in my chest. "I just wanted you to believe. I just wanted you to believe in me." I felt tears stinging in the corners of my eyes. "But you're just like the rest. Do you really think I want to spend the rest of my life seeing people die?" I snapped.

"Charley, I'm just trying to protect you," he said. "That's all I've ever wanted to do. You're my little girl."

"I'm not six anymore," I said, heart still thumping.

"I know," he said. "But you will always be my little girl. I can't help feeling like that. I just don't want to see you being used."

"Who by?"

"By that cop," he said, inching closer still. "Don't you see, Charley? He will just bleed you for information about what happened to that girl you say was killed last night. That's what the police do—it's their job."

"Tom seems nice," I told him. "He could have arrested me. He could've taken me into custody and interrogated me."

"And he still might, Charley," my father warned. "All I want for you is to have some fun."

"So you keep saying," I said.

"You should be out with friends, not creeping around in the dark, looking for places where young girls have died. I think this has more to do with the death of Natalie than you might want to admit."

Then something struck me as hard as my father's unkind comment. What if Natalie had been killed by the same person as Kerry? They had both died on the railway tracks, at night, and both had been near some kind of outbuilding. Was there a connection? The phone call I'd received at the funeral. Had it really been Natalie trying to make contact with me?

NATALIE CALLING!

NATALIE CALLING!

NATALIE CALLING!

My flesh turned cold and felt as taut as a bowstring. My heart sped up and I looked at my father.

"What?" he asked, looking back into my eyes. "What's wrong now?"

I couldn't tell him. He would just get angry again and tell me I was making connections that weren't really there. I swallowed hard. "The flashes aren't connected to Natalie's death. I've been having them since I was six. Since Mum died."

He looked at me. He was so close I could smell the car-cleaning fluid he hadn't yet wiped from his hands.

"Dad, how did Mum die?"

"Don't go there," he said. "I know what you're going to say, Charley, but you're wrong."

"What's to say that Mum's death didn't trigger something inside of me?" I said. "I was so young I barely remember her. Any memories I do have of her are just like those flashes—broken."

"And that's why your mum's death hasn't got anything to do with this," he said, and I saw him tense up again. He'd always been reluctant to talk about her as I'd been growing up. But maybe her death did have something to do with my flashes.

I took his hand. Mine trembled and I knew he felt it. "Why did Mum kill herself?"

"Because she was unhappy," he said.

"But what did she have to be unhappy about?" I asked. "She had you, and she had me."

"It wasn't enough," he whispered.

"Why?"

"I don't know."

"Did she leave a note?" I asked.

"A note?"

"Saying why she wanted to kill herself."

He shook his head.

I drew a deep breath. "How did Mum die? You've never told me and I've always been too scared to ask."

"So why ask now?"

"Because, as I keep trying to tell you, Dad, I'm not a little girl anymore," I whispered.

"But . . ." he started.

"How did she die?"

Dad squeezed my hand and said, "She died just like Natalie and Kerry did."

"How do you mean?" I breathed.

"Beneath a train."

CHAPTER 10

TOM—MONDAY: 21:54 HOURS

I reached the police station with only minutes to spare before my night shift started. The station wasn't big, just two floors of offices and a holding area containing six cells. The town of Marsh Bay was small, set on the southwest coast of Cornwall. It wasn't busy like Truro and didn't attract the number of vacationers St. Ives or Penzance did.

I'd heard that Marsh Bay was pretty quiet all year round and practically dead in the winter. It could be so quiet that force headquarters had discussed the idea of closing Marsh Bay Police Station altogether and centralizing us all. But as yet that hadn't happened.

I liked the notion of being moved to a busier town after my attachment came to an end at Marsh Bay. It would be a good way of gaining experience, especially for someone young in the service, like me. But transfers weren't always easy to come by. Nowadays, most forces wanted to shed officers, not recruit them. So for the time being I was stuck in Marsh Bay, but I intended to make the most of it.

The CID office was on the ground floor, at the rear of the building. The whole department consisted of four officers, and that included Harker. Taylor was the skipper and Jackson the detective constable. There was another, Kent, but he was long-term sick, and that's how I had got my attachment; I had been brought in to cover his post until he returned to work.

Detective Chief Inspector Parker and Detective Superintendent Cooper were based at force headquarters in Truro, and should we ever stumble across a serious crime like a murder, then they would put in an appearance and extra resources would be drafted in from there. But until that day, we were pretty much left to our own devices, and Harker had built his own little kingdom within the CID at Marsh Bay Police Station.

I entered the CID office. Jackson was sitting at his desk, feet up, thumbing through a file. He glanced at me, then went back to the paper-work. Taylor was standing by the coffee machine in the corner.

"Want one?" she asked me, filling a large mug.

"No, thanks, Sarge," I said, shaking the rain from my jacket and hanging it off the back of my chair.

"Lois," she said, coming over and standing next to me as I sat at my desk.

"Sorry?" I asked.

"That's my name." She smiled. "I prefer it to sarge, skip, or boss. We're a small team. Like I said last night, you're among friends here, Tom."

I glanced over at Jackson and wondered. "Thanks, Lois," I said, feeling uncomfortable calling my sergeant by her first name. At training school and when I worked in uniform, I had always called my supervisors by their title, and I had grown used to it. Maybe it was different in CID, but I could never imagine Harker letting me call him by his first name, whatever that might be.

"Get much sleep?" she asked.

"Some," I said. I thought of Charley and what she had told me. My heart raced and I found it difficult to look at Lois.

"You look beat," she said, then took a sip of coffee.

I looked away. She seemed rather too interested in what I had been doing today. Did she know that I'd taken Charley for breakfast? I started to panic. Had someone seen us? Did she know? Did they all know?

"Just tired from last night, I suppose," I said, switching on my computer. "I couldn't get it out of my head. What with having to go and tell the Underhills that their daughter was dead."

"Not up to the job?" Jackson asked from behind his file.

"I'm up to the job," I said.

"We'll see," Jackson said, closing the file and placing it on his desk.

I almost wanted to laugh. His marine-style haircut glistened with gel, and he wore the tightest T-shirt I'd ever seen—it could have been sprayed on. He obviously wore it to show off his muscles. He could've been mistaken for a lifeguard—all that was missing were the skimpy shorts and flip-flops.

"What's that s'posed to mean?" I asked, wishing now that Lois had made me a cup of coffee so I could hide my grin behind it.

"What's the joke?" Jackson asked.

"Nothing." I smiled.

He gave me a distrustful look and said, "You know what? I don't think you're too tightly wrapped, kid."

"Cut it out," Lois said. "Give the guy a break. Tom just needs time to settle in."

"Well, he'd better settle in real quick," Jackson said. "Kerry Underhill's ex-boyfriend is in the interview room."

"Her boyfriend?" I asked. "What's her boyfriend got to do with this?"

"While you were stressing yourself out over the Underhills, me and the skip were out knocking on doors," Jackson said smugly.

"We went and spoke to the landlord of the Pear Tree Inn, where Kerry had been drinking last night with some friends," Lois explained. "It seems that she was having quite a good time until her ex-boyfriend, Jason Lane, put in an appearance. The landlord said it got quite nasty between them. He was just about to throw Lane out when Kerry stormed off."

"Has Lane got any priors?" I asked, wondering if he was who Charley had claimed to see in her flashes. I was desperate to know more about him. What did he look like? How old was he? What color car did he drive? But I had to be careful; I didn't want Lois or Jackson to become suspicious. They couldn't know that I had any information from a source that would be considered unnatural—*supernatural*!

"Just a bit of drugs and an assault," Jackson said, tossing the file he had been reading onto my desk.

I opened it and scanned Lane's old arrest record. He was last brought into the station eighteen months ago for possession of cannabis. I read the arresting officer's notes and my heart leapt into my throat: Lane had last been arrested out at that old disused house by the railway tracks.

I closed the file and looked at Jackson. "So you still think that Kerry Underhill took a shortcut across the tracks?"

Jackson ignored my question. "We viewed the CCTV from inside and outside the pub. You can see the row taking place. Lane looks to be quite agitated and at one point he even raises his hand at her."

"Does he hit her?" I asked.

"No," Lois said, putting down her mug of coffee and taking some statements from her desk. "You don't see him hit her on tape at least. But according to these statements we took from Kerry's friends, he did get nasty with her and called her all sorts of names."

"Like what?" I asked.

"The usual stuff," Lois said, glancing down at the statements. " 'Filthy bitch' looks like a favorite."

The word *bitch* made the hairs at the nape of my neck stand on end. The man in Charley's flashes had called Kerry a bitch, too.

"Kerry left the pub first," Jackson said. "You can see that on the CCTV. She turns left in the direction of home and the railway tracks, but then we lose sight of her. Lane leaves a few minutes later but goes to the parking lot at the back of the pub, where he gets into his car and drives away. That's the last we see of him."

I didn't know how hearing all of this made me feel. Part of me felt excited that what Charley had told me was true, but another part of me felt sick because I knew what had happened once they had both left the pub. But if Lane didn't admit to it, how would I ever prove it without saying what I had done and how I had implicated Charley? I looked at Jackson. "So you don't believe Kerry took a shortcut anymore?"

Jackson smiled at me and said, "I'm even more convinced of it."

"How do you work that out?"

"Can't you see what happened last night?" he sighed, as if he were trying to teach a child the ABCs. "Kerry goes out for the evening with her friends. Matey-boy Lane shows up. They get into a row and she storms out. He then follows her in his car. He tells her that he's sorry and just wants to talk to her. It starts to rain, so not wanting to walk home, she gets into his car with him. They drive around, and the row flares up again. He then tells her to get out, dropping her near the railway tracks. It's now pouring with rain and freezing cold, so Kerry decides to take the shortcut, collapses or trips because of too much booze, and *wham!* She gets hit by the train. End of story, case closed."

"Is that what you think happened?" I asked Lois.

"It looks that way," a voice says before she can answer. It was Harker, standing in the open doorway of his office.

"But—" I started.

"But what?" Harker asked.

"If it's such an open-and-shut case, why bring in Jason Lane for questioning?" I quizzed.

"To cover our arses," Jackson said.

"To cross all the *t*'s and dot all the *i*'s," Harker said.

"Was she drunk?" I asked Harker.

"Still waiting for the toxicology reports. The autopsy was done earlier today."

Then, with my heart starting to thump and that sick feeling in the pit of my stomach again, I said, "What about Kerry's mobile phone?"

"What about it?" Jackson asked.

"Has it been found?"

"Nope."

My heart began to slow, but there were a couple of questions I needed to ask, to fully put my mind at rest. "Has anyone tried to triangulate it to find out its location? Has anyone been in contact with the phone company to try and get a printout of any texts or calls that might have been made?"

"Faxed over the data protection forms earlier, but the phone company reckons it might take a few days for them to get back to me," Jackson said. "As for trying to trace the phone, it was probably smashed to pieces beneath that train, and you know as well as I do, if the battery is dead or missing, they won't ever be able to track it."

Charley had said that the killer had thrown it away. But how could I tell them I knew that?

"Is there something on your mind?" Lois asked, tearing me from my thoughts.

"Huh?" I said, desperate to hide the worry that she had obviously seen on my face.

"It looks like something's troubling you." She smiled, but I couldn't be sure if it was genuine or not. It was one of those smiles that said, *Come on, Tom, you can tell me you took that pretty young girl to breakfast and she told you lots of stuff about what really happened to Kerry Underhill. The pretty girl knows what really happened up at the railway tracks because she saw it in her head like lightning bolts. Go on, you can tell me all about what she saw. I won't be angry with you, because I'm your friend.*

Is that what she was really thinking behind her smile? "No, there's nothing wrong," I said. "I'm fine."

"Good," Harker said, "because I want you to go and speak with Jason Lane. See if you can't get him to tell us what happened last night after he left the pub. Jackson will go with you."

Jackson was already heading for the office door. "C'mon," he said. "Let's go and see what this dimwit has to say for himself."

Jason Lane wasn't anything like I had expected. Kerry seemed to have come from a good home with respectable parents. I doubted if they would have approved of Lane if they had ever met him. He sat on the opposite side of the interview room table from Jackson and me. His acne-scarred face was tilted downward so he didn't have to look at us. His long greasy hair hung in his eyes, and his nose piercing glimmered in the light from the overhead fluorescents. He had an untidy goatee with flecks of ginger in it, and his leather jacket was so worn and faded that it was no longer black but a washed-out gray. The guy looked a mess, and I saw that he wasn't in control. He slumped forward in his chair, and in the confines of the poky interview room, I could smell the distinctive scent of weed.

"Are you ready?" Jackson asked him.

"Ready for what?" Lane mumbled without lifting his head.

"To talk about what happened last night," Jackson shot back, and I could sense he was going to enjoy interviewing Lane. He was also going to take great pleasure in showing off his interview skills to me. Jackson laced his fingers behind his head, and leaned back in his seat. "Wakey-wakey, sunshine."

Lane said nothing.

"Have it your way, numbskull, but you don't get to leave here until you've told us what happened to Kerry last night," Jackson said, as if he had all the time in the world.

"But . . ." I said, "you're not actually under arrest. You're free to go at any time, though we would like you to stay and help us figure out how Kerry came to be on those railway tracks last night."

Jackson scowled at me and opened his mouth as if to say something, when Jason spoke.

"I can't believe she's dead," he whispered. His voice sounded broken, as if he had been crying.

"What do you expect if you dump your ex-girlfriend in the middle of nowhere in the dark and the—" Jackson started.

"I didn't dump her anywhere," Lane croaked, and this time he did look up. I could see his eyes were red and sore.

"What happened?" I asked, keeping my voice quiet.

"We had a row in the pub." He sniffed, wiping his nose on his jacket sleeve. "She left and I went after her."

"Tell us something we don't already know," Jackson said with an impatient sigh.

"I went after her because I felt bad for upsetting her . . ." Lane started.

"I'd feel bad if I called my ex-girlfriend an effing bitch and waved my fist in her face." Jackson sneered.

I shot a glance at Jackson. He continued to lean back in his chair, and I could see he was enjoying seeing Lane distressed. I turned back to look at Lane. "Go on, Jason."

"We broke up a few months back," he explained, looking up at me through his straggly fringe. "Kerry didn't like some of the people I hung out with. She said I was different when I was with them—you know—I used to act like a tool. So I finished with her, I put me mates first. I soon realized that she was right, of course, and I tried to get back with her, but she'd moved on and wasn't interested. I hadn't seen her for a few weeks, not until last night. I didn't know she was going to be in that pub. When I saw her, I couldn't help myself, I had to go and speak with her. But her friends started to butt in—you know, bad-mouthing me, piling on and stuff. They never liked me. Kerry started to join in and I lost my temper, that was all."

"So what happened after you left the pub?" I asked, not giving Jackson the chance to cut in.

"I drove around for a bit," Lane said, and sniffed again. "But I couldn't find her. I took the route that she would have taken home, but she'd gone. It was like she had vanished."

"Bullshit." Jackson sat forward. "Why are you lying to us?"

"I'm not lying," Lane said, still refusing to look at Jackson.

"Yeah, you are, and that causes me a problem."

"What problem?" Lane asked, his voice dropping to a whisper again.

"You'd only be telling lies if you had something to hide," Jackson said.

"I haven't got anything to hide," Lane said, looking down at the table.

"So what happened?" There was a moment's silence before Jackson said, "I'll tell you what happened, shall I? You went after her. You got her into your car—perhaps she didn't come willingly? Then once you had her trapped, you drove her out to some desolate spot like that deserted lane. And let's be honest, Jason, you would have known that place would be deserted as you've spent enough time up there smoking crack—you've even been arrested up there."

"That's not what happened," Lane said.

Jackson wasn't listening. "So you've driven up to that remote spot and you've begged her to go back out with you. She refuses and you get angry—you've already told us that you got angry with her. You told us that, didn't you, Jason?"

"Yes." Lane nodded. "But . . ."

"And we know that you've got priors for violence. You've been nicked in the past for assault . . ." Jackson continued.

"But . . ."

"So Kerry tells you to get lost and that just makes you even angrier," Jackson went on. "You lean over and try to kiss her, put your hand up her skirt to show her what she's been missing. But Kerry won't have any of it because she knows what a loser you are. All her mates know what a loser you are. They've just been laughing at you, mocking you. How dare they? You're going to show her that you're not a loser. You're going to show that bitch that you're not some kind of joke. You're going to show her what a real man you are. But she manages to escape. You go after her and she runs in fear. Kerry's scared of you, so in a panic, she runs through the dark, blinded by the rain. You run faster, calling her a bitch and waving your fists just like you did in the pub. But this time it's worse for poor Kerry, because it's just you and her and she doesn't have her friends' protection. And being the pathetic coward that you are, you hound her down onto those railway tracks. Then, when she thinks that she has escaped you, she looks back to see if you're still behind her and in doing so, she trips and falls. But she can't hear the train coming toward her, because all she can hear is you screaming 'Bitch! Bitch! Bitch!'" With each word, Jackson slammed his hand down on the table. "That's what happened, isn't it?" he screamed. "You're as guilty as if you pushed Kerry in front of that train with your own hands!"

"No!" Lane cried out, covering his ears with his hands. "I never touched her. I promise."

"You're a liar," Jackson said coolly. He got up and went to stand menacingly behind Lane. "You're so doped out of your skull, you wouldn't know the truth if it came and bit you on the arse."

"It's not true." Lane started to sob. "I would've never hurt Kerry. I loved her."

"What color is your car?" I asked Lane, just wanting Jackson to stop. This wasn't an interview; it had become an interrogation and I didn't want any part of it.

"Red," Lane whispered, tears running down his face.

"What has that got to do with anything?" Jackson grunted at me.

I ignored him and said to Lane, "What were you wearing last night?"

"What I'm wearing now," he sniffed, and by the look of his disheveled state, I got the impression he was telling the truth. I glanced under the table at his feet.

"We know what he was wearing," Jackson sneered. "We can see that on the CCTV, and the color of his car."

I stood up and opened the interview room door. "Jason, you're free to go now. I'm done."

Lane stood. Jackson shoved him back into his seat. "You might be done with him, but I'm not," he said.

"He's telling us the truth," I said.

"And how do you figure that out?" Jackson snapped.

How did I know that? Despite the kid having some minor convictions for drugs and an assault that took place during a drunken brawl outside a nightclub in Truro, Lane wasn't a killer. He was pathetic. But not only that, the car Charley said she had seen parked in the lane had been white, not red. It was unlikely Lane was responsible for the death of Kerry Underhill, and I couldn't sit back silently and watch Jackson persecute him.

"Can I have a word outside?" I asked Jackson.

"Stay put," Jackson said to Lane.

We left the interview room. I closed the door and we eyed each other in the corridor.

"What's your problem?" Jackson said. "I was just about to get him to cough and you started going on about the color of his frigging car and the clothes he was wearing."

"It's important," I said.

"Important, my arse." Jackson's face was red. "Listen to me, Columbo, you don't just walk in here and start throwing your weight around. I've been in CID for nearly six years—"

"So you keep saying," I shouted. "But you're wrong about him."

"I'm not."

"Just take a look at his boots, for crying out loud. It was raining last night and that dirt road was covered in mud and puddles. If Lane had chased Kerry like you reckon he did, then they would be covered with the stuff. But his boots are clean."

"So he washed them." Jackson took a step closer, but I stood my ground.

"Lane doesn't even bother washing his hair, let alone his freaking boots! Can't you see that he is genuinely upset by Kerry's death?"

"Give me a break; that's just an act," Jackson roared, his face so close to mine I could smell stale cigarette smoke on his breath. "You don't really buy the tears and the sniveling, do you? That's not a result of him crying; that's from all the shit he's snorted up his nose. The guy's a drug addict, for Christ's sake."

"He does a bit of blow," I said. "He's not on crack."

"I couldn't give a toss if he's stuffing Smarties up his nose and shooting crack through his veins. What matters to me is what happened to that girl last night."

"You've suddenly changed your tune," I said. "I thought you couldn't wait to write the whole thing off as an accident."

"That's before I got hold of Lane," Jackson said. "He has something to do with that girl's death and I'm going to tear him up for toilet paper."

Before I'd had the chance to try and convince Jackson he was wrong, Harker appeared in the corridor, looking grim. "What's going on down here? The custody sergeant said he can't hear himself think for all the shouting and hollering you two are doing."

"You'd better speak to Poirot," Jackson said, hooking his thumb in my direction.

"Henson?" Harker said. "What's the problem?"

"There's no problem," I said.

"Yes, there is. He's the problem," Jackson said. "He thinks he knows everything. I was seconds away from getting Lane to admit to taking that girl up to the tracks last night, when he has to go and poke his nose in."

"Did you?" Harker asked me, fixing me with his icy stare.

"Lane's innocent," I told him. "Jackson is wasting his time."

"See what I mean, boss?" Jackson groaned. "He reckons Lane couldn't have been involved because he hasn't any mud on his boots. I think the kid has been watching too many episodes of *Sherlock*."

"Is this true?" Harker asked me.

"What, that I've been watching too many episodes of *Sherlock* or that Lane is innocent because he hasn't any mud on his boots?" I regretted the words as soon as they left my mouth; I sounded like a wisearse just like Jackson said.

Harker pointed a bony finger at me. "You need to cool off."

"I don't need to cool off . . ."

"This isn't a debate," Harker said. "This is an order. Take the night off and go home."

"But—"

"Home!" he almost snarled. "Get some sleep. You look like a sack of crap."

Without saying another word, I skulked back to the CID office, snatched my coat from the back of my seat, and left the station.

I drove out of the parking lot, hardly remembering a time when I had felt so frustrated and angry. Why wouldn't anyone listen to me? Why wouldn't anyone believe what I was saying? Because I couldn't prove any of it, that was why. And what did I really know anyhow? Just a bunch of stuff that some pretty girl had told me over breakfast. Perhaps Harker had been right to send me home. Maybe I did need to cool off. Maybe it was me who had put his personal feelings before the case he was investigating. I had let a little flirting with a pretty girl go to my head. Why was I prepared to believe her and not my colleagues? Because something told me she was telling the truth. I had to know. I headed back toward the tracks and the little house on the hill.

I parked my car along the dirt road, then made my way down toward the railway tracks. It was full dark and the crescent moon did little to light my way. I took my police-issue flashlight from my coat pocket and peered to the left.

The freight train had long since gone and trains were once again thundering past in both directions. It was as if what had happened to Kerry Underhill the night before had already been forgotten, and the trains were back to carrying their freight across the country while the world slept.

Both sides of the track were covered with deep foliage. The first time I'd been here, it had been dark, and rain had been driving through the tall, leafless trees. The second time, I had come across Charley. Now that I was alone, I had a chance to have a good sniff around.

I forced my way through the undergrowth to the right of the area that led down to the tracks. Nettles and thorns snagged at my clothes and scratched at my hands. It didn't look as if anyone had been here before me, so Kerry Underhill must have gained access to the tracks through a hole in the fence near to where she was hit by the train.

I turned around and saw something through the close-knit trees. It was the house Charley had spoken about. Even though it sat on a small hill, it was so well hidden that from this side of the tracks, it couldn't be seen. I pushed on through the bushes and thorns until I found a narrow path. I followed it up the hill and through the trees until I stood before the derelict-looking building. I shone the flashlight over it. The glassless windows stared back at me like dead men's eyes. What had looked like a hovel from the tracks was in fact a small house that looked as though it hadn't been lived in for some time. It was covered in wild ivy and moss, and the bricks were yellow and green with age. The roof slanted inward at one end where too many slate tiles had fallen away. Perched on the roof was a broken-down chimney, exactly as Charley had described.

Just the sight of it made my heart quicken and my flesh turn cold. The front door was open, like an oblong slice of darkness in the front of the building. I stood before it, and with the sound of a crow squawking in the distance, I shone my flashlight into the darkness.

The floor was covered in mounds of bricks and rubble and there were several old beer cans and broken bottles littered about. I didn't need to be in CID to realize that the discarded syringes said this place had been frequented in the past by drug users—Lane and Co. There was a scratching sound in the corner. As my eyes became accustomed to the gloom, I saw a long black shape scurry along the back wall.

Rats! I hated them. Copper or not, I made my way from the abandoned house and back down the path. I hadn't gone far when I looked back, and already the old building was barely visible through the trees. All I could make out was that tumbledown chimney sticking up from the roof like a broken finger.

I reached the end of the path and got back on the dirt road. I looked left and could see my car parked several yards away. Unless you knew the location well, you would never have known about that tiny path that wound its way up the hill. Whoever had dragged Kerry to her death must have been local. They would've known about that hidden path. Lane would have known about it. My heart began to sink in my chest.

Perhaps Jackson had been right about him. If I'd never met Charley, then I would be thinking just like Jackson. Lane would be my prime suspect, too. But I had met her and she had told me something different, and I just couldn't shake that off, no matter how hard I tried.

Back in my car, I pulled my mobile from my pocket. The screen on the front flickered into life, then died. I tapped it against the dashboard. The phone hadn't worked properly in months and I knew I needed to get a new one. But it was one of those "pay as you go" phones and was cheap. I liked cheap—when it worked. I hit the phone harder against the dashboard and it flickered into life.

I texted Charley. Even before I'd hit SEND, I'd decided to bring Charley back out to the crime scene.

But was it a crime scene? I wondered, driving back to my apartment for some much-needed sleep. *Had a crime been committed?*

Perhaps Charley would be able to help.

CHAPTER 11

I lay on my bed, feeling too numb to move or even to sleep. To hear that my mum had killed herself by being hit by a train just like Natalie and Kerry was like being punched in the stomach. I closed my eyes and all I could see was my father slowly walking away from me.

"You can't just tell me that and walk away," I'd called after him.

"I never wanted to tell you, Charley," he said, pausing by the door to look back at me. "I wanted you to believe your mum had taken some tablets and fallen asleep. It was never my intention to let you know that your mum had . . . well, you know now, so no more secrets."

"But why?" I'd asked, looking at him. "Why did she do it?"

"Why did she drink so much?" He shrugged. "Why would I come home from work and find you screaming in your crib, with the same diaper on that you'd been wearing when I left for work eight hours earlier? Why was your mum crashed out on the sofa? Why did she have to climb into a bottle of vodka every day? I don't really know the answer to any of those questions even though they've haunted me for the last eleven years."

"You make her sound like a monster," I whispered, my heart feeling as if it had been crushed underfoot.

"No, Charley, your mum wasn't a monster," he said, still looking at me from the doorway. "Your mum was sick—she had an illness . . ."

"But didn't she love me?" I asked, unable to stop my lower lip from trembling however hard I bit into it. "I've always wondered that. If Mum had loved me, she would never have left me."

I could see he was struggling to find the right words.

"Like I said," he sighed, "it wasn't you or me that she was running away from, it was her illness, those monsters within her—that's what she was running from."

I heard the front door close and I was on my own in the semidark kitchen. I went to the sink and splashed water onto my face. It felt ice-cold and stung my cheeks.

Through the window, I saw Dad rubbing at a dent in the trunk of his car with his fingertips. His face looked ashen and his eyes dark. I felt bad for him. It couldn't have been easy raising me on his own, knowing that one day he would have to tell me what had really happened to my mum. How did you plan for something like that?

Maybe the death of Natalie and the girl in my flashes had opened up old scars, although I doubted if they had ever truly healed. Or maybe recent events had provided him with an opening he had always searched for but had never quite found. When would have been the right time to tell me what really happened to my mum?

I'd left my dad to tinker with his car, like he so often did these days, and gone to my room. When it got dark, he'd set off to cabbie for the night, picking up the drunks from the pubs, bars, and nightclubs.

I rolled over on my bed and looked at my iPhone. The battery was almost dead, but I couldn't find the strength to climb from my bed and recharge it. I felt like it was me who needed recharging. I checked for any unread messages. I don't know why I bothered, to be honest. No one sent me texts these days, not since Natalie had gone. I thought of my father and wished we hadn't fought.

As I looked up at that pink lampshade, the one that I had stared up at for as long as I could remember, I couldn't really blame Tom for not believing in my flashes. How could he make sense of what I had seen if I didn't really understand myself? Why did they come? Why had the flashes of Kerry been so strong—so intense? They had never been that strong before.

Perhaps it has something to do with mum, I thought. The flashes had started soon after she died. I didn't know what they were back then— just very vivid dreams—nightmares. I would wake, sobbing, my head throbbing. Dad would come to my bedroom and comfort me. But some nights when those flashes had been really bad and I just couldn't be settled, he would lift me into his arms and let me sleep next to him. I would lie in the dark and listen to the sound of him snoring. Other kids had counted sheep; I had counted my dad's grunts and snorts until I drifted off.

My iPhone beeped. I went to my messages and could see that I had received a text from someone. At once my heart leapt. Had the text come from Natalie's phone? I opened the text and squinted at it.

The text read:

> *I'll pick you up at 9 2morrow morning. Wrap up warm and wear some wellies! Tom.*

Scraping my hair behind my ear, I couldn't help but feel relieved the message was from Tom. But why did he want to meet up with me again? Was this a date? I doubted it. Who wore wellies on a date?

I'll be waiting, I wrote. Smiling, I sent the message.

CHAPTER 12

TOM—TUESDAY: 07:30 HOURS

The alarm clock woke me at 7:30 a.m., but after having only a few hours' sleep, I stuck my hand out from beneath the covers and switched it off. I hadn't slept well again. My tired mind scrambled with thoughts of Charley, dead girls under trains, and the sobs of a heartbroken mother.

Just five more minutes, I told myself, and promptly went back to sleep. I woke again at 8:36 and, seeing the time, scrambled from my bed and into the shower. I was going to be late to pick up Charley. Being late wasn't a good idea. I wanted to spend as much time as I could with her before I had to prepare for my evening shift.

I shaved with my hair still dripping wet, then threw on a clean but unironed shirt and a pair of jeans. As I raced from my apartment and into my car, I checked my watch. 9:03. *Damn!*

Careful not to trigger any speed cameras, I sped across town toward Charley's. The December sky was gunmetal gray. It was bitterly cold. I switched on the heater, but it just blew more cold air into my face. There was no rain, though, and for that I was grateful. I passed houses already decorated with Christmas trees and lights and they looked warm and inviting.

My mother and father's house always looked inviting at Christmas. But I wouldn't be going home. It wasn't that I didn't want to see them; it was the thought of my father leading me into his study and trying to persuade me to leave the police and join his law firm, again. I didn't want to spend my Christmas arguing with him.

As I drew closer to Charley's house, the realization of what I was about to do hit me. To take a civilian—a seventeen-year-old girl—to a potential crime scene was madness. And it wasn't just me who'd think so. Harker and all my other colleagues would be aghast if they ever found out. But what if Charley was right? What if Kerry Underhill had been taken against her will up to the railway tracks and killed? That would be a murder, right?

Nevertheless, if it were ever discovered that one of the investigating officers had taken a young woman out to the crime scene on the off chance she had received premonitions in a series of flashes, they'd be lucky if they spent the rest of their career slopping out the holding cells.

"I must be mad!" I said aloud, and sped up.

But who would ever know that I had taken Charley there? No one would. And what if she was right and the flashes were true? What if Charley saw some clue—something that would explain what had really happened to Kerry Underhill? What did I do with that information? I wouldn't be able to hide it, especially not if the girl had been attacked—murdered. I'd terminated the interview with Lane because of what Charley had already told me. And ending that interview had got me into a whole lot of hot water with Harker.

Half of me just wanted to stop, reverse, and head back to bed, pull the duvet up over my head and go back to sleep before I did something I might later regret. But the other half wanted to know what had really happened to Kerry Underhill. With Jackson desperate to stamp DEATH BY MISADVENTURE all over the case file at the earliest opportunity, I couldn't get what Charley had told me out of my head. I couldn't ignore it.

Besides, by taking Charley to the scene, I was hoping she'd reveal more clues, and those and her behavior might show me whether the flashes she saw were a glimpse of real events or just a figment of her imagination. I pressed down on the accelerator.

I parked the car at the curb and got out. Charley's father was in the drive again and was checking out what looked like a dent in the trunk of his car.

"Problem?" I asked, walking toward him.

"No problem," he said, glancing at me, then back at the dent.

"Back into someone?" I asked, not because I was really interested; I was just trying to make conversation with the guy. I'd got the feeling the day before that he didn't like me much. Was it because I was a copper or because he thought I might be dating his daughter?

"Someone backed into me," he said.

"I hope you exchanged details," I joked.

"No," he sighed, and his hostility appeared to soften. "It happened in Sainsbury's parking lot. Came out with the groceries to discover someone had hit the car. They never do leave their details, do they?"

"I guess not." I shrugged. "Is Charley in?"

"Where else would she be?" he muttered, and I detected that coolness toward me again.

I didn't want to fight with him. "I thought I might take her for a bite to eat—you know, breakfast."

He shot me a distrustful look, but before he could say anything, Charley appeared at the front door.

I looked at her and smiled. She had done as I suggested and was wearing a thick warm-looking coat. The collar was pulled up about her throat. Her auburn hair spilled onto her shoulders, and with the pale winter sun shining, her hair almost seemed to glow red. Even though she wore just an overcoat, jeans, and Wellington boots, Charley looked stunning. It was everything about her. Her thick mane of curly hair, brilliant green eyes, the little speckling of freckles which started on the bridge of her nose and covered her high cheekbones.

"Okay?" I asked her as she came toward me down the drive. I had that horrible uncertain feeling as I wondered again if I was doing the right thing. Did Charley even want to see me again? But when she smiled, I knew that she was as glad to see me as I was to see her.

Her father looked at us. "I thought you were taking my daughter out for breakfast? She's dressed as if you're taking her on some kind of hike."

"Just to McDonald's," I said. It was the best I could come up with.

"McDonald's?" Frank tutted with a shake of his head. "You fellas really know how to show a girl a good time these days." He looked at Charley. "Remember what I told you."

"Yes," she sighed.

Although I didn't know what it was he'd said, I suspected it was some kind of warning about me.

"Just remember," he said again, walking back to the house. Then he was gone, closing the front door behind him.

"What was that all about?" I asked.

"It doesn't matter now," Charley said.

"Okay." I shrugged but secretly wondered if it did matter.

"So has Mackey-Dee's flooded?" Charley smiled.

"What?"

"Why did you ask me to wear these things?" she said, staring down at the green wellies.

"I'll explain in the car."

CHAPTER 13

So where are you really taking me?" I asked as Tom steered the car away from the curb.

He looked pale and tired, and his knuckles shone white where they gripped the steering wheel. "Are you all right?"

Tom stared straight ahead. "I couldn't stop thinking about what you told me. The stuff you said about Kerry Underhill and the house on the hill with the broken-down chimney."

"What about it?" I asked.

"I went back to that dirt road, back to where Kerry Underhill met her death," Tom said. "It really wasn't that I didn't believe what you told me. I never thought you were a liar. It's just I couldn't believe you could know that stuff about her—about what happened to her."

"Isn't that the same thing?" I asked.

"No," he said. "I didn't for one second think you were making up stories. I'm not like those other people—like your father. I just couldn't believe you could've seen what happened to her, if that makes sense."

"Not really," I sniffed, and stared out the windshield.

"If I thought you were just telling me a pack of lies, Charley, I could have arrested you yesterday morning."

"What for?" I glanced at him.

"For wasting police time?" he said, looking ahead at the road.

"It was you who invited me for breakfast, remember?" I said. I knew he was clutching at straws. "You don't look as if you've had much sleep. I've been playing on your mind, haven't I?"

"Don't flatter yourself," he smirked.

"I didn't mean it like that." I smiled back. "You've just got to know if I was telling the truth."

"And were you?"

"I guess you're going to find out one way or another today," I said, looking at the flat, pale sun as it slipped behind a scrub of cloud.

"I want to take you back there, not because I don't believe you," he whispered as if he was telling me a secret that he didn't want anyone else to hear.

"Why, then?"

"Because you might be able to see more. Maybe by visiting the place where Kerry died, you might have more of these flashes you say you have . . . You might *see* more."

"More of what?" I asked, my stomach knotting.

"Think about it for a moment," Tom said. "If you saw all of that stuff in the flashes you had in your bathroom, miles away from the death, what might you be able to see if you were closer—if you were right where Kerry Underhill died?"

"I don't think I like the sound of this, Tom. I don't even know if it works like that. I've never done anything like this before. The flashes have come to me at home, school . . . Trying to make them come where a death has actually occurred scares me."

"You don't have to be scared," he said, glancing at me again. "I'll be with you the whole time. I won't leave you. And if it doesn't work, we haven't lost anything."

"It's not being on my own that scares me." Now it was my turn to whisper. "I'm scared of what I might see."

"If you start to see stuff that you can't handle, I'll get you out of there. I promise," he said.

Then, thinking of the warning my father had given me about Tom being a cop, I said, "How good will it look for you at work? I mean if you could solve this case, find out the truth about what had happened to Kerry—that would be good for you, right?"

"Is that what you think this is all about?" he asked, sounding hurt. "Climbing the ladder?"

"Isn't it?" I said, trying to read him.

"No, it's not," he said. "If what you saw is true, there is someone out there who hurt Kerry Underhill and maybe your friend Natalie, too. He might not have pushed them both in front of trains, but he had something to do with their deaths. And whoever he is, he needs to be caught. He's responsible for Kerry's death. I couldn't give a shit what my colleagues think of me, or I wouldn't be here with you right now. What's important is getting some answers for the Underhills and for their daughter, Kerry."

"Okay, I'm sorry," I said.

"Don't be sorry," Tom told me. "I'm the one who should be sorry. I should've thought more about how this might make you feel. I'm being selfish, but not for the reasons you thought. If you would rather go and get something to eat, I'll understand."

I didn't answer him at first. I did want to help. I did want to find answers for Kerry and maybe Natalie, too. But I had questions of my own that needed answering, like was my mother's death connected to my flashes in some way? Had I had such vivid images of Kerry's death because she died in similar circumstances to my mum? Was it Natalie who had tried to contact me in the graveyard? Maybe by going to where Kerry died, I might find the answers to my own questions.

"It's okay. I'll do it," I said.

The dirt road was narrower than it had seemed in my flashes. Tom stopped the car and we sat silently together. My heart was racing so fast that I thought it just might burst from my chest at any moment. A wind had picked up and I could see the tree branches bending back and forth.

"Are you okay?" Tom asked, placing a gentle hand over mine. I didn't brush it away. "You don't have to go through with this if you don't want to."

"No, I want to," I told him, and opened the car door. It was freezing cold, so I pulled my coat tight about me. My hair blew around my face and shoulders and I wished that I'd tied it into a ponytail before I'd left home. Tom came around the front of the car.

"Well?" he asked me.

"Well, what?" I said.

"Do you see anything yet?"

"It doesn't work like that, Tom," I said. "I told you, it might not work at all."

"Okay," he said.

"Just give me a minute or two." The pains that warned me the flashes were coming crept up the right side of my face.

Tom walked past me and pointed to a nearby hedgerow. "I found this . . ."

"Stop!" I snapped, raising a hand. "Don't tell me anything."

"Okay." He sounded like a scolded child.

I heard a rumbling sound. At first I couldn't tell if it was coming from inside my head or farther away. I closed my eyes, but there were no pic-tures—no flashes. The rumbling came again, this time louder, nearer. I opened my eyes. A train.

It was the distant sound of a train thundering toward us. To hear it reminded me instantly of the images I'd seen the other night. My head snapped backward as if someone had yanked on my hair, and the searing bolt of pain streaking across my brain told me the flashes were coming.

CHAPTER 14

CHARLEY—TUESDAY: 10:43 HOURS

"A re you all right?" Tom's voice was fearful. "What's happening to you?"

"Don't touch me!" I hissed, one hand clamped to the side of my head, the other pushing him away. "Keep away, Tom."

"Charley . . ." he said, but his voice was drifting away, as if he were shouting from the bottom of a deep well. He was drowned out by the sound of that train inside my head. It was so loud it was as if I were being dragged under its wheels.

Flash! Flash! Flash!

Those bright white lights exploded inside my head and in them I saw the train bearing down on me. The front of it almost seeming to grin, like a huge steel monster coming out of the darkness. The train driver's face swam in an inky pit of black, his eyes wide. I was suffocating beneath the stench of grease and oil. There was an ear-piercing screech of brakes and suddenly my whole body was on fire.

The flashes stopped. I opened my eyes to see Tom standing beside me, his face sick with worry. I looked at him, the palms of my hands pressed against the side of my head, my eyes watering.

Tom took a piece of crumpled tissue from his pocket. "Here, use this."

"Thanks," I said, wiping the tears away.

"Are you okay?" he asked.

"Just give me a moment," I said, screwing up the piece of tissue. I looked hard at him. "Scared?"

"Well, yeah," he whispered. "You don't look very well, Charley. Perhaps we should stop?"

"I'm used to it," I said.

"Did you see anything?" he asked.

"I saw the train just as Kerry would have done. It was like I was lying right in its path as it raced toward me."

"Has that ever happened before?" he asked me.

"Yeah, but not so intense."

"How do you know it was Kerry's eyes you were looking through?" he asked.

"Who else could it have been?" I said.

"I don't know," he said. "Did you see anything else?"

No sooner had Tom spoken than something new happened. It was as if his car were flashing with bright white light.

"Do you see that?" I breathed, walking back toward his car.

"See what?" he asked.

"Your car. Look at your car, Tom."

"What about it?"

"It's sparkling," I murmured.

"Sparkling?"

"Yeah, like it's been showered with glitter." I held my hand up in front of my eyes to stop them from being blinded by the bright white lights that popped and glimmered all around it; they looked like a million swarming fireflies. "It looks beautiful." I had never seen anything like it before.

"Charley, there are no lights," Tom said from behind me, and just like before, his voice faded away, as if snatched by a gust of wind.

I continued toward the car, one hand held over my eyes, the other stretched out before me.

Flash! Flash! Flash!

Tom's car wasn't there anymore. In those rapid, fleeting pictures inside my head, I saw another car. It was white. The passenger door was open. There was the sound of someone pleading—Kerry. It was Kerry I could hear.

Please let me go! she sobbed.

Flash!

I saw hands yank her by the wrist from the passenger seat. I felt a spike of pain in my own wrists, as if invisible fingernails were cutting deep into my flesh. Another blinding snapshot of her face. Her pretty eyes pleading with him. Another burst of white. Fingernails clawed at the side of the car. I saw her fingers scraping away the paint with a sound like metal scraping over ice. A chill ran up my back and I felt sick. Then the flashes and bright lights disappeared.

"Charley?" Tom said.

"Whoever brought Kerry up to this place parked right here," I said, pointing at his car.

"How can you be so sure?" he asked.

"I saw lights around your car and in them images of a different one. I couldn't be sure of the make, but it was white. I saw Kerry being dragged from it. I saw her scratch at it with her fingernails. Get someone to check under Kerry's nails."

"For white paint?" Tom said.

"Yes," I said. "I saw it. The paint would have come from his car."

Tom reached into his coat pocket and pulled out his notebook. I turned back to look at Tom's car, but it just sat there in the gloom beneath the bruised sky. There were no more lights—or so I thought. In the hedgerow, I saw them again. They were neon white, the size of bottle-caps, blinking on and off as if trying to grab my attention.

I walked around the back of Tom's car and headed toward them. "Can you see the lights this time?"

Tom looked up from his notebook. "What did you say?"

"You can't see them, can you?"

"See what?" he asked, coming toward me.

"More lights," I whispered.

They hovered around a gap in the bushes and nettles. I went toward it, and my head jerked to the right. More flashes. Mud. Puddles. Kerry's dirty sneakers being dragged through them. I opened my eyes, pushed the undergrowth apart, and the lights disappeared as quickly as a set of Christmas tree lights being switched off.

A narrow path spiraled into the gloom on the other side of the bushes.

"I found this earlier," Tom whispered behind me. "It leads to . . ."

"Shhh," I said. "Don't tell me."

"Sorry," he said.

I made my way up the path, more lights appearing in the distance as if showing me the way. All the while my head thumped, as though my heart were inside my skull instead of my chest. Every few feet the flashes would shatter like shards of glass inside my head, each one a picture of Kerry being dragged through the undergrowth. She cried out, her shrill voice all around me.

There was music, too—faint—in the distance. Ellie Goulding singing "Burn." Kerry's phone lighting up the night.

Please let me call my mum, Kerry called out.

Shut up, you silly little bitch! the man spat.

My blood felt as if it had turned to ice in my veins. The vision's clarity took my breath away. I felt it deep inside, and my mind screamed in trauma. This was much worse than I had ever felt it before.

I opened my eyes to see the building with its tumbledown chimney.

"This is the place I saw." I gasped, not knowing how I should be feeling. As Tom said, I would never have known this place existed if I hadn't seen it in those flashes. What I'd seen was real.

My head hurt, but not as bad as before. The pain was a dull thud, like a toothache. The lights that blinked on and off all around the house eased the pain. I didn't understand why, but whatever the reason, I was grateful for it, although they couldn't take away my feeling of shock.

Being able to stand before the ruined house showed me what I saw in my flashes was real, but it didn't fill me with joy and relief. I felt as if my skin was peppered with goose bumps even though it felt hot. It was as though I was burning from inside out. Was it because I was standing so close to a place I had seen in my flashes?

The world swayed, then swam back into focus again. The very air around me felt charged with static electricity. I felt sick, as if I'd gone around too many times on a merry-go-round.

In my flashes, the tiny, derelict house hadn't been illuminated by bright white lights that flickered all around it. The house seemed trapped in a snow globe, and every so often, some invisible force took hold of it and gave it a good shake, causing a snowfall of light to shower down all around it.

"Do you want to take a look inside?" Tom asked me.

"Yes," I said, slowly making my way toward it. The air fizzed in my ears. I felt unsteady on my feet.

As I moved closer, the lights began to dim, flicker out. I looked up as the last of them winked out, and all I could see was the endless murk of the winter sky.

The doorway to the house looked like a gap in a row of front teeth. I walked toward it. With Tom at my side, I reached the opening, then paused. Something felt different, wrong.

The flashes had been so vivid this time, so much so that they shook me to the core, but inside I felt an emptiness, as if I had lost something.

I waited for the flashes to come again, but in my heart, I knew they had gone.

CHAPTER 15

What's wrong?" I asked.

Charley stood before the open doorway of the house, kneading her temples with her fingertips. "The flashes . . ."

She looked bewildered, like a child who's lost sight of her mother.

"What about them?" I said.

"They've gone," she said, screwing her eyes shut.

"Gone where?"

"How should I know?" Charley shot a glance at me, lowering her hands and folding her arms across her chest. "It's not like they go anywhere . . . but I feel different somehow, hollow."

"But you said they had gone."

"I know what I said." She glared, looking as frustrated as I felt. It was as if we had got so far and now the information had dried up.

"Can't you *see* any more?" I asked. "Aren't any more pictures going to come through?"

Charley looked lost somehow, disturbed. "I'm not some kind of freaking tap that you can turn on and off!"

Her hair blew about in the nagging wind. Nearby tree branches screeched and the hanging door of the house slammed closed. Both of us flinched backward. It was as if it were telling us there was no more to be seen—no more secrets to be given up. Charley shivered, with fear or the cold, I couldn't be sure. She looked lonely, even though I stood just feet away.

I fought the sudden urge to go to her, wrap my arms about her slender frame, and hold her tight. I couldn't. She was a potential witness to a crime. Witness? Crime? Who was I trying to kid? I couldn't be sure of either. The only thing I could be sure of was that if I was caught with Charley anyplace near where Kerry Underhill had died, my feet wouldn't touch the ground as Harker kicked my arse out of CID.

"I'm sorry," Charley said. "The flashes have stopped."

Or had they ever really been there? I wanted to say, but that would've just been cruel. Yet I couldn't help thinking it as I stood and looked back at Charley. Slipping my notebook into my pocket, I didn't know who was kidding themselves more—me or her? Charley for believing she could see what had happened to Kerry Underhill, or me for even entertaining the idea.

Lowering my stare, I said, "C'mon, let's get out of here."

"Why?"

"You said your flashes had stopped, so what's the point?" I said, maybe a little harsher than intended.

"So you've finished using me, is that it?" Charley said, her green eyes bright with anger. No, it wasn't anger I could see, it was hurt.

"It's not like that . . ."

"Then what is it like?"

"I should've never brought you out here," I said. "C'mon . . ."

"You don't get to just walk away, Tom," she snapped. "If my flashes were still shining brightly in my head, you wouldn't be going anywhere right now; you'd be standing there scribbling away in your little note-book. Taking down every little thing I told you."

"I've heard enough," I said.

"Enough of what?" Charley asked. "Enough of me telling you how it is, or just enough of *me*?"

Taking a deep breath, I looked at her. "Any other time, any other situation, I couldn't imagine myself ever having enough of being with you, Charley. But it isn't like we've met in some bar or out with friends. We met stomping all over a crime scene, for Christ's sake. Don't you get that? Don't you see I could land in the shit for bringing you within a mile of this place?"

"So why did you?" she yelled, clenching her hands into fists. Before I'd had the chance to defend myself, she said, "Look, don't even bother trying to explain, Tom. It looks as if my dad was right about you. You did just want to use me. I should've listened to him."

Charley turned and hurried away.

"Hey!" I yelled. "Where are you going?"

"Home," she called, sounding as if she was crying.

I went after her. "Let me give you a lift."

"I'd rather walk."

"Charley!" but she was gone, disappeared among the hedgerows and bushes.

I forced my way through the undergrowth. I had brought her out here, so it was down to me to make sure she got home safely. Reaching the dirt road again, I looked left and right, but she was nowhere to be seen. "Charley!" I called out again, but there was no reply.

I sat in my car, the engine idling. Should I go in search of her? I wanted to. I was worried. I tried to push away thoughts of Kerry Underhill being dragged along the dirt road. Was there a killer out there? I only had Charley's word that there was, and the train driver's description of how he had seen Kerry lying in an odd pose between the tracks. There was still a chance that the killer was Jason Lane, and he would have no reason to harm Charley.

The temptation to just go home, climb into bed, pull the blankets over my head, and forget about her was huge. But I knew in my heart as soon as my eyes were closed, I would see Charley lighting up the darkness of my mind. I drove out of the narrow lane and back onto the country road. I had several hours to kill before my night shift started and they seemed to stretch out before me like a desolate road.

I would go back to my flat, but not yet—I needed to clear my head. As if on autopilot, I drove down the country roads toward the coast. As I drew near to the jagged cliffs that dropped away into the ocean, the wind buffeted the side of my car. I drew to a stop on a flat piece of ground. Grass flecked with sand blown up from the shoreline lay on either side. Seagulls squawked overhead as they circled high above, their beady black eyes constantly in search of food. I could hear the waves crashing against the granite rocks below.

Settling back in my seat, I switched on the CD player. "I Will Wait" by Mumford & Sons seeped from the speakers. I adjusted the volume so the music became nothing more than a distant sound track to my thoughts. Charley was the first to fill my mind. If I were to be honest, she hadn't left it since she had marched away in tears. Could I blame her for being upset—*angry*—with me?

No, not really. I had used her in my own way and I couldn't deny that. It wasn't as if I wanted to intentionally hurt her, but I had done it all the same. That's what happened when you were trying to prove yourself—people had the habit of being stepped on and squashed. Isn't that how anyone reached the top of their profession? I should know. I had seen my own father climb over enough people to become a partner in the firm of lawyers he worked for.

He had been relentless in his pursuit of being the most notorious defense lawyer in London. I stared up and watched the seagulls, remembering how my father had never wanted me to be a police officer. He had wanted me to join the firm—but there had been another firm I'd rather be a part off. I had never been able to understand how he defended some of his clients.

To most right-thinking people, their guilt was obvious, but my father would fix me with his stare and tell me that everyone was entitled to a defense—that those he represented had a voice. But the victims had a voice, too. I couldn't help but remember how my father had chuckled when I told him I wanted to join the police service. I could still hear him laughing now, and I turned up the volume on the CD player sandwiched into the dashboard of my car.

You'll never really help anyone by joining the police, he had said, and smiled. *It's a thankless task.*

But I wanted to prove him wrong. I wanted to be able to help Kerry Underhill and not the man who had hurt her. That was the difference between me and my father. But in my desire to prove my father wrong, I had hurt someone very special and quite possibly put her in danger. Whether or not Charley really could see what had happened to Kerry Underhill—that's not what made her special. It wasn't why I felt a connection with her. I wasn't the only one who had something to prove to their father.

With Charley at the forefront of my mind, I pulled my mobile phone from my coat pocket. The screen flickered again, so I bashed it against the dashboard.

"Charley." I sighed, thumbing through my contact list in search of her number. My thumb hovered over it. Her name and number stared up at me. Taking a deep breath, I placed the phone back on the dashboard. I didn't want to add to the hurt I'd already caused . . . but I needed to know if she was okay.

If Charley was to be believed, there was a murderer at large and I had left her all alone. I took the phone from the dashboard again.

For God's sake, Tom, grow some balls, I heard my father whisper as if sitting in the backseat.

And however much the memory of his voice got my back up, he was right—I needed to grow some and fast. I had left Charley alone out here where a murderer was killing young girls. What sort of cop would do a thing like that? Not a good one.

I pressed Charley's number with my thumb.

"The person you are calling is unable to answer . . ."

Charley was either in a dead patch or . . . I started up the engine. The clock on the dashboard read 15:47. It was beginning to get dark. Flipping on the headlights, I sped back toward the road and away from the cliffs. I needed to find her—make sure she was safe. But where to start? Most of the roads out here were nothing more than a winding maze.

Trace the route she would have taken from the dirt road and then follow it back into town, I told myself. Charley would be just fine, and once I knew she was safe, and I had taken her home, I would still have enough time to go back to the railway track and the dilapidated house and look for some clues the old-fashioned way. Kerry's phone still hadn't been found. Charley had said the man who took Kerry had thrown it into some nearby bushes . . .

I had to try and forget what Charley had told me and get on with some solid police work, but I knew in my heart I couldn't. With the last of the wintry daylight fading fast, I raced back in the direction I had last seen Charley. I drove the desolate and winding roads, my fingers gripping the steering wheel. I leaned forward in my seat and scanned the road for any sign of her. The daylight was fading with each passing moment. I drove around and around, peering left and right into the gloom.

Could she have reached home already? I doubted it.

It was as if she had vanished. My heart started to race. I licked my dry lips. How could I have been so stupid—so cruel to someone I'd promised to help? What if Charley had gone back to that ruined building? What if she had stumbled across . . . what if? I saw Charley peering out at me from beneath the wheels of a train . . . her eyes blank . . .

I shook my head, desperate to rid my mind of that hideous image, then realized I was back near the dirt road that led down to the railway tracks.

Killing the engine, I climbed from my car. It was almost full night now, so I took a flashlight from the trunk and switched it on. A thin beam of light cut through the darkness. A train thundered past in the distance. Pulling up the collar of my coat, I set off in the direction of the tracks.

I hadn't gone very far when I heard the sound of a girl scream in the distance. I stopped dead. Whoever it was, they sounded terrified. The scream came again and I raced through the dark toward it.

CHAPTER 16

I didn't know how long I'd been wandering round the narrow country roads that crept away from the area where Kerry Underhill had died. All I knew was that I felt cold and pissed off. It had been Tom's idea to come out to the house, not mine. It was me who was doing Tom the favor, not the other way around.

It was bitterly cold and I longed to go home and sink into a nice hot bath. But I couldn't go home. My father would be there and the first question to trip off his tongue would be, "How did breakfast go?"

What was I to tell him I'd been doing for the last few hours? "Breakfast was great, Dad. I ended up back up at that derelict house seeking out dead people in my flashes. Oh, and by the way, you were right about Tom; he was nothing more than a user."

I couldn't bear to get into another row with my dad and I didn't want to see the *I told you so* look in his eyes. Even if it meant freezing to death, I wouldn't go home just yet. I needed time to get my head together.

Most important, I needed to figure out why the flashes had suddenly stopped. I'd never had any control over them—they controlled me. It was the flashes that decided to come; I had never been able to summon them. And that's why I was never going to get my dad or someone like Tom to believe me. I sounded like a cheap fairground fake. I could give generalizations, nothing really specific. But I had seen the white car the killer had driven and the paint under Kerry's fingernails. Hadn't that been specific enough for Tom? Obviously not; he had wanted more. But was there any more to see? Would my flashes show me any more about the killer and what happened to Kerry?

The longer I walked, hands thrust into my coat pockets and head tilted down against the wind, the more my own frostiness melted toward Tom. Now, I wasn't going soft on him because of his roguish grin, deep dark eyes, and black messy-looking hair; it was more than his obvious good looks and cocky charm. I sensed that, deep down, he did believe me. His feelings of frustration weren't so much to do with me as with his desire to solve the case. It seemed to really matter to him that he find out what had happened to Kerry Underhill. Despite his cockiness, there was a part of Tom that cared or a part of him that needed to prove himself to someone. I understood all about that. I didn't know very much about the police, only what I had seen on TV, but I don't ever remember seeing anyone as young as Tom on any of the shows. The cops who always solved the cases were old with silver-white hair and acted grumpy and pissed off the whole time. They usually had a problem with drink and even bigger problems with their wives. Most of them smoked like it was going out of fashion and they looked red-faced and stressed-out the whole time. Tom didn't look like any of those coppers I'd seen on TV. Maybe he *was* trying to prove himself. Maybe, like me, he was having problems fitting in? Hadn't Tom told me he was new to the area and had just joined the CID? I knew what it felt like having to prove yourself the whole time. I would be doing exactly the same thing when I returned to college after the Christmas break. Now that Natalie was gone, I would be going back to college alone. It would be like my very first day. Trying to make a friend in the sea of faces that watched me as I passed down the corridors, sneering and pointing, laughing at the most recent posts on Facebook and Twitter. I knew what it felt like to be the odd one out, and perhaps Tom understood that, too. It wasn't as though I had a whole bunch of friends texting or calling me, inviting me out to Christmas parties.

Why did I even bother having a phone? I wondered, taking it from my pocket. I went to my contacts and looked at the three names. Dad. Natalie. Tom. There were just the three, and one of them didn't even count anymore. My thumb hovered momentarily over Tom's name. My heart sped up a little.

Should I call him? And say what?

I shoved the phone back into my coat pocket and walked among the mulch that had formed at the edges of the twisting country roads. With my fingers brushing against the phone in my pocket, I thought of Kerry's phone and how the killer had thrown it away. Despite what my dad or Tom thought, I knew the phone would still be lying up near that house somewhere. I had seen it in my flashes. If I could find it, that would prove I was right, wouldn't it? Even if no one else believed in me, I needed to believe in myself. Perhaps that was the trick? Perhaps that's what I'd been missing—something the flashes had been unable to show me. Didn't I have to believe in myself first, before I could expect anyone else to?

I walked on. It was getting dark and, now not feeling so bad about heading home and facing my father's questions, I looked up to get my bearings. I gasped to find myself standing at the entrance to the dirt road that led off to the railway tracks and the tumbledown house. It was as if I had wandered around in a big circle and come back on myself, or the house had somehow drawn me back. It wasn't quite ready to let me loose yet. I looked back over my shoulder in both directions. The road was deserted. So, lowering my head against the howl of the wind, I made my way back up the dirt road. There were no lights this time, just the growing darkness that fell about me like a thick shroud. I made my way up the path that twisted its way like an ancient spine. With hands in pockets, I stood and looked at the derelict building through a gap in the trees. It almost seemed to be peeking back at me, its windows like soulless eyes.

The door slowly swung open as if inviting me in. Instead of inching backward, I walked toward it, heart racing. That throbbing pain began to build in my head again. Then, instead of my head jerking backward as it so often did when the flashes came, I lunged forward as if being shoved from behind. It was like the house wanted me.

Flash!

I could see Kerry in the corner. Cowering. Her knees drawn up to her chest.

Flash!

Please, she whispered, her voice floating around me like a chill wind.

Flash!

You are going to die tonight, the man said. His voice was soft, gentle, as if he were trying to soothe her.

Flash!

Kerry's eyes, huge and tearful. Terrified. *Please don't hurt me.*

Flash!

I'm not going to hurt you, he said, in the same comforting tone. *But you will die.*

Flash!

Please let me call my mum. Kerry's mouth. Lipstick smeared.

Flash!

Shhh, he soothed. His hand gently stroking her hair.

Flash!

Please don't touch me. Kerry's hands pulling her clothes tight.

Flash!

I'm not going to touch you. I just want to be with you for a while. His hands held out before him. Open palms. Shielding his face from me.

Flash!

Why? Tears on her cheek. Rolling like liquid glass around the corners of her mouth.

Flash!

How can I mourn for someone I don't truly know? he whispered. A faint smile, but gone too soon for me to really see.

Flash!

The sound of a child crying in the distance. Why is there a child crying?

Flash!

Tiny white shoes. A child in a car. Crying.

Flash!

Then, as soon as they had come, the flashes were gone. Those images were dragged so violently from me, I staggered backward into the darkness of the house and screamed. I turned around and around in the dark, desperate to find the entrance and get out. It was as if the place was haunted by the ghost of Kerry Underhill. But it wasn't Kerry I was afraid of. It was that man. Slithering around in the darkness, just dying to reach out and touch me. I screamed again.

Hands gripped hold of me.

"Get off me!" I shrieked, my head feeling as if it was being crushed.

"Charley," a voice said.

"Let go!" I cried out.

"Charley, it's me! No one is going to hurt you."

I opened my eyes to find Tom holding me to his chest.

"Get off me." I groaned, gently pushing him away. My head rolled on my shoulders and I felt sick. With the house seeming to sway back and forth, I staggered to the doorway. The cold night stung my face.

"What did you see in there?" Tom panted.

"Just give me a minute," I gasped. The sick feeling in the pit of my stomach started to ease a little.

I got myself together and looked at Tom. "What are you doing here?"

I saw the concern in his eyes. "I came looking for you."

"Why?"

He looked away. "I thought that you were right. We should find Kerry's phone."

I took a deep breath; that hadn't been the answer I was hoping for. Nevertheless, it was clear that somewhere deep down, Tom did believe me. "The phone I told you the killer had thrown in the bushes?"

Tom looked back at the house. "What else did you see?"

"He took Kerry in there. He took her into that house before she died down on the railway tracks."

"Why? Did he hurt her . . . ? You know . . ."

"No," I said, shaking my head. "I don't think so. I don't think that's his thing. He wanted to talk to her—get to know her."

"Did you see him?" he asked, pen poised. "What did he look like?"

"I didn't see his face," I started. "I told you that."

"But you saw Kerry?"

"It's like I only get to see the person who's dying or dead already," I told him. "The flashes show me them. The lights I saw earlier. It's almost as if they're some kind of energy left behind by Kerry—a trail for me to follow—if that makes sense."

"Not really," Tom said, sounding disappointed I didn't have a description of the man who had brought Kerry up here.

"But I can tell you that whoever this man is, he isn't married and is probably over the age of thirty, white and clean shaven."

"I thought you said you didn't see him?" Tom asked, confused. "How do you know he's single?"

"I saw his hands," I told him. "He held them up in the air as if to prove he wasn't going to hurt Kerry. I could see he wasn't wearing a wedding ring, but there was a mark to show he once had, and his hands were white. His voice came through muffled and almost kind of distorted, but it wasn't a young voice. It was too deep."

"Did you see anything else?" Tom asked, taking out his notebook again.

"Only the fear in Kerry's eyes," I whispered, picturing them again in my mind.

"You said he didn't hurt her," Tom said. "But she ended up dead."

"He told Kerry she was going to die, but he wasn't going to murder her."

"So why bring her up here to this place?" Tom wondered.

"He told Kerry he wanted to spend some time with her, before she died," I explained, and I shuddered as I heard his voice in my head again, his breath warm against my ear instead of Kerry's. I suddenly felt a chill and pulled my coat tight about me.

"Why would he want to get to know her?" Tom asked.

"I know it sounds weird, but he said he couldn't truly mourn someone he didn't know," I told him.

Tom went to say something, but before the words had even left his mouth, the lights started to appear again. This time, they weren't winking on and off around the decrepit house, they were near to the ground, leading away from it, like the emergency lights you see running down the aisle on a plane.

"What is it?" he whispered.

"Shhh," I hushed. "They're back."

"Who's back?" he asked, and I caught him glancing around, with a look of worry on his face.

"The lights," I said, following them.

CHAPTER 17

CHARLEY—TUESDAY: 17:48 HOURS

I followed the lights with Tom close behind me as they led me back through the undergrowth. My breath came in wispy clouds and disappeared into the night. My hands were numb with cold. Bushes and shrubs brushed up against me on either side of the path. I was glad Tom was with me again. The thought of being out here alone and following the lights made my flesh prickle with fear.

This is the way he dragged Kerry, I thought as a rapid series of flashes popped inside my head. I saw Kerry's hands, floppy like a rag doll's. She stumbled and he yanked her to her feet. It was like she was drunk. She mumbled incoherently and I could smell something a lot like whiskey. It smelled sickly sweet and stronger than any drink I had come across before. Its potency made me screw up my nose and feel sick, and then I got a taste of it in the back of my throat. It burned as if I had swallowed acid. And just like Kerry, I gagged.

My head thumped like a wild heartbeat. Ahead of me, I could hear the sounds of trains racing past. The lights began to fade, winking out like dying stars. The bushes thinned out and I found myself by a fence. On the other side of it, I could see the railway tracks. There was a hole in the fence.

"This is where he brought Kerry," I told Tom.

"We thought she got onto the tracks farther back," Tom said. "That's where the search took place."

"You searched the wrong area," I said. "It was here."

"How can you be so . . ." he started, but his voice was drowned out as the flashes came with a vengeance.

Flash! Flash! Flash!

They were white and blinding. I dropped to my knees as if my legs had been swiped away from beneath me. There was Kerry, lying by the hole in the fence, semiconscious. The man was beside her, hidden by the overgrown bushes covering the embankment. He gripped her shoulders as if getting ready to move her at any moment.

There was a faint sound in the distance.

The sound grew louder—growing nearer and nearer with every passing second. I could feel his excitement building into a frenzy inside him. Starting in the pit of his stomach and spreading out like electricity through his whole being.

He swooped Kerry up into his arms and, stooping low, carried her through the hole in the fence. Reaching the tracks, he knelt and placed her over the rails, then folded Kerry's arms over her chest and looked down at her.

The sound grew even louder, though Kerry couldn't seem to hear it. Perhaps she was too drunk and just wanted to sleep, hoping that when she woke from her nightmare, the man would be gone.

Then, drawing one long finger almost lovingly down the length of her white cheek, the man whispered, *You're just like the rest of them. You look so beautiful lying asleep in the dark, Kerry.* Then leaning forward, he kissed her gently on the cheek. *Sweet dreams*, he whispered, then turned and fled back across the tracks and through the hole in the fence.

"Wake up!" I screamed, just wanting to reach out and shake Kerry awake.

Flash! Flash! Flash!

I was no longer on the tracks. I was in a car, sitting in the backseat. I could hear a child crying beside me. But I couldn't turn to see; I could only stare at the back of the killer's head. He sat rigid and motionless. There was the sound of thunder again, but it wasn't the sound of an approaching storm I could hear. There were no rain clouds in the sky tonight—only stars. It was the sound of a train and the killer could hear it, too.

The flashes almost seemed to scream inside my head as the sound of the train's horn blared in my ear. Then I understood why the killer was sitting in the dark near the tracks. He was listening to the sound of the approaching train. He was waiting for the sound of the horn, because at that point he knew the train was just about to strike the girl. He knew in the next second she would be dead, the wheels slicing through her body like blades.

It was awful.

Suddenly, I felt the shock impact and my whole body turned to shreds as if it was I beneath the train.

Slowly, the killer turned the ignition key. The car purred into life and drove up the dirt road and into the night.

CHAPTER 18

Charley dropped to the ground by the hole in the fence. My first instinct was to go to her, but she had told me not to touch her. Perhaps it disrupted her flashes in some way. I was glad now that I'd decided to come back. Not because her flashes appeared to have returned with a vengeance, but because I could be here to help her. Comfort her and know she was safe.

Her eyelids flickered, as if she was having some kind of seizure. Every time her eyes opened, I could see only white; the pupils were rolled back into her skull. Her head snapped left and right as if she was watching something unfold that only she could see. Then she reached out with her hand as if trying to grab someone or something.

"Wake up!" she screamed.

Her arm dropped to her side again, and she slumped forward, like a puppet whose strings had been severed.

"Charley?" I said, crouching beside her, hand hovering, not knowing if it was safe to touch her.

"Sick," she breathed, trying to stand.

"You feel sick?" I asked, helping her up.

"He's sick," she gasped, sounding short of breath.

"What do you mean?"

"He's deranged," Charley murmured. "Sick in the head."

With my arm wrapped about her shoulder, and her head resting against me, I helped her up the path and back up the dirt road toward my car. "What did you see?" I asked.

"He just wants to hear the train approach and kill them," Charley said, and instead of pushing me away, she pulled me tight. "He gets a kick out of the anticipation of knowing that she's going to be hit by the train. He waits in his car, listening for the sound of the train and the impact."

"But why not just kill Kerry himself?" I asked, pushing aside brambles and thorns with my free hand.

"He doesn't want to physically hurt them. Not with his own hands. He told Kerry he wasn't going to hurt her, but he still wanted her to die. He justifies what he does to them by not murdering them himself."

Halfway up the embankment, I took Charley by the shoulders and looked at her. "Charley, you keep saying *them*. You think he's murdered before?"

"Yes," she said, looking down and nodding her head slowly.

"How can you be so sure?" I asked, my stomach beginning to knot. "Did you see them?"

"No," she said, still refusing to look at me. "It was the way he spoke. As he stood looking down at Kerry after he had placed her on the tracks, he said, 'You're just like the rest of *them*. You look so beautiful, lying asleep in the dark, Kerry.'"

"You say this guy laid Kerry on the tracks?" I asked, remembering how the driver had said it looked like the girl was asleep.

"I think the killer got Kerry drunk on whiskey or something stronger, a concoction perhaps. I could taste it during the flashes. It really made me want to gag. Once she was literally legless, he carried her down onto the tracks, placed her arms over her chest . . ."

"What did you say?" Tom cut in.

"The killer placed Kerry's arms over her chest," she repeated. "Is that important?"

"The driver of the train said he thought it was strange how the girl had been lying across the tracks with her arms folded," I said, staring at her, ever more convinced she was telling the truth, however weird it was, and ever more guilty that I had grown frustrated with her earlier that day. I ran my fingers through my hair. "For Christ's sake," I groaned.

"What's wrong?" she asked.

"If what you are saying is true, we could have a serial killer on the loose, and there's not a damned thing I can do about it."

"I thought that's why you brought me up here," Charley breathed. "I thought you wanted me to tell you exactly what happened up here so you could go catch the man who did this. This is a good thing, isn't it?"

"No, it's not good, because I can't keep this to myself, but I can't tell anyone, either," I snapped. I wasn't angry at Charley, I was angry with myself. "If I keep it to myself, then that just leaves this guy out there to kill more young girls, and if I tell the guv . . .'"

"Surely he'll be pleased. Isn't it a good thing you can provide him with clues?" Charley asked, turning and heading back toward the car.

"What am I meant to say, Charley?" I said. "Pop my head around his office door and say, 'Oh, by the way, guv, you know that poor cow Kerry Underhill? Well, this guy actually dragged her up onto those tracks. But first he took her to this little house where he spent time getting to know her. He got her drunk. And, oh yeah, he drives a white car; he's white European and single.'"

"It's all true," Charley said.

"I guess it is, but isn't my DI just going to be the slightest bit curious as to how I know all this stuff?"

"Tell him the truth."

"No way," I barked.

"Oh, okay, I see," Charley sighed. "Frightened he might think you're some kind of a Looney Tune? Well, get used to it Tom. I've spent a lifetime feeling like that."

"It's not that," I protested. I didn't want to get into another row so soon. "Like I told you before, if anyone in the police were to discover I'd brought you out here, I'd be in deep shit."

"Even if it meant finding the killer?" Charley asked me.

"Charley, you don't know the people I work with like I do," I tried to explain. "They wouldn't believe a word of what I told them even if I explained how I'd come by the information. They wouldn't just boot me off the force because I'd brought you out here; they would get rid of me because they would think me unstable."

"So what are you going to do?"

"I don't know," I whispered, my mind racing over the possibilities and the consequences of each one of them. "I need to think about it."

"Well, don't think about it for too long," Charley shot back. "There's a killer out there somewhere."

Before I had the chance to say anything else, Charley was heading away from me again. I walked in silence behind her, my brain feeling as if it had been scrambled. Why had I brought her out here?

Because if I were to be honest with myself, maybe the reason was that, deep down, she had been right—I hadn't believed her. But now that I did believe, what did I do with the information she had given me? Write it all down and send it anonymously to Harker? He would probably just chuck it in the trash. The police were always receiving crank information from members of the public. Some of them even confessed to crimes they hadn't committed. Maybe the search teams had found something?

Perhaps they had found the path up to the house? But so what if they had? That route could have been walked by anyone—trespassers, graffiti artists, people taking a shortcut . . . There had to be a way of slipping this information into the inquiry. There just had to be.

As I walked with my head down, chin almost touching my chest, I heard Charley say, "What about Kerry's phone?"

"Phone?" I asked, still distracted by my own thoughts.

"You told me the reason you'd come back here was to look for it. Do you know the number?" Charley asked.

"Yeah, her mum gave it to me," I said, taking my notebook from my pocket and thumbing through it. I read it out, then looked up at Charley; I could see that she was typing it into her phone.

"What are you doing?" I cried, snatching for it. But I was too late. Charley had hit the DIAL button and had brought the phone up to her ear.

"Calling Kerry's phone," she said.

"Have you lost your mind?" I cried, reaching for her phone again. "If Kerry's phone is found, it will be handed over to the tech guys and they will download the SIM card."

"So?" Charley asked me, her phone pressed to the side of her head.

"They'll check all the numbers that have called her phone," I snapped. "And they'll be particularly interested in the calls made to her phone since her death."

"Well, let's just hope we find it first," Charley said. "I saw the man throw it away. So it'll be out here somewhere. If I get through to it, then we might hear it ringing and we can find it."

"Charley, just hang up!" I shouted at her.

"Wait a minute," she said. "It's ringing."

"Charley, hang up!"

"Shhh," she said, putting a finger to her lips. "Can you hear it?"

I listened, but all I could hear was the branches of the trees swaying overhead, and the trains roaring past in the distance.

"Charley, I can't hear anything," I told her. "Please hang up. I'm in enough shit—"

"Shhh!" she hissed. Then, speaking into the mouthpiece, "Hello? Hello? Who's there?" She took the phone from her ear. "Tom, somebody has Kerry's phone."

"What are you going on about?"

"Somebody answered her phone."

"What?" I breathed, praying it hadn't been discovered by the search team already.

"Tom, someone definitely answered Kerry's phone, because I could hear what sounded like someone shoveling earth."

CHAPTER 19

Who d'you think answered Kerry's phone?" I asked as Tom started the car. "It sounded like they were shoveling mud or something." I remembered the grave diggers at Natalie's funeral and shuddered.

"How should I know?" He moaned, switching on the wipers against the rain. "Knowing my luck, it was probably one of those tech guys at headquarters, or worse, Harker. I can see that phone now, sitting on his desk with an exhibit label hanging from it."

"I'm sorry, Tom," I said, glancing at him. He did look stressed.

"It's not your fault," he sighed. "You were only trying to help. But if they analyze that phone, then your number will come up."

"Who's to say it's the police who have the phone?" I said, trying to ease his mind.

"What do you mean?" he asked, leaning forward in his seat as the rain bounced off the windshield.

"I saw that man throw Kerry's phone away, right? The phone could have been found by anyone."

"That place is pretty remote," he said.

"Maybe, but that old house looks like it's used by kids as some kind of camp. You must have seen the empty beer cans and all the other junk that's been left up there," I said. "It could've been found by them."

"I guess," he said, stopping at a set of traffic lights. "That could be an important piece of evidence."

"You might never find it," I said. "Whoever has it now, they'll probably remove the SIM card and put their own card inside. What's the difference between that and it getting crushed by that train? You wouldn't have the phone anyway if that had happened."

"I guess," he said again, and moved the car forward, heading in the direction of my home.

"I saw a child. It was crying," I said.

"Sorry?" Tom said. "What?"

"I saw a child in those flashes."

"A child?"

"I could hear it crying in the distance. Then it was beside me in the killer's car."

"He brought a kid along with him?" Tom asked. "Is that what you're saying?"

"I don't know. Those flashes came so quickly. I don't know if the child I could hear crying was something to do with what that man did to Kerry, something he has done in the past, or something he's planning to do in the future."

"This just keeps getting worse and worse," Tom moaned.

"There was something else, too," I said.

"What?"

"When we first got up to that dirt road—"

"Before you stormed off." He half smiled at me.

I rolled my eyes and continued. "I told you I had flashes as if I were looking through Kerry's eyes as the train struck her," I said.

"I remember," he said, nodding his head thoughtfully. "What about it?"

"Kerry wasn't looking at the train when it hit her," I told him. "She had her eyes closed."

"That's what the driver said," Tom said. "He said she looked as if she were asleep."

"So whoever's eyes I was looking through, they weren't Kerry's," I whispered. "They were somebody else's."

"Whose?" Tom asked.

"I don't know," I said, and turned to look out the window again. But I feared that perhaps I had been looking through Natalie's.

Tom parked outside my house. The rain hadn't eased and it lashed at the car. It reminded me of when I was a small girl, huddled in my bed feeling snug and warm as the rain beat against my bedroom windows.

"Are you okay?" Tom asked, leaning out of his seat toward me.

"Sure." I smiled faintly at him. The pains in my head had almost gone now.

"You look tired," Tom said, taking my hands in his.

That was the second time he had held them. I didn't pull away. "Those flashes kind of take it out of me," I said. It wasn't just the physical exertion, but the mental strain, too. Seeing such upsetting images today was even harder to deal with than usual. "I think that's why the flashes stopped coming earlier today. I think my mind has some kind of pressure valve and it switches off when it all gets too much. It's happened before, now I come to think about it. It's a natural sort of protection, I suppose."

"Perhaps," Tom said, still holding my hands and looking me straight in the eyes. "Charley, I'm sorry about how I behaved today. It wasn't really you I was mad at."

"Who was it, then?"

"It doesn't matter now," he said.

I looked straight back at him and met his stare, "I think we're more alike than perhaps we know," I whispered.

"Perhaps." He smiled.

There was a pause—a silence—that could have only been filled with a kiss. But instead, I broke his stare. "I think I'll have an early night."

"I wish I was joining you," he said.

"What did you say?" I smiled, glancing back at him.

"I didn't mean it to sound like that," he said, and smiled back. I loved the crooked grin he so often had and that mischievous twinkle in his eyes. "What I meant to say was, I wished I was going home to get some sleep instead of having to go start my night shift."

We looked at each other. There was another pause. Then, leaning in, he kissed me gently on the lips. I kissed him back. His lips were soft against mine, and I felt my heart start to race.

Tom eased back and our lips parted. "I'm sorry," he said.

"Why?" I whispered, part of me hoping he would kiss me again.

"I'm a police officer and . . ." he started.

"And what?" I pushed. Did he regret kissing me?

"It's just I don't act very professionally around you," he said, looking away. "It's like we keep a secret now. A secret about what really happened to Kerry Underhill and what just happened between us."

"Does that worry you?" I asked him.

"No, and that's the problem," he said. "It's kind of exciting. I find being with you exciting, Charley. When we went our separate ways today, I was mad at myself because you were right; I was using you. But I never meant to. So I told myself I would continue to investigate the case in a more conventional way instead of relying on you. Then, when I found you back at the house in the midst of your flashes again, I got a real kick out of working with you as we tried to solve what happened. It was like we were a team."

"Do you want to be on a team?" I looked at him.

"Yeah." He grinned at me. "I want to be on your team."

CHAPTER 20

I arrived at the police station with just over ten minutes to spare. I'd stopped off at home to change out of my jeans. But my smart work shoes no longer gleamed; they were caked with mud from where I had been trampling up and down the dirt road with Charley. The hems of my trousers were flecked with mud.

Guessing I'd already failed to make a positive impression on Harker since my arrival at Marsh Bay, I hurried to the locker room. Like all locker rooms, it smelled of sweaty socks and stale deodorant. I yanked open my locker door and reached inside for the tin of boot polish I had stashed there. Unscrewing the lid, I sat down and kicked off my shoes. I looked at them and knew I'd need a hammer and chisel to remove the thick lumps of mud. If Harker and the others saw it, they'd start asking questions. What would I say? That I ran cross-country to work?

I banged the flats of the soles together, and some of the mud came away in thick chunks and covered the tile floor. The sound of my pounding the soles of my shoes together sounded like cannon fire in the tiny room.

I stopped, fearing that it might bring someone to the locker room to find out what all the noise was. But I was too late; the door swung open and Jackson strolled in. He was wearing shorts and a white vest that clung to him with sweat. I suspected he had been in the gym again, admiring his muscles. He looked at me and then at the mud on the floor.

"I hope you're going to clean that shit up," he said.

"It's mud, not shit."

"I'm sorry, I thought it was more of the shit that keeps falling out of your mouth," he said, closing the door behind him. He folded his meaty arms over his chest. I put my shoes down and stood up. I would never match Jackson's colossal size even if I spent the rest of my life lifting weights and eating cans of spinach, but at least now I came somewhere close to matching his height.

"I don't talk shit," I said. "You know what I said about the Underhill girl was right."

"All I know is that you've come into this station all guns blazing and trying to make a name for yourself," he said, stepping away from the closed door and toward me. He puffed out his chest like a gorilla spoiling for a fight. Is that what he wanted? Did he want to fight me? He was a cop and so was I. We didn't beat each other up. That was for the school yard, right? He came close enough for our noses to almost touch. Beads of sweat glistened on his forehead and upper lip. He stank of sweat.

"You need to take a shower and cool off," I said.

He grabbed my collar and slammed me back into the locker. I was momentarily stunned. Not because I was hurt or in pain, but because this was something that would happen in school. But why was I surprised? Jackson was nothing more than a bully.

He had one hand pressed against my chest; I glanced down and couldn't help noticing the indentation on his finger where there had once been a wedding ring. I pushed him away and stepped aside.

"Grow up, Jackson," I said. "You're behaving like a freaking child."

He came toward me again, his lips a grim line, his eyebrows knitted together over the bridge of his nose as he glared at me.

"The only one who needs to grow up around here is you, Henson," he snarled. "You think you know it all. You think you can come in here and make me look like a jerk in front of scum like Jason Lane."

"He hadn't done anything wrong," I reminded him. "He was just a scared kid . . ."

"He's an animal," Jackson seethed.

"Despite what you think of him, he has rights," I told him.

"See, there you go again." Jackson grimaced. "You think you can tell me how to do my job. I was arresting scum like Lane while you were still having your diapers changed by your mum."

"And I was learning about the Human Rights Act at training school while you were beating the hell out of some petty thief," I shot back.

"You think you're so damn smart, don't you?" Jackson said, getting even more in my face.

I didn't budge. I hit back with just two words.

"Natalie Dean," I said.

Jackson's eyes widened as if I had just punched him in the face.

"Natalie Dean," I said again, sensing his weakness. "You dealt with her case, didn't you?" I didn't know this for sure, but I sensed it by the look of shock in his eyes.

"You don't know squat, Henson," Jackson barked.

"She died just like Kerry Underhill, didn't she?" I said, taking a step closer. "She was killed by a train and, let me guess . . . you wrapped the job up just like you want to wrap up Kerry's death. You wanted to put it down as a death by misadventure."

"You weren't there, Henson," he said, his voice full of bitterness. "So you know nothing."

"Let me see," I said, as if pondering the facts. I stalked across the locker room like Sherlock Holmes. "Natalie Dean was found lying across a set of railway tracks late at night. She had been drinking and the driver said she looked as if she were asleep. Then Jackson-of-the-yard showed up and worked his detective magic . . ."

"Natalie Dean had enough booze in her veins to fill a brewery," Jackson cut in.

"And took a shortcut home across the tracks, where she fell down and was run over by a passing train," I finished for him.

"So?" Jackson shrugged his giant shoulders. "What's your point?"

"My point is that you haven't been investigating these deaths properly," I snapped at him. Now it was my turn to be angry. "Two girls die in exactly the same circumstances just a few weeks apart and you don't see any connection?"

"Kids are always screwing about on the tracks," he shot back. "They're always taking shortcuts across 'em. It's no big deal."

"No big deal?" I gasped. "Two young women just lost their lives. Maybe you should go and see Mrs. Underhill and tell her that her daughter's death was no big deal."

"Stop trying to put words in my mouth," Jackson growled. "You know that's not what I meant."

"No, I don't know what you meant," I said. "But one thing I do know is that you're meant to be a police officer, Jackson. That's meant to stand for something."

"Don't you dare stand there and preach to me," Jackson boomed, the veins on his neck throbbing.

"And don't you dare try and tell me that there is no connection between the Dean and Underhill cases," I roared back. "You should have told me about the Natalie Dean case. We're meant to be on the same team. But you couldn't tell me, could you, Jackson? Because the guv might have gone back and looked more closely at the Dean case. He might have seen what an incompetent job you'd carried out. The guv might have seen at last what a joker you really are . . . Or is there another reason you didn't want the guv or anyone else to look too closely into the deaths of Natalie Dean and Kerry Underhill?"

"What's that supposed to mean?" Jackson hissed.

Before I'd had the chance to explain what I meant, and I wasn't sure that I could, the door to the locker room flew open. Harker stood in the open doorway, his face ashen and his cold eyes boring into mine.

Pointing a finger at me, he said, "You, my office, now!"

CHAPTER 21

I pushed the front door open, stepped out of the wind and rain and into the hall. My father appeared as soon as I closed the door. It was like he had been waiting for me. He looked me up and down, his eyes narrowing into slits. He saw the mud caked over my wellies, the dead leaves stuck to my coat, and the twigs trapped in my hair.

"I thought that copper was taking you for breakfast, not camping. You've been out with him all day."

"His name is Tom," I said, kicking my boots free.

"So?" he said, watching me pull twigs and leaves from my hair. "Where have you been? Not McDonalds, that's for sure."

I pulled off my damp coat and hung it up. As I brushed past him, he took me by the arm and swung me around to face him.

"Where have you been?" he asked.

170

I couldn't lie to my father. I didn't want to. I had nothing to hide and I'd done nothing wrong. "Tom took me back to where that girl . . . Kerry—"

"See, I told you."

"You told me what?" I asked, knowing exactly what he was going to say next.

"The cop is using you, Charley," he insisted. "Can't you see that?"

"He just wants to help catch the man who killed that girl, and so do I," I said, shaking free of his grip. "Besides, I think whoever killed Kerry Underhill also killed Natalie."

He drew a deep breath. "Just listen to what you're saying. Natalie died in a tragic accident. She wasn't killed by anyone. You're making links to stuff that isn't really there. You're seeing all these strange things inside your head and then trying to make connections with what's happening in the real world."

"No, I'm not," I said.

"At first you said you saw a girl called Kerry being murdered. Now you're saying your friend Natalie was killed by the same person? What, is this guy now suddenly a serial killer? It just doesn't make sense, Charley, and it's got to stop."

"It does make sense. If only you could see what I see in my flashes, then you'd believe me, like Tom does."

He looked at me as I placed one foot on the stairs, and I could see him fighting to stay calm. He took one of my hands in his and held it gently. "Charley, this copper . . . Tom . . . he doesn't really believe you. He fancies you, that's all. I don't blame him for that. He's a young man and you're a beautiful girl—of course he's going to like you."

I remembered how Tom had kissed me. It was more than him just trying to make a pass at me. The kiss had been gentle, like it had meant something.

"Charley, some guys will say anything to please a pretty girl. If he really believed you, then he wouldn't be sneaking you up to where that girl was killed. He would be taking a statement and making it official."

"He can't tell anyone, because no one will believe him . . ." I started.

"And that's the point I'm trying to make, Charley," my father said, gently squeezing my hand. "How can he get his mates in the police to believe when he doesn't truly believe himself?"

I didn't want my father to put doubts in my head about Tom. He did believe me. Tom had risked a lot to take me up to the scene again. He wanted to find the killer just as much as I did. He'd said we're a team.

"You're wrong about Tom," I whispered, slowly sliding my hand free. "He does believe me, Dad. I just wish you did."

I turned my back on him and climbed the stairs to my room. I didn't look back. I heard him grab his coat from the hook, then the front door opened. A rush of cold air swept up the stairs after me, and then the front door slammed shut, rattling in its frame.

I showered, washed the mud from my hair, changed into my pajamas, then climbed into bed. As I knew they would, those images of what I had seen up on the dirt road kept going around and around in my head. To try and block them out, I listened to "The One That Got Away" by Katy Perry on my iPod. I loved the song. I stuck it on repeat, but it still did little to block out those pictures.

I sat up and drew my knees up under my chin. Why had my dad said that stuff?

Because I'm his daughter and he's worried.

Was Tom really using me? Did he really believe in my flashes? I picked up my iPhone to text him. I needed some reassurance:

Thanx 4 believing in me x

I waited for Tom's reply with the phone still in my hand. A few minutes passed.

Then a few more.

Would he text back?

Perhaps he was too busy at work.

Maybe my father was right.

But Tom had kissed me.

The phone vibrated. I opened the message. My heart felt like it had stopped. I dropped the phone.

With my hands covering my eyes, I peered through my fingers and read the message.

> *Don't cut me off*
> *Not like Natalie*
> *Don't lose the connection*

I picked up the phone with my fingertips. The number was the one Tom had given me—the number I had called from my phone. With my heart now racing like a trip hammer in my chest, I knew the text had come from Kerry.

CHAPTER 22

Harker slammed his office door with such force the framed pictures of himself receiving commendations shook on the walls. He marched around his desk, loosened his tie, and sat down. His shock of white hair shone beneath the glare of the fluorescent strip lighting. Harker couldn't have been any older than forty-five, but the wrinkles around his eyes and across his forehead made him look older.

"Sit down," he barked, flapping his hand toward a chair. "I was just in the middle of my supper when you started to kick off," he said, picking up a half-eaten sandwich and taking a bite. Mayonnaise oozed onto his chin. He wiped it away with a piece of crinkled tissue paper. "So what *is* your problem?"

"Jason Lane isn't responsible for taking Kerry Underhill up to the railway tracks," I said.

"What makes you so sure?" he asked, chewing the remains of his sandwich.

How did I answer that? I didn't think the "no mud on the sneakers" routine would work, either. "Just a gut instinct, I guess. My copper's nose," I said eventually. "He seemed really upset during the interview last night."

"I'd be upset if I thought I was responsible for that poor cow's death," Harker said. "If Jackson is right and Lane did take the girl against her will, then he's in a whole load of crap."

"He didn't do it," I told him. Jackson and Harker were wasting their time while the real monster was out there, perhaps even preparing to take his next victim. If that happened—if another girl lost her life and I hadn't done anything to stop it, how could I live with that?

"Well, there's the trick. If all we've got to go on is your gut instinct, then that isn't good enough." He screwed up the greaseproof paper his sandwich had been wrapped in and threw it in the trash can on the other side of his office. "I need evidence."

"Yeah, I know all that, but this is different," I said, my stomach knotting as if I was just about to sit for an exam I hadn't bothered to study for.

"Oh? How come?" Harker said, doing that thing with his bushy eyebrows again.

I took a deep breath, then said, "Kerry was taken up to the railway tracks by a man, but it wasn't Lane."

"Who, then?" he asked.

I knew I had his full attention. I whistled through my teeth, my heart racing, but I had to say something. "What I can tell you is the man drives a white car, and there will be scratches down the back somewhere. Kerry struggled with him and scratched the paint. There will be white paint under her fingernails—"

"Whoa! Whoa! Whoa! Stop right there," Harker cut in. "Where did all this come from?"

I shook my head and said, "Just let me finish."

He stared at me blankly for the next ten minutes or so, while I told him everything Charley had seen in her flashes.

Once I'd finished, there was an awful silence, louder than any noise. Just when I thought I couldn't bear it any longer, Harker spoke.

"So how do you know all this?"

Now came the hard part. "My . . . a girl I know told me."

"Your *girlfriend*?" Harker asked.

"She's not my girlfriend," I said, not able to meet the intensity of his stare.

"I couldn't give a crap if she's your mother. How in the hell does she know?" Harker snapped.

"I took her up to that place . . ." I said, but it was barely a whisper.

"You did what?" Harker roared, shooting up out of his seat. It was then, seeing his reaction, I fully understood the seriousness of what I had done.

Then I began digging an even deeper hole for myself to be buried in. "Charley . . . that's her name . . . sees things."

"Are you putting me on?" Harker asked, sounding as if he were catching his breath.

"It's true," I said, now looking at him. "Charley has flashes."

"Flashes?" Harker roared. "What are *flashes*?"

"They're like pictures inside her head." I tried to explain, desperate to find the right words—words that didn't make me sound as if I were losing my mind.

"So let me get this right," Harker said, coming around his desk to stand over me. "I've had two of my best officers interviewing witnesses today, collecting CCTV, and gathering evidence—doing real police work, when all the time I should've called up your girlfriend and got her to solve the case with the help of these *flashes*?"

I looked at him, not knowing what to say.

"Have you lost your freaking mind?" he snapped, eyeballs bulging. "I took a chance on you the other night. I listened to what you had to say over Jackson, an experienced officer, and I was pleased to say your hunch was right. There was more to Kerry's death than her just taking a short-cut. But now you have the nerve to question the ability of one of my officers, compromise the investigation into the death of a young woman on the say-so of your girlfriend?"

"She's not my girlfriend," I said. "But what Charley sees is true. You have to believe me. Lane isn't part of this and you're just wasting time."

"How dare you!" Harker bellowed, looking as if he wanted to punch me. "How dare you sit there and tell me that I'm wasting my time. The only time I've wasted recently is giving you the opportunity of coming onto my team."

"But what I'm telling you is true," I insisted, taking my pocket notebook from my coat. "No one has found Kerry's mobile phone, right?"

"Take some advice, Henson," Harker said. "Don't make this any worse for yourself."

"No, listen to me," I said, sounding too needy. "Charley told me that in her flashes, she heard Kerry's ringtone. She said it was an Ellie Goulding song called 'Burn.'"

"So not only does your girlfriend see things, she *hears* things, too!" Harker groaned in disbelief. "I tell you what, Henson, I can't believe I'm *hearing* this bullshit from a so-called professional copper!"

I found the Underhills' home phone number in my notebook and dialed it on Harker's desk phone.

"What do you think you're doing?" Harker seethed, trying to snatch the phone from my hand.

I pulled away, praying that either Mr. or Mrs. Underhill answered the phone before Harker wrestled it from me.

"Hello?" It was Mr. Underhill.

"Hello, Mr. Underhill," I said, looking at Harker. "It's Constable Henson; we met the other night."

"Yes, is there some news?" Mr. Underhill asked hopefully.

"I'm sorry, there's no news," I said into the phone. "We are having problems finding Kerry's mobile. I was wondering if it had something unique about it. For instance, did it have a distinctive ringtone?"

"I'm not sure," he said. "Let me ask my wife."

In the background, I could hear him talking to Mrs. Underhill.

Harker continued to stare at me, his face flushed.

"Constable Henson, are you still there?" Mr. Underhill asked.

"Yes, I'm here," I told him and switched on the speaker so Harker could hear what Mr. Underhill said.

"My wife thinks Kerry downloaded a song by a singer called Ellie Goulding," he said, his voice wobbling.

"Can your wife remember which song?" I asked.

" 'Burn,' " Mr. Underhill said. "It was Kerry's favorite."

"Thank you," I whispered, glancing at Harker.

"Is there a problem?" Mr. Underhill asked.

"No problem," I assured him. "Thank you, you've been a great help. Someone will be in contact with you shortly."

"Okay, thank you," he said, and the phone went dead.

I replaced the receiver and looked at Harker. "How would Charley have known that?" I asked him.

"Millions of girls probably have that ringtone," he snapped.

"Don't you think it's just a bit of a coincidence?" I asked.

"I'll tell you what I think, shall I?" Harker said, closing the gap between us. "I think you're so desperate to impress that you'll do or say anything to score points against Jackson."

"That's not true," I insisted.

"I don't really care what you believe *is* and *isn't* true," Harker said. "I want you to get your stuff together and go home. Take a few days annual leave and have a good long think about what you've done. And while you're off, make sure you iron your uniform, because you won't be coming back to CID. You're off the team."

"But—"

"Just get out of my sight," Harker said, and I thought I detected the slightest hint of disappointment in his voice.

With my head hung low, I walked to the door. I opened it just an inch, and then looked back at him. "Jason Lane wasn't involved in Kerry's death; it was someone else and he's done this before. Other girls have died in the same way."

"Bull," Harker said, sitting back behind his desk. "We would know about them if there had been others."

"No, you wouldn't," I said, looking straight at him. "Because there are too many officers out there like Jackson who are all too eager to put the deaths down as suicide or accidents for an easy clear-up. Go and check out the case of a girl named Natalie Dean."

Harker sat back in his seat, his face hard and tired. "Have you finished?" he asked me.

"Yes," I said.

"Then piss off. I'm sick of looking at you." Harker picked up some of the paperwork that littered his desk and started to thumb through it.

CHAPTER 23

I hadn't really slept, so when the first rays of light crept around the edges of my curtains, I had to force myself out of bed. My iPhone was in the dresser drawer, where I had hidden it the night before after receiving that text from Kerry.

It was that one single text that had kept me drifting restlessly in and out of sleep all night. Had that text really come from her? But she was dead; I had seen it happen and Tom had seen her body.

Perhaps she hadn't sent it? Maybe whoever had found her phone sent it as some sick joke? But I doubted that. Why pick my number? And how would that person know about the missed call I'd had from Natalie at the funeral? Had Natalie been trying to call me? She was dead, right? I'd seen the grave diggers shoveling earth into her grave. The text message I'd received last night hinted I had now lost the connection with Natalie.

But the thought that kept me awake the most was my fear it had been the killer who had sent me the text.

Everything seemed different in the pale winter sunlight bathing my room. How could the killer have sent that message? He didn't know anything about me. How would he have known I'd seen what he'd done to Kerry in my flashes? God, I couldn't get my own father to believe me, let alone a complete stranger.

But where does that leave me? I wondered, putting down the hairbrush and staring at myself in the mirror. I eased open the dresser drawer. My iPhone lay among my underwear. I picked it up, fearing there might be another text from Kerry. I turned it over and looked at the screen. No new messages, not even from Tom. I thought of him and guessed he would be heading home to his flat, tired after his night shift.

I opened the message and read it again.

Don't cut me off

Not like Natalie

Don't lose the connection

Those words had burned themselves into my mind throughout the night. Should I tell Tom about it?

No.

He was already stressing himself out about the phone. If he thought I was receiving texts from *someone*, it would only cause him more anxiety, and he had his position in the police to think about. Should I tell my dad? Ask for his opinion? No, I thought again. Like Tom, he was pretty wound up by the whole thing and would blame Tom even more for getting me involved. I decided, for the time being at least, to keep the message to myself.

My thumb hovered over the REPLY button. Then before I could change my mind, I quickly wrote, *Who are you?*

I closed my eyes, took a deep breath, and hit SEND.

Almost at once, I regretted sending it. What had I done? But in my heart I knew why I had sent that message. I wanted to know if it had really been Kerry. Was there another dimension to the flashes? After all, I had seen those lights up at the shack; they had led me to it. Something inside me said it had been Kerry who had left that trail of lights. So perhaps the text was the same kind of thing? Was Kerry trying to make contact with me? Maybe she was going to lead me to that man? If she did, no one would ever be able to doubt me again.

I sat in my room and listened to Bruno Mars sing "Grenade" on my iPod, my phone in my hand, feeling half scared yet half hopeful that Kerry would make contact again. Shadows stretched across my bedroom walls as the day passed like a haze around me, as I listened to songs play on my iPod, my eyes fixed on it.

I don't know how long I sat there, and I would have probably remained like that for the rest of the day had it not been for my father shouting up the stairs at me.

"Hey, are you going to put in an appearance today or what?"

I looked down at the phone one last time, and then put it in my pocket. I turned off my iPod and went to the top of the stairs.

"At last, the creature from the black lagoon has risen," my father said, staring up the stairs at me. He seemed to be in a much better mood than the night before. Perhaps he had done some thinking and calmed down a little.

"I was planning on having a lazy day," I told him.

"Every day is a lazy day for you," he said. "Are you going to come down or what?"

"Nah, I was going to—"

"I went out and got a Christmas tree first thing this morning." He smiled. It seemed like ages since I'd seen him do that. "Want to help me decorate it?"

Of course I would want to decorate it! He knew how much I enjoyed putting up the Christmas decorations. Some of my happiest memories were of me and my father sitting by the tree and covering it with tinsel, bows, and lights. He would drink a can of beer or two, and I would sip pink lemonade from a tall glass that was only got out at Christmas. I'd always felt very grown-up drinking from that glass, because usually I drank from my plastic cup, the one with the picture of Miss Piggy on it.

"So what do you reckon?" he asked.

"Got any pink lemonade?" I smiled.

"Bottles of the stuff," he said with a wink.

"How can I refuse?" I said, heading down the stairs. Then, halfway down, my phone vibrated. With a trembling hand I pulled out the phone. One new message. With my eyes half-shut, I opened the message and breathed out. It was from Tom.

Hey, Charley, only just got ur txt. Think my phone is on the blink. Last night didn't go well. Have been kicked off CID. Will call you later. Tom X

Why has Tom been kicked off CID? I wondered, putting my phone away.

"Everything okay?" my father asked.

"Sure," I said thoughtfully. I feared Tom was in trouble at work because of me—because I had called Kerry's phone. More than ever now I wished I hadn't responded to that text I'd received last night. I hoped that whoever had Kerry's phone didn't answer it.

I reached the bottom stair and, trying to kid to my dad that everything was okay, I said, "So where's the lemonade?"

He laughed and went to the kitchen. We spent the rest of the morning and afternoon decorating the Christmas tree. To be with my dad like that was wonderful, just like it used to be—before the flashes had taken over.

CHAPTER 24

Sleep hadn't come easy, so I had spent most of the night playing *The Last of Us* on the PS3 until I finally crashed out at around seven a.m. Childish, I know, but a good way to unleash my frustrations and anger. Each zombie I shot, I pretended was Jackson.

Did I regret telling Harker what I had? No, not really. I had to say something. That idiot Jackson was going to terrorize Lane into confessing to something he hadn't done. Someone like my father would have a great time tearing the confession to pieces—Lane had been stoned at the very least. I doubted very much he had been fit for the interview, voluntary or otherwise.

Charley said whoever had taken Kerry against her will to the railway tracks had committed similar acts before or was going to do so again in the future. I couldn't live with that on my conscience, even if it did mean

I wasn't part of CID anymore. They could shove it. I had told Harker the truth, and he could either act on that information, despite how he had come by it, or he could sit back while more young girls lost their lives. I believed Charley, even if he didn't.

As I sat in the dark and my thumbs worked themselves into a frenzy over the PS3 controller, I knew that even though I wasn't returning to CID, what I had told Harker about Charley would be all around the station. Coppers loved to gossip, and what they didn't know, they made up. Maybe now was a good time to put in for that transfer to a busier station.

At about seven in the morning, I couldn't fight the tiredness anymore. I switched off the PS3, curled up into a ball, and I fell asleep on my tiny couch. I dreamt I was being chased along a set of railway tracks leading into the mouth of a giant tunnel. I kept looking over my shoulder but couldn't see who it was running after me. The sound of my heart beat in my ears, and I was breathless and drenched in sweat. I reached the mouth of the tunnel. The darkness inside was impenetrable, blocking my passage like a black wall. There was a sound coming from the other side—a girl calling my name. I knew it was Charley.

Charley! I called out to her.

Please, Tom, she screamed. *Help me!*

I pounded against the unbreakable darkness with my fists. There was a sound behind me. I spun around, half expecting to see whoever had been following me. But the noise was the sound of a train speeding over the joints in the tracks.

Clackerty-clack! Clackerty-clack! Clackerty-clack!

The train raced toward me, its headlights seeming to smile at me from the darkness.

Clackerty-clack! Clackerty-clack!

My nose filled with the smell of diesel fumes, and my ears filled with the sound of the train rushing toward me.

Clackerty-clack!

The shrill horn split my ears. I covered my face as the train struck me . . .

. . . I woke, sweat dripping from my hair, my throat raw and my heart pounding. I was in my flat. There was no train, no tunnel, no Charley. But I could still hear the sound of the horn. I shook my head and the sound changed, becoming a series of beeps. I looked down and saw my mobile winking on and off at me from the floor. Empty Coke cans rolled away as I fumbled for it. I switched off the beeping and sighed with relief.

One new message. It was from Charley.

Thanx 4 believing in me x.

I looked at my watch. It was just before five p.m. Charley had sent the message just before midnight last night, and it had only just come through. The phone was a piece of junk, and I'd known for some time I needed a new one. Something that wasn't the size of a brick.

I sent a text back to Charley and told her I'd been busted out of CID.

I'd call her later. After the text had disappeared from my phone, I tossed it across the room and went for a pee. My bladder felt the size of a blimp. I stared in the mirror; I looked rough. No, *rough* wasn't the word. I looked as if I'd spent a night in that broken-down house with Lane and his friends getting wired.

I stuck my tongue out and grimaced. It was gray. I took hold of my toothbrush, deciding I needed to freshen up. With it hanging from the corner of my mouth like some weird-looking pipe, I went to the kitchen and made myself a strong black coffee. As I sloshed boiling water into the mug, the buzzer on my front door sounded.

Charley? I wondered. Part of me hoped so.

I hit the intercom button and stifled a yawn. "Yeah, who's there?"

"It's Harker."

I flinched away from the intercom. What did he want? Had he come around to tell me that not only was I off CID but I'd been booted out of the job altogether?

"Henson, are you there?"

"I'm here," I said. "What do you want?"

"I need to speak to you."

"What about?" I said, my stomach starting to churn over again.

"Are you going to let me in or not?" he snapped. "It's freezing cold out here."

I took a deep breath and hit the door's RELEASE button. "Come up," I said. "The door's open."

He must have run up the two flights of stairs to my apartment, because he was already at my door by the time I opened it. He stood in the hallway, his hands thrust into his overcoat pockets. I couldn't help but notice he looked as beat as I did; I guessed he hadn't slept well, either.

Perhaps he was so consumed with guilt for kicking me off the team that it had kept him awake. Somehow I doubted it.

"Can I come in?" he asked.

"Sure," I said, stepping aside.

Harker walked into the living room, which doubled as a dining room. He looked with distaste at the discarded Coke cans and McDonald's wrappers lying strewn across the carpet and kitchen table.

"Excuse the mess. I must remember to sack my housekeeper." Harker didn't look amused. "So have you come to give me another kicking? Like the one you gave me last night wasn't bad enough?"

"I'll have a black coffee. No sugar." He shoved the cheeseburger wrappers out of his way and sat down at the table. "I'm not here to apologize for what I said to you last night," he said, rubbing his hands together as if trying to warm them. "What you did was bloody foolish and could've not only got you in the crapper, but all of us."

"So why are you here?" I asked, placing a steaming mug of coffee in front of him.

He took a sip, then said, "After you left, I thought about what you said. I've spent most of the night pondering everything you told me."

"And?" I asked, sitting down opposite him.

"You said Kerry would have white paint under her fingernails." He stared hard at me.

"Did she?"

"Yes." He nodded. A length of hair flopped over his brow. "Only I knew about that. I received the autopsy report from the pathologist after you left. So the question is, how did your girlfriend know about it?"

"Charley," I said.

"What?"

"Her name is Charley."

"So how did *Charley* know about that?" he asked, his right eyebrow cocked. "She was either there and witnessed it happen or, however improbable, she saw it in those flashes, as you like to call them."

"It's Charley who calls them that," I told him. "And no, she wasn't there."

"How can you be so sure?" he asked me.

"Because she was at home throwing a fit in her bathroom."

"A fit?"

"It happens sometimes if the flashes are particularly intense," I explained. "She has these terrible headaches, too. I'm guessing her father will be able to vouch that she was at home."

"Okay, so Charley wasn't there—up at the scene," Harker said, and took another sip of his coffee. "However much it pains me to say this, I don't know how Charley would have known about the paint beneath the victim's fingers."

"So you think that Kerry is a *victim* now?"

"Look, Tom, I haven't come around here to fight with you or go over old ground," he said.

"So what have you come round here for?"

"I want to know more about Charley and what she told you."

"Why?" I shot back.

Sliding his hand inside his coat, he pulled out a beige-colored folder and laid it on the table.

"What's that?" I asked.

"You told me Charley said there had been others." He opened the file. "So I went back through the files and looked into the deaths of young women that had occurred near to or on that same stretch of railway."

"And what did you find?" I asked him, now finally coming awake.

"Possibly seven others spanning the last ten years or so," he said.

"Possibly?"

"Three of them were definitely suicides," he explained. "They had known mental health issues and all left suicide notes, so they can be ruled out."

"And the other four?"

"All died in very similar circumstance to young Kerry," he said, pawing over the sheets of paper in the file. "All of the girls were young women with no recorded tendencies to commit suicide. There were no previous issues of depression, self-harming, the usual stuff that you would expect to see. I have copies of their medical records. There were no family issues, and all, prior to being found dead on the railway tracks, seemed happy with their lives. One of them had only recently got engaged. Another had just won a place at a prestigious university. And just like you said, one of the girls was named Natalie Dean."

"So let me guess," I remarked. "All of them were recorded by the coroner as death by misadventure. Young girls who had all taken shortcuts across the railway tracks late at night?"

"Yes," Harker said bluntly. "But you've got to understand, none of these deaths would have raised any suspicion."

"Really?" I said, trying not to sound too cocky.

"Really," he grunted. "These deaths were spread over more than ten years. They were dealt with by different officers. CID was only notified about two of the deaths. The drivers all said that the young girls were just lying across the tracks like they had collapsed. All of them were overflowing with alcohol. It just kind of made sense to think they had fallen down drunk and got killed."

"Or perhaps they were carried unconscious onto the tracks?" I said.

"None of the drivers reported seeing anyone else near to the scene," Harker barked.

"Just out of interest," I said, leaning across the table and thumbing through the paperwork, "who was the investigating officer on the two cases that were brought to CID's attention?"

"Jackson," Harker said.

"I might have known." I half smiled.

"Jackson is a good officer," Harker snapped.

"He's a joker," I said back. "Why do you protect him?"

"Be careful of what you are suggesting, Henson," Harker said, fixing me with his cool stare.

"I'm not suggesting anything," I said. "But the guy is incompetent."

"He's not the one who let his girlfriend prance about all over a potential crime scene," he reminded me.

"So if you're still pissed off at me for taking Charley up there, what are you doing here now?" I asked him.

"I'd like her help," he said without any shame at all.

"Help with what exactly?" I asked, not believing what I was hearing.

"If these young women died because someone placed them on those tracks in front of trains, then that's murder in my book, and I want to catch him before he does it again."

"So you do believe her."

"We'll see," he said, standing up.

"What does that mean?" I asked him.

"I'd like to meet her."

"Why?"

"I have something I want to show her," he said.

"What is it?"

"Are you going to introduce me to Charley or not?"

CHAPTER 25

CHARLEY—WEDNESDAY: 19:08 HOURS

My afternoon decorating with Dad was just like it had always been. I was happy that for one afternoon it was just us—me and my dad. I sat cross-legged on the floor, watching him hang decorations from each corner of the living room ceiling. He didn't stop until the room looked like a winter wonderland.

"Okay," he said, placing his hands in the small of his back and stretching, "just one last thing. You know what to do."

This was my favorite part. I reached into the cardboard box we stored the decorations in and pulled out the fairy. She was shabby-looking, but I wouldn't dream of replacing her. While I straightened her hair and dress, Dad put on his Elvis Christmas CD. It was the same every year and had been for as long as I could remember.

So as Elvis started to sing "White Christmas," I reached up on tiptoes and placed the fairy on top of the tree.

"Doesn't it look cool?" I sighed.

"We certainly did a good job," he said, and squeezed me tight. We stood together, the Christmas tree lights twinkling on and off and Elvis playing in the background. I couldn't help but feel happy. I still doubted my father believed in my flashes, but perhaps he had realized being mad at me the whole time was the wrong approach.

"So what are you hoping Santa will bring you this year?" he joked.

I looked at him. "For us to be friends?"

He loosened his arm from around my shoulders, his face crestfallen. "We're more than just friends, Charley."

"I know, but we seem to argue so much these days," I said. "I don't want to fight with you over Christmas. I don't ever want to fight with you again. Can we just agree to disagree about my flashes?"

Dad looked at me and then sighed. "Okay, okay. If it will make you happy, then I'm happy."

"Perhaps Tom could come over . . ."

"Don't push it," he said, jabbing a finger at me.

"You'd really like him, if only you gave him a chance," I said.

He glared at me for a long moment. Was he going to get mad again? His shoulders tensed and the muscles in his jaws flexed as if he was about to shout at me.

"Please?" I whispered.

Then his face relaxed and the knot in my stomach loosened.

"Okay," he sighed, with a shrug of his shoulders.

"Yes! Dad, you're the best," I said, pulling him close and kissing him on the cheek.

"You'd better tell him to bring some beer," he grumbled, crossing the room to the window.

"I'll tell him." I smiled, skipping about the room.

My father pulled back the curtain and looked up at the sky. "Looks like it might just snow. I'd better go and rustle up some fares before it starts to come down."

"Okay," I said. "Do you want me to save you some dinner to warm up later?"

"No, it's okay," he said, putting on his coat. "I'll get something while I'm out."

"Are you sure?"

"Sure," he said, kissing me on the forehead. "I'll catch you later."

As he opened the front door, a blast of icy air blew into the hallway. I shivered.

"Thanks, Dad," I said.

"What for?" he asked.

"You know what for," I said, and smiled.

"No worries," he said, and disappeared out into the cold.

I heard his car drive away, and snatched my phone from my pocket. I opened my contacts list and pressed Tom's name, but all I got was a recorded message telling me the number was unavailable.

I punched out a message: *Call me X*, then went to the kitchen. My stomach rumbled and I couldn't stop thinking about cheese on toast. I had only just got the bread from the cupboard when my phone buzzed. I yanked it out of my pocket. One new message. I opened it.

Charley, help me!

I reread the message, mouth dry and tasting of roadkill. Where had that taste come from?

"Leave me alone," I whispered. "Please just leave me alone, whoever you are."

The phone buzzed so violently it flew from my hand and spun across the kitchen floor, coming to rest by a chair leg. Unable to move, I stood and looked down at it. I saw the message box had lit up again. With my head in my hands, and that disgusting taste in my mouth, I screwed my eyes shut, hoping it would make the nightmare go away.

Buzz! Buzz! Buzz!

With my eyes closed, I inched my way across the kitchen toward the phone. The buzzing grew louder, like a swarm of bees circling my head.

I prodded the phone with my foot, hoping that would somehow make it stop. It didn't.

I opened my eyes. A new message burned across the front of the screen.

Charley, please talk to me

"I don't want to, Kerry." I breathed. I knew what she wanted—she wanted to talk about what had happened to her. But was it really Kerry who had sent the message? Or was it some sick joke?

I picked up the phone with trembling hands. Part of me expected the flashes to come, but they didn't. Then the phone buzzed again. I felt I was being watched, so I looked behind me. There was no one there.

I opened the message.

Charley, we really need to talk. Follow the lights.

Biting my lower lip so hard I drew blood, *Talk about what?* I typed.

Within seconds of hitting the SEND button, the phone started to ring. My Coldplay ringtone echoed off the kitchen walls, sounding as if it were coming from far away, like the other end of a tunnel. I looked down at the screen. I recognized the number flashing across it. It was Kerry's. With my thumb twitching so badly I had to draw breath to calm myself, I pressed ANSWER and slowly raised the phone to my ear.

There was a faint scratching sound, like fingernails clawing at the underside of a coffin lid. That had been the sound I'd heard the night before. It hadn't been shoveling at all.

"Who is this?" I whispered, eyes screwed tight, heart racing in my chest.

There was a voice, but it was barely a whisper. It came again, this time louder but still unrecognizable. It sounded like whoever was trying to talk was choking on a throat full of dirt. My skin broke out in goose bumps, and shivers raced up and down my spine.

"Who's there?" I whispered, eyes still shut. "What do you want?"

There was a sound of choking in my ear and I started to cry. I was trembling with fear. Scared my legs would buckle beneath me, I dropped to my knees on the kitchen floor, cradling the phone to my ear. The line went dead and with it went the disgusting taste in my mouth.

Now all I could hear was my own racing heartbeat.

CHAPTER 26

A knock at the front door made me scream aloud. I wiped away the tears from my cheeks and approached the front door. The knocking came again, slow and deliberate. I closed my eyes and saw Kerry standing outside, her fingernails black with mud, earth dribbling from the corners of her dead, bloated lips.

"Who's there," I whispered, my voice wavering with dread.

The knocking came again.

"Hey, Charley," a voice said. "It's me, Tom."

"Tom?" I gasped, running to the door and yanking it open.

He stood in the dark. There was someone with him, a man I didn't recognize. Snow fell in powdery flurries.

"Hey, Charley, is everything all right?" he asked.

"Yeah, I'm fine," I lied. I didn't want to explain in front of the stranger.

"Can we come in?" Tom asked.

I stuffed the mobile phone into my pocket and stepped aside. "Sure."

The tall guy brushed snow from his shoulders and stepped into the hall.

"Charley, this is my inspector, Detective Inspector Harker," Tom said.

"Very pleased to meet you," Harker said, holding out his hand.

I took it and he pumped it up and down. His grip was strong. Was he here because he had discovered I'd called Kerry's phone? Tom had told me there would be trouble. What would they both say if they found out I'd been receiving and sending texts, too? What would they say if I told them I just had a call from that phone and thought I heard someone choking . . . suffocating. What would either of them say about that?

Harker released my hand, but not once did he take his eyes off mine. I started to feel uncomfortable.

"Do you want a coffee?" I asked Tom, trying to think of something to say. "You look frozen."

"No, I'm fine," he said. "Guv?"

Harker shook his head.

"Come through to the kitchen," I said. "I was just about to have some cheese on toast, but I'll wait."

"Please, don't let me interrupt your tea." Harker smiled.

"It's okay," I said.

There was an uncomfortable silence. We all sat down at the table. The silence continued. I looked at both of them; I couldn't bear the tension. "Am I in some sort of trouble?"

"No," Tom said quickly. "No, nothing like that."

"Like what, then?" I asked.

"Tom has told me about your . . . your *flashes*," Harker said. "*Flashes*— that's what you call them, isn't it?"

"Yes," I said, looking straight back at him. Then, as if he had slapped me hard across the face, my head rocked to the right.

Flash! Flash! Flash!

I saw a black leather purse.

Flash!

Do you want a lift? a man's voice whispered in my ear.

Flash! Flash!

Trust me.

Flash!

Get in, love.

Flash! Flash! Flash!

The sound of a car door opening. The same car as before.

Flash!

My brain felt as if it was swelling inside my skull. There was a crippling pressure on my forehead, and my face began to prickle, as if burning. I heard the sound of chair legs scraping as Tom ran to the sink for a towel.

"What's happening?" Harker said. "What's wrong with her?"

"It's the flashes!" Tom said, stuffing a cool wet towel into my hands. He gently eased my head back as I placed the towel to my face.

Flash! Flash! Flash!

Where you heading? I heard the man's voice again. It was muffled—barely there—but I could hear it.

Flash!

I don't know you, another voice said. This one female. Young.

Flash! Flash!

I'm not going to hurt you, the male voice said, and in the flashes I could see he was holding something in his hand. Bright. Silver.

Flash! Flash! Flash!

A girl in a car. Pretty. Very pretty. Hazel eyes. Light brown hair.

Flash! Flash!

What's your name? he asked her.

Flash!

Alice. She smiled. *Alice Cotton.*

Flash! Flash! Flash!

The pictures and voices disappeared as quickly as they had come. I opened my eyes; the kitchen seesawed. Tom hovered at my side, wringing his hands. Harker was still seated opposite me, his face grave.

"Are you okay?" Tom asked.

I nodded slowly.

"Maybe this wasn't such a good idea," Harker said, getting up from the table. "I think I should go."

"If you go now," I whispered, "you'll never really know what happened to Alice Cotton."

"What did you say?" Harker said, flinching, his gray eyes growing wide beneath those bushy eyebrows.

"That's why you came here, wasn't it, inspector?" I said, forcing myself to my feet and staggering around the table toward him. "You wanted to see if I could tell you about Alice."

"Who's Alice?" Tom asked, but neither I nor Harker answered him. We were too busy staring at each other. It was like Tom didn't exist anymore, like he was someplace else.

"That's right isn't it, inspector?" I said, reaching for his coat . . . I was exhausted. "You would only believe me and Tom if I could pass some kind of test. That's why you brought Alice's purse with you."

"How do you know about—"

I lunged for him, and he flinched away. But I had hold of his coat. Fearing I might just drop to the floor at any moment, I used what little strength I had left and slipped my hand inside his pocket. My fingers brushed over what I was looking for. I pulled the black leather purse from within his coat and held it up in my trembling hand.

"Alice Cotton's purse," I whispered, my legs buckling as the flashes came again.

I fell backward, eyes closed. It felt as if I were falling down a bottomless well. My head hurt, feeling like it was being crushed in a vice.

Flash! Flash! Flash!

Don't hurt me, Alice whispered in my ear, her breath warm against the side of my face. *You said I could trust you.*

Flash!

I'm not going to hurt you, Alice, the man said, running his finger down the curve of her neck.

Flash! Flash!

Beer cans, cigarette ends, rubble and earth. They were in the tumble-down house.

Flash! Flash! Flash!

I can get you money, Alice said. *My dad is very rich.*

I don't want his money, the man roared. *I just want to get to know you. Here, have a drink. This stuff is nice and strong. It'll help you relax. Take your fears far, far away.*

Flash!

How? Alice asked, drawing her knees up to her chest. I could sense her fear. I knew what she feared the most. What she feared more than death. *Please don't hurt me.*

Flash! Flash!

Talk to me, he said, his voice soft again. *Tell me about you. I want to know everything.*

Flash! Flash! Flash!

I want to see you! I screamed inside my head. Just show me your face!

Flash!

The sound of trains close by. The fence with the hole. Alice lying comatose on the ground in front of it.

Flash! Flash! Flash!

I heard the man's heart as he listened to the fast-approaching train. I felt his excitement; my body tingled with it.

Flash! Flash!

He picked her up and carried her through the hole in the fence. His heart was beating as fast as the approaching train.

Flash! Flash! Flash!

Alice stirred. The smell of alcohol on her breath so overpowering, I wanted to cover my nose.

He lay her down, folding her arms across her chest as if she was asleep.

Flash!

Sweet dreams, he whispered, stroking her unblemished cheek.

Flash! Flash! Flash!

Bright lights, but not the flashes. The front lights of the train bearing down.

Flash! Flash!

In his car now. Sitting behind him, there's the sound of a small child sobbing beside me.

Flash!

Keys swinging from the ignition as he sits and waits in the dark—listening to the sound of the approaching train.

Flash! Flash! Flash!

Alice opened her eyes at the very last minute. A drunken gurgle of a scream in the back of her throat. The noise was deafening. I wanted to cover my ears. Knowing that Alice was dead, the killer twisted the keys in the ignition. The engine rumbled into life. And the killer slowly drove away in his car.

CHAPTER 27

CHARLEY—WEDNESDAY: 20:47 HOURS

I opened my eyes to find myself slumped across the table. My head was thumping, as if it had been repeatedly punched. I looked up to see Harker standing by the sink, his coat open from where I had snatched Alice's purse. Tom was sitting beside me, his face white with worry.

"Charley, is it over?" he whispered, taking my hands in his.

"Yes," I nodded, trying to straighten up in my seat. I felt sick, and my throat was raw. "Water," I croaked.

Harker filled a glass and placed it on the table in front of me. "What did you see?" he said.

I took a sip of ice-cold water. "I saw Alice Cotton," I whispered, my throat still feeling sore.

"Where?" Harker asked impatiently.

"She was taken by that man, the one who took Kerry," I said.

"How do you know it was the same man?"

"Because he took her to that run-down house," I told him. "Then down onto the tracks."

"But why did she just lie down?" Harker said. "Why didn't she get up—run away?"

"She wanted to, but if you were picked up off the streets at night and driven to some remote house in the middle of nowhere, terrorized into believing that you were going to be raped and murdered, and given strong drink, you'd have to struggle to run, too. He gets them so drunk they are practically unconscious. I could taste the alcohol. It was strong, like several drinks had been mixed together. It made me gag. Both Alice and Kerry were too drunk to run away," I told him.

"When was this?" Tom cut in. He looked at me, then at Harker.

Harker ignored him. "Did you see what this man looked like?" he said.

"No," I said. It was on the tip of my tongue to tell them Kerry wanted to lead me to him, but I couldn't face having to explain how I'd come by that information. I would tell Tom at some point, but not in front of Harker. I didn't like him. And besides, he'd probably take my phone as evidence or something. Dad had given me my iPhone as a birthday present and there was no way I was going to let Harker have it.

"How does this man manage to get the girls to go with him?" Harker asked. "How does he get them into his car? Does he get them drunk first?"

I thought of the flashes I had just seen, and I could hear Alice's voice again, as if she were standing right next to me. "You said I could trust you," she'd said.

Then I remembered seeing the man holding something out, showing it to Alice as she walked along the street next to his car. It was bright and shiny. Realizing I had seen something similar before, I turned to Tom. "Get your ID card out."

"What?" Tom said.

"Just give it to me," I said.

Tom took his ID card from his pocket and opened it, revealing the silver police badge. With my skin turning cold and my heart racing, I turned to Harker. "This is how he gets the girls into his car. He shows them one of these. Your killer is a police officer."

The silence that followed was deafening. It seemed to go on forever. I handed Tom his ID card. He sat numbly, looking at it.

"That is a serious accusation," Harker eventually said.

"I know," I said, and took another sip of water.

"Are you sure about what you saw?" Harker pressed me, again making me feel like I was the suspect.

"I'm as sure as I can be," I said. "But it would make sense, don't you think? I mean, why else would girls like Kerry and Alice get into a complete stranger's car late at night?"

"Charley's right, guv," Tom whispered, as if it was a secret that he didn't want to be overheard. "It was raining the night Kerry was taken.

She wouldn't have thought it strange if a copper pulled up beside her and offered her a lift home. That's what a good copper would do. Kerry wouldn't have been suspicious, she would have been grateful; especially after the row she'd had in the pub with her ex-boyfriend. A friendly copper would have been a welcome sight."

"I don't know," Harker said, shaking his head. "A police officer? Who?"

"You're the detectives," I said.

Harker shot me a quick glance. "This isn't something to be taken lightly. Anyway, we only have your word for it. This is only something that you claim to have seen in your . . ."

"So that isn't Alice Cotton's purse, then?" I hissed, pushing it back across the table toward him. "Alice Cotton wasn't killed by a train? She didn't have light brown hair and hazel eyes? Her father isn't a wealthy businessman? Do I need to go on?"

"No," Harker said, shaking his head. It was the first time since meeting him I'd managed to break his stare. He looked down at the purse and put it in his pocket.

"So where do we go from here, guv?" Tom asked, sounding out of breath.

But before Harker had had a chance to answer, my dad appeared in the kitchen doorway. "What the bloody hell is going on here?"

We all looked at him.

"Who are you?" he barked at Harker.

"I'm Detective Insp—"

"And what are you doing in my house?" he shouted, looking at my flushed face and the wet towel strewn across the kitchen table.

"Charley has been helping us—" Tom started, getting up from his seat.

"What you mean is that you've been using my daughter again," Dad snapped at him. "Jesus, can't you see what happens to her every time she has those flashes?"

"Listen, Mr. Shep—" Harker said.

"No, you listen!" Dad barked. "This is my daughter you're messing with. She's not some kind of freak show you can use to help solve your crimes. You're the bloody police—you solve 'em!"

"That's what we're trying to do," Tom insisted.

"What, by getting my daughter to make herself ill? You really are a selfish bastard."

"Please, Dad," I said, tugging at his arm. "Let me explain."

Dad gripped me by the shoulders. "Charley, you can't see it, but he's just using you. He is using your so-called ability to see things to help him climb the promotional ladder. And when he gets to the top, he will drop you faster than a sack of shit."

"That's not true," Tom shouted.

"Why else would you be hanging around with a seventeen-year-old girl?" Dad hissed. "Or perhaps there's another reason?"

"Don't be so disgusting," Tom said. "Charley is my friend."

"You have a funny way of treating your friends," Dad spat, and squared up to him.

I wedged myself between them, pushing them apart.

"Please, Dad," I cried. "I want to help Tom. I want to help him find the man who killed Kerry."

"But it's not your job!"

"I can help," I insisted. "Every time I see those flashes, I see a little more about that man. I know it won't be long until I know who it is and where to find him."

"And that's what frightens me, Charley," he said. "This man, whoever he is, is dangerous. I don't want you to end up on those tracks like your mo . . ."

There was a brief moment of silence, broken by Harker. "Come on, Tom. I think we should leave," he said, heading back down the hall toward the front door.

"But—" Tom started.

"Just get out." Dad glared at him.

Tom reached forward and kissed me on the cheek. "I'll call you," he whispered.

"You'll leave my daughter alone," Dad told him, following Tom and Harker to the door. "If I ever see you around here again or find out you have contacted my daughter, I will report the both of you to your superiors. I'll tell them what you did here tonight. Now get out!"

CHAPTER 28

T hat went well," I said, climbing into the car.

"I guess he has a point," Harker said, starting the engine and pulling away from the curb.

"Looks like I won't be seeing Charley again," I said.

"That should be the least of your worries," Harker said.

"But I do worry," I told him. "I like Charley a lot. I was hoping to spend some time with her over Christmas. You know, take her out some place nice. Now I've gone and messed everything up."

"You'll get over it," Harker said, concentrating on driving. The roads were fast becoming slippery with snow.

"I don't want to get over it," I told him. "Anyway, I don't even know what I'm doing discussing this with you; it's my personal life."

"You started it," he said, shooting me a glance.

"I never."

"Yeah, you did," he said drily. "You involved your personal life the moment you took Charley up to that old house."

"Whatever." I shrugged, turning to look out the window at the falling snow. It annoyed me that he was right.

"So what do you reckon?" Harker asked me after a few moments of silence.

"About what?" I asked.

"Do you think we have a killer in our midst?" he said. "Do you really think this man is one of us—a copper—not just someone using fake ID?"

"Charley hasn't been wrong yet," I said, watching the snow swirl through the night sky.

"That's what scares me," Harker muttered. "Got any ideas?"

It was the question I hoped he wasn't going to ask me. Slowly, I turned to look at him in the gloom of the car.

"Well?" he pushed.

"Jackson," I said.

"You've got to be joking?" Harker said, almost steering us into the curb.

"I'm not joking," I told him. "He's the one who couldn't wait to brush Kerry's death under the carpet as an accident. And when the evidence started to show otherwise, he leapt on Jason Lane. He was the one who quashed the other two cases that came CID's way."

"But when would he have had the opportunity?" Harker asked. "He was at work the night Kerry died."

"Are you sure about that?" I asked. "You were out of the office with Lois, and I made my way down to the tracks on my own. Jackson was already there when I arrived. And that's another thing. Charley said Kerry scratched this guy's car, which was white. We have a whole yard of white police cars parked at the back of the station. Jackson could've taken one of them."

"I don't know," Harker sighed. "I don't like pointing the finger at one of our own—one of *my* own—one of the team."

"Is Jackson married?" I asked.

"No," Harker said. "Got divorced recently. Why do you ask?"

"Charley told me that during one of the flashes, she saw the killer's hand. He wasn't wearing a wedding ring, but she could see a mark on his finger where one had once been. I noticed the other day Jackson has the same type of mark on his finger . . ."

"So he's divorced. So are many men living in Marsh Bay," Harker reminded me. "It's not enough."

"Have the printouts from Kerry's phone arrived yet?" I asked Harker.

"I don't think so," he said.

"Jackson said he faxed off for them. It's not as if he needs the phone to get that information, so why haven't they shown up yet?"

"Maybe they have," Harker said.

"Maybe they were never requested?" I said. "And what's with this

Alice Cotton? You never mentioned her back at my flat. How long ago did she die?"

Harker took a deep breath, and then said, "Last year."

"Last year?" I cried. "Natalie Dean's death was just three weeks ago! You told me that these deaths had been spread over ten years or more."

"And they have been," Harker said. "Except for the Dean girl."

"And let me guess—it was put down as either a suicide or a death by misadventure?"

"Yes," Harker said, and I could feel the embarrassment seeping from him. "You've got to understand, Henson, I was on annual leave. Jackson dealt with the case in my absence."

"So that's why CID was called out to the death of Kerry Underhill," I gasped. "Someone thought it was strange that two girls had died in a matter of weeks in the same circumstances and in the same place." Then, staring at him, I added, "That's why you called SOCO and the search team in. It wasn't to do with anything I said. You thought there was something not quite right, too. You didn't believe Jackson's theory, either."

"Okay, smart-arse," Harker snapped. "You don't have to be so damn cocky about it. Yes, I did think it was strange, but not too strange. I mean, there are regular spots where people kill themselves. Take the Forth Bridge. How many people have jumped from there over the years? What about that town in Wales? Bridgend. A place that would normally see two or three suicides a year had about twenty-five in two years and all of them by hanging. But did it all point to a killer? No. This sort of thing has been happening for centuries. One person kills himself, another hears about it and does the same—it becomes kind of contagious. It's known as the suicide cluster phenomenon. And I bet you didn't know about that."

"No," I admitted.

"Okay, so there were two deaths in the same place within a few weeks of each other," he said. "But it didn't start me thinking *serial killer*. There could have been a number of reasons."

"Like what?"

"Internet suicide cults, for starters," he said.

"You didn't really consider that, did you?" I asked him.

"Why not?" he growled. "It seems a more logical explanation than a seventeen-year-old girl witnessing the deaths in a series of flashes inside her head."

"Okay, you've made your point," I said. "But it still doesn't rub out what Charley told us about the killer being one of us."

We drove in silence, until Harker turned the car into the station parking lot.

"What have you brought me here for?" I asked. "I'm off the team, remember?"

"You're back for now or until I decide to kick you off again."

"Thanks, you're all heart," I said, though I was secretly really grateful. "Did you tell anyone else that I took Charley up to the railway tracks?"

"No," he said. "That stays between you and me."

"Okay. Thanks. So, what now?"

"I want you to check all the police car logs for the night of Kerry's death," he said. "I want to see which car it was that Jackson booked out. I want to see if there are any scratches on it. Then I want you to lean on the mobile phone company and get that printout."

"So you do believe that Jackson is the killer?" I asked him.

"No, I don't," he said back.

"Then what's the point in me checking the car logs?"

"Because I want to prove to you that Jackson wasn't involved and that he's a good copper," he said, fixing me with his cold stare. "What are you waiting for? Carry on."

I swung open the car door and got out; the snow was coming down harder now, covering the roof of the station and the cars in the yard. Just as I was about to walk away, Harker called to me.

"Henson!"

"Yes, guv?"

"You know if you're really stuck for something to do over Christmas, my wife usually does a pretty good spread," he said. "You'd be welcome."

At first I didn't know what to say. I was surprised and touched by his kind offer. "Thanks, guv, but I'll be okay."

"Think about it," he said as he marched away in the opposite direction.

CHAPTER 29

That's the last time he shows his face around here," my father bellowed, storming down the hall and back into the kitchen.

"You can't stop me from seeing him."

"I can do what I want," he seethed. "I'm your father and you'll do as I say."

"But I like him, Dad."

"Don't make me laugh," he snapped. "You're seventeen, for crying out loud. What do you know about anything?"

"I know enough to know that Tom believes in me," I snapped back.

"He's using you, Charley, can't you see that?"

"So you keep saying!"

"Why can't you like boys your own age? Tom's too old for you," he said.

222

"You are kidding me?" I spat. "Have you any idea what most boys my age are like? All they're interested in is a quick fumble!"

"Not all boys are like that," he grunted.

"Oh, no?" I said. "Why don't you go and take a good look around the shopping center on a Friday night. You'll see them all there clutching their packets of ten Marlboro Lights and bottles of Smirnoff Ice. All they want to do is get soused and lay the nearest thing in a skirt."

"Don't you dare use that language in front of me!" he shouted. "I'm your father. Show some respect."

"Well, it's true," I shouted back. My head was hurting so much I was beginning to feel sick. "Tom's not like that. He treats me nice."

"Jesus." My father sighed with disbelief. "You really are the softest touch walking the face of God's earth. Dragging you up to the place where some girl was killed is treating you nice, is it?"

"I was just trying to help. Don't you care that there's a killer out there?"

"It's not our problem. It's nothing to do with us."

"Don't you see, Dad? This thing that I can do—these flashes—doesn't have to be a curse." I tried to reason with him. "I might actually be able to help people."

"The only people you'll be helping will be those two coppers, to reach the next rank up," he said. "Can't *you* see that?"

"I think Mum has something to do with the stuff I see."

He looked at me, agog. "What are you talking about?"

"Mum died on the railway tracks, right?"

"So?"

"Well, don't you think it's more than just a mere coincidence that my flashes have grown stronger—become more vivid—since other girls started to die on the tracks?" I said in one breath. "Maybe Mum is trying to tell me something."

"My God, Charley," Dad cried. "I don't believe I'm hearing this."

"Maybe the man who is killing these girls had something to do with Mum's death," I suggested.

"Charley, your mum suffered from depression. She was ill. She took her own life—she wasn't murdered," he said.

"Well, connection or not, I'm going to find this man," I insisted. "I'm going to stop him killing any more girls and find out if he is connected to Mum's death."

Dad took a deep breath and shook his head. "Charley, I give up. I can't deal with this right now. We'll talk about this again when we've both had a chance to calm down."

"I'm not going to change my mind," I said, placing my hands on my hips and staring at him.

Pouncing forward, my dad gripped me by the wrist and started to yank me out of the kitchen.

"What are you doing?" I yelled.

"Saving you from danger," he said, pulling me up the stairs.

"Let go of me!" I screamed. I gripped the banister and dug my heels into the carpet. "I'm not in any danger! You don't even believe there's a killer."

"You're right," he heaved, prying off my fingers and pulling me farther up the stairs. "But if I'm wrong, I won't forgive myself if I don't protect you from yourself and those coppers."

"Please, Dad," I yelled, feeling scared. "I'm not a child anymore."

"Then stop bloody behaving like one." He dragged me toward my bedroom door, my fingernails clawing at the wallpaper. He pushed into my bedroom and threw me onto my bed.

"It's not like you can lock me in my room like I'm some kind of kid," I hissed, leaping toward the door.

"It's a lot like that," he said. He pulled the key from the lock on my side of the door, slammed it, and locked it from the other side.

I banged my fists against the door. "Let me out! Let me out!"

"I'm not having you end up like your mother, Charley!" he panted from the other side of the door, catching his breath.

"What are you talking about?" I demanded, hammering my fists so hard my hands began to hurt.

"I'm just trying to help you," he said. "I love you. I've got to go out to work, but I can't leave you alone knowing you might go back up to those tracks. I just can't take that risk."

I heard the sound of his footfalls as he headed back downstairs. The front door opened and then slammed shut behind him.

I stood in my bedroom, listening to the sound of his car drive away. I started to cry. I couldn't believe what my father had done. He had made me feel childish and stupid, like a little girl again. When was he going to realize I wasn't a little girl anymore? When was he going to realize he couldn't keep on trying to protect me like he had failed to protect my mother?

Sitting down on the edge of my bed, I wondered if that was what my father's irrational behavior had really been about. Did he wish he'd locked my mother away the day he'd left for work only to come home and find that she had gone—that she had taken her own life?

My breath still stank of something close to roadkill. Feeling as if I needed to cleanse myself somehow, I pulled some fresh clothes from my wardrobe and put them on.

My brain felt as if it had been wrung out by a pair of invisible hands. It was oozing with everything that had happened in the last hour or so. I knew I could help people. I believed that now. If I didn't use my flashes in a positive way, then what was the point of them? They just became a curse. If only I could find out the identity of this man, lead Tom and his inspector to him. If I could do that, and Tom still hung around, Dad would be able to see Tom wasn't just using me and that I wasn't a danger to myself or to anyone else. He would see how I could use the flashes to help others. Despite what Dad thought, I was almost certain the flashes were connected to the death of my mum. If this man was identified and a connection found, then perhaps my dad's guilt would be lessened.

Sitting on the edge of my bed, I tried to brush the smell of decay from my hair. I scraped it into a ponytail, then picked up my tainted clothes. My jeans were tangled around my T-shirt, and as I pulled them apart, my phone fell onto the floor. The screen started to glow as my Coldplay ringtone started to play. The song was "Fix You" and the words were about lights guiding someone home so that they could be fixed.

Slowly reaching down, I picked up my phone. Would Kerry be able to guide me—would she be able to fix me?

"Hello?" I whispered.

All I could hear was the sound of fingernails clawing against wood.

I screwed my eyes shut. It almost sounded like someone trying to climb out of their coffin.

"Charley?" Kerry's voice startled me.

"Yes," I gasped. The overpowering smell of rotting flesh and decay was back again, washing over me.

"Want to see the lights?" Kerry asked, her voice sounding as though she had a mouthful of mud and grit.

"Yes," I whispered, fighting the urge to throw up. Hot bile gushed into my throat.

"Come to the house," she breathed.

The line went dead.

CHAPTER 30

Lois was in the office, a steaming mug of coffee in front of her. She was busy typing at her computer.

"Okay?" I said, taking off my jacket and sitting at my desk.

"Still snowing, is it?" she asked, smiling.

"Yeah, how did you guess?"

"You're covered," she laughed. "Either that or you're going prematurely gray."

I smiled back at her, and ran my fingers through my hair. "Busy?" I asked.

"Just typing up some of Kerry Underhill's friends' statements," she said, going back to her work.

"Where's Jackson?" I asked her.

"Out, hitting up CCTV," she said without looking up.

228

"What, at this time of night?"

"Jason Lane says he stopped to fill up his car at that twenty-four-hour gas station, out on Gospel Road," she explained. "Reckons it was around about the same time the train driver saw Kerry lying on the tracks. If he's on CCTV, then Lane's in the clear. The railway tracks are about five miles from that gas station."

"Jackson still reckons Lane's involved, then?" I asked her.

"I guess," she said, her keyboard clacking as she continued to type. "Anyway, where did you get to last night? You shot off pretty quick."

"Had gut ache," I lied. "Must have been something I ate."

"Well, next time just let me know, okay?" she said, peering over the top of the computer screen. "I am your skipper."

"Sorry," I said. "I did tell the governor."

"He must have forgotten to mention it," she said.

Seeing that her head was firmly buried in her work, I slowly got up from my desk and crossed the office. As casually as possible, I lingered by Jackson's desk. I glanced back at Lois. Her back was to me. Taking my chance, I quickly thumbed through the pile of paperwork in Jackson's tray.

"Looking for something?" Lois asked.

"I don't suppose you know if that printout from Kerry's phone has turned up yet?"

"Haven't seen it," she said.

"Has Jackson mentioned it?"

"Not that I remember," she said, her smile fading. "Tom, are you okay?"

"I'm fine." I smiled, stepping away from Jackson's desk. "Why do you ask?"

"It's just that you seem on edge or something."

I patted my stomach, feeling bad about lying to her. "Like I said, gut ache."

"Okay, if you're sure that's all that's wrong," she said.

"I'm sure," I breathed, and left the office.

I made my way to the small briefing room. It was empty, just as I hoped it would be. A long table ran the length of the room. Attached to the far wall was a board hung with keys to the station vehicles and their corresponding logbooks. The station had five marked vehicles, and two unmarked allocated to CID. The keys to one of these vehicles were missing. I checked the logbook and could see it had been signed out at 22:13 by Jackson. That was okay, it was black. Not the vehicle I needed to check. The second unmarked vehicle was blue, so no point in checking the logbook for that one.

Only two sets of keys remained; the other marked vehicles were obviously out patrolling the streets of Marsh Bay. But all of the logbooks were present. I took the first one down and opened it. I scanned the pages to see who had booked the vehicle out three days ago, Sunday night. Rogers from D relief had used it. Replacing the book, I picked up another and opened it. Little had signed for that one on Sunday night. I took hold of the third. There, next to Sunday's date was Jackson's signature, timed at 22:02. The vehicle had been signed out two minutes after his shift started.

Where had he gone in such a hurry? I wondered.

I replaced the logbook and looked for the keys. They were missing. The vehicle was out, so I wouldn't be able to check it for scratches until it was returned. Taking down the logbook again, I checked to see who had logged out that particular vehicle on Monday morning. Perhaps they had noticed some scratches on the paint. It had been signed out by Jones at 07:13 at the start of her early turn.

I knew Sarah Jones from training school. She was a good copper and if anyone would have noticed any damage to the police car, it would have been her. I took my mobile phone from my pocket, scanned my contact list, and dialed Sarah's number. All I got was an unobtainable-number tone.

"Bloody thing," I hissed, ending the call.

There was a landline on the desk, so I dialed her number and got a connection straight away.

"Sarah speaking," she said.

"Hey, Sarah, it's Tom Henson from work."

"Hi, Tom. Don't tell me, all rest days have been canceled for tomorrow."

"No, it's nothing like that," I laughed.

"Thank God," she sighed. "I've got something on tomorrow I can't cancel. So why the call? It's late, you know."

"Sorry to bug you. You know you booked out vehicle Romeo Two-One, on Monday morning?"

"Yes, what have I done? Damaged it or something?"

"No, not you, but I think someone did. I don't suppose you noticed any scratches on the paint, near the back of the car, when you booked it out?"

"Not that I remember," she said. "But hang on, there was something."

"What?" I asked, my heart leaping into my throat.

"It's probably nothing."

"Go on," I said, gripping the phone so tightly I heard my knuckles crack.

"Keep this between you and me, okay, because I don't want to get him into any trouble or anything," she said.

"Get who into any trouble?"

"You know, that tall guy from CID, the one who loves himself—Jackson," she said. "I could see from the logbook that he was the last one to use the vehicle. Well, since that guy got divorced, he thinks he's a real ladies' man. He's made a pass at me once or twice . . ."

"What was strange about the vehicle?"

"Well, he'd obviously had a woman in the car with him," she said, and my heart began to speed up.

"What makes you say that?" I asked, trying to be cool about it.

"The car stank of Chloé perfume," she said. "I recognized it straight away because I have a bottle."

"Are you sure?" I asked.

"Positive. As I said, the car stank."

"Thanks, Sarah," I said.

"Thanks for what?" she asked.

"It doesn't matter," I said, and hung up the phone.

CHAPTER 31

I stood and peered out my bedroom window in search of the taxi I'd booked. I'd been mindful not to book a cab through the same firm my father worked for; I didn't want him turning up. As soon as Kerry had ended the call, I'd thrown on some warmer clothes, coat and gloves, then taken the twenty I had saved from my jewelry box.

There was no sign of the taxi yet, so pushing the window open, I swung one leg out over the window ledge. Turning onto my stomach, I pushed the other leg out and hung precariously out of the window. If my father were to come home now, he'd probably think I wanted to do myself in, or had gone totally mad at the very least. I lowered myself out of the window, the wind howling about the eaves and blowing snow into my face. I felt the tips of my sneakers touch the roof of the porch above the front door. I hoped it would support me. Carefully, I eased myself down until all my weight was on it, then reached up and pushed my window closed.

I jumped down into the snow, landing with a heavy thud and rolling over onto my back. I'd winded myself, but that was the worst of it. Pulling myself to my feet and sucking cold night air into my lungs, I went and stood beneath a tree by the curb outside the house.

Desperate to be gone before Dad returned home, I peered around the tree trunk, hoping for a sign of the cab. There was a glow of headlights as a car turned into the street. It slowed, then stopped just outside the house, snow swirling in the glare of its headlights. I patted my coat pockets just to make sure I had my phone and flashlight with me, then crept from behind the tree and made my way as quickly as possible to the taxi.

"Taxi for Charley?" the driver asked me, rolling down his window.

"That's me," I said, and climbed in the passenger seat.

"Where to?" he asked.

It was then I realized I didn't actually know the name of that dirt road. I tried to remember the route I had walked the other night. I was sure the dirt road was off Oakgrove Road.

"Could you take me to Oakgrove Road, please," I said. "I'll give you directions from there."

"Are you sure you want to go all the way out there?" the driver asked me, turning out of my street.

"I'm sure."

"It's just it's fairly remote . . . and on a night like this . . ."

"Just take me there, please," I said. I turned to look out the window.

"Okeydokey," the driver said.

The silence made me feel uncomfortable, but we were soon heading out of town and working our way down the narrow roads that led in the direction of the derelict house. The snow didn't seem to want to let up, and on several occasions the driver had to slow the vehicle to a near crawl to navigate his way around the twisting bends.

Through the window I saw wide, open fields, now covered in white. I looked at the digital thermometer on the dashboard and it read minus two degrees. The taxi driver was right; I must be mad to make this journey on such a cold and bleak night. But he wasn't any better, risking bringing his cab all the way out here. With the snow falling as fast as it was now, he might never get back to town himself.

I peered through the darkness as we reached a junction. The driver turned right onto Oakgrove Road. I looked from left to right, but with the snow coming down, it was hard to see anything clearly. Then, just as he was about to drive past it, I saw the tiny road to my left.

"Stop," I said. "This is the road."

The cabbie slowed the car and peered at the narrow lane I'd pointed to. "I'm sorry, love, but I'm not risking taking my car up there. Not in this weather. I'll never get out again. I must have been mad to bring you this far."

"It's okay," I told him. "I can walk the rest of the way. How much do I owe you?"

The driver checked the meter. "Eight-forty."

I dug around in my coat pocket and pulled out the twenty. "Take ten." I felt grateful to him for driving me out so far.

"Thanks, sweetheart." He took the money and handed me my change. "Look, I don't know what's brought you out to such a god-forsaken place like this, and I know it's none of my business, but I don't mind waiting."

"How long have you got?" I asked him, grateful for his offer.

The cabbie rolled down his window and looked up at the snow-laden sky. "About five minutes, ten at the most. After that, those roads back to town will be treacherous."

"You'd better get back," I said. "I have no idea how long I'm going to be."

"Meeting someone, are you?" he asked, rolling up his window to stop the snow blowing in.

"Something like that," I said, reaching for the door handle.

"Boy trouble?" he asked. "I've got a daughter about the same age as you. I understand."

"I don't think you do," I said, pushing open the door.

"I wouldn't want my Casey coming out here alone on a night like—" he started.

"My boyfriend is a policeman, so if I can't get back, I can always call him," I said. Tom wasn't technically my boyfriend of course, but I hoped that might change one day. "I'm sure he'll be able to come out and pick me up."

"Okeydokey," he sighed. "As long as you're sure?"

"I'm sure," I told him, and closed the door.

I stood with the snow falling all around me and watched the cabbie drive away. Once the taillights of his car had disappeared around a bend in the road, I turned and faced the narrow entrance to the dirt road.

Flashlight in hand, I started off up the narrow road toward the house. I shone the light from side to side, its narrow beam reflecting off the snow that covered the ground. Plumes of breath puffed from my mouth and nose. The world seemed deathly quiet; the only sounds were my beating heart and the powdery snow crunching with every step I took.

I'd trudged about halfway up the road and had hoped I would have seen those lights again to show me the way. Everything looked different now that it was covered in snow, and I couldn't be sure where to leave the lane and find the path that led to the house. I shielded my eyes and looked back, wondering if I had passed it already. I didn't know. I kept moving, the taxi driver's words now ringing in my ears, *Are you sure you want to go all the way out there?*

Now I was here, alone and in the dark, I wasn't so sure, and I began to regret telling the cabbie not to wait for me. This had all seemed like a good idea back at home in the warmth and safety of my bedroom. I had been angry and confused. I'd wanted to prove to Dad I could use the flashes to help people and that he couldn't hold me prisoner.

But more than that, I wanted to prove to him that Tom wasn't using me. In my heart, though, I knew it was me I was trying to prove it to. Those years of taunts, the teasing, the bullying on Facebook about my flashes had hurt me more than I dared to admit. I was tired of being known as some kind of daydreamer, fantasist, witch—*freak*! I knew the images I saw in my flashes were real, a window to events that had happened. I knew the phone call from Kerry was real. I had heard her gasping for breath.

So if I could come away from the old house tonight with the name of the man who had killed Kerry, Alice, and my friend Natalie, if I could identify the killer for the police, no one would ever be able to doubt me again. I would have proved to everyone that what I saw was real. I could help people and my flashes would be a gift and not a curse.

With my head bent low, I pushed forward through the driving snow. I'd walked another twenty yards or so when I saw a patch in the bushes where the brambles had been snapped and broken. At once I recognized it as the place where Tom and I had gone the night before. I made my way toward it. Holding the flashlight in one hand, I used the other to push apart the bushes. I stepped through and in the beam of light I saw the tiny winding path leading up to the house.

I was surprised not to see the lights Kerry had promised, but maybe they would appear once I was at the house. A thought occurred to me. Would Kerry appear, too? And if she did, would she look nightmarish, as if she had just crawled out from beneath that train? Had she dragged herself back up the hill to the house, her broken and twisted body snaking behind her, leaving a crimson trail of blood and mud in the snow? I shuddered at the thought.

In the distance, through the trees, I could see that broken chimney pot and I pushed those images of Kerry from my mind. I made my way toward the house. It stood before me, leaning to one side as if it had spent too many nights standing in the cold and the wind. The snow-covered ground before it was fresh and untouched. There were no other footprints than my own.

The wind blew hard through the nearby trees, and the branches creaked like the bones of the elderly. I started to feel spooked, but it wasn't just the sound of the wind in the trees—I felt as if someone was watching me. The lights had yet to appear, so I made my way inside.

The smell of stale beer, pot, and urine wafted into my nose again, just as it had before. In the silence, I could hear the sound of water dripping down the moss-covered walls. There was a noise, a scratching sound, in the far corner. I spun around to see a pair of orange eyes peering out of the darkness at me. I gasped and dropped my flashlight. It rolled away, and in the light that it cast across the house, I saw a fox go tearing past me and out into the night. Then the light went out. I looked back to see the fox's tail swish around the doorway and a shadow fall across the snow outside.

The shadow was far too big to belong to the fox and it was moving toward the house, not away from it. Somebody was coming.

"Kerry, is that you?" I called out, frantically searching the floor for my flashlight.

From outside I could now hear the sound of approaching footsteps in the snow.

"Hello?" I called out again, my fingers at last brushing over my flashlight, which had rolled away into the corner. I snatched it up and switched it on. Nothing. The bulb had broken.

The sound of the footsteps outside stopped. With my heart racing in my chest, I looked up to see the silhouette of a man standing in the doorway of the shack. I stumbled backward in fright.

"Hello, Charley," he whispered.

CHAPTER 32

Harker was sitting in his office. I knocked once on the door and entered without giving him the chance to answer. I put the logbook on his desk. He looked at it, then up at me.

"Well?" he asked, raising one of his eyebrows. "Did you find the phantom scratches?"

"They're not phantom," I told him. "And no, I haven't found them—not yet anyway."

"So what's with the logbook?" he asked.

"Jackson did sign out a marked police car on Sunday night. He took Romeo Two-One."

"So?"

"As you can see, he signed it out just two minutes after turning up for his night shift," I said.

"What are you suggesting?" Harker asked me, picking up the logbook and studying it.

"Does a CID officer usually take a marked vehicle out on patrol?" I asked. "And why the rush? He had only been in the station two minutes, not even long enough for him to book on duty with the control room."

"Maybe he had an urgent statement booked that he needed to get out and take?" Harker said thoughtfully.

"What, at that time on a Sunday night?" I cried. "Not likely. Anyway, how do you account for the car smelling of women's perfume?"

"What?" Harker said.

"As you can see, the vehicle was next booked out by Jones at a quarter past seven on Monday morning. No one had used it since Jackson," I explained. "I've just spoken to Sarah Jones and she says she remembers getting in the car the next morning and that it stank of perfume. Now, why would that be? I wonder."

"Do we know what perfume the Underhill girl wore, if any?" Harker asked.

"Not yet," I said. "But I'm about to check with . . ."

"And even if she did, what does that prove?" Harker cut in. "Half the women in town probably wear it." Harker snapped the logbook closed. "Where's Jackson now?"

"He's gone out to collect some CCTV . . ." I started.

Then, from behind me someone said, "No, I'm right here."

Jackson stood in the doorway. "What's going on?" he asked.

243

"I've got a bloody good mind to ask you the same question," Harker barked at him. "Where have you been?"

"To collect some CCTV for the Underhill job," he said waving a silver disc in the air. "Look, what's this all about?"

Harker stood up and came around from the other side of his desk. "Did you take a marked police vehicle out on patrol on Sunday night?"

"No," Jackson said, his eyes narrowing as he glanced at me. Then, as if sensing that everything wasn't quite right, he said, "I can't remember. You know what it's like; all the days just seem to roll into one."

"Then let me refresh your memory," Harker yelled, snatching up the logbook and throwing it at Jackson. "Don't you lie to me. I want the truth or I'll come down on you so hard, so help me God."

Jackson opened the logbook and flicked through the pages. I could see he wasn't really reading the pages; he knew his name was going to be in the book. "Oh, that's right, I remember now. I took a marked vehicle as someone hadn't put the keys for the CID cars back on the hook."

"Why were you so keen to get out that night?" Harker shot back, and all the while I kept watching Jackson. His face had gone white and that air of cockiness had melted away.

"I had a job I had to attend to," Jackson said.

"What job?" Harker snapped.

"Um," Jackson mumbled.

"I want the truth!" Harker roared, just inches from Jackson's face. I saw Jackson flinch away. "Why did that police car stink of perfume? Who did you have in that car? Was it the Underhill girl?"

Jackson's eyes bulged in their sockets. "What?" he gasped. "Is this some sort of joke?" Then, looking at me he said, "This is your doing, Henson. It's you who's put these doubts about me in the guv's head. Don't think I don't know what you're up to. I've met smarmy little pricks like you before. You're just trying to make a name for yourself. Well, don't think you're going to get away with it."

"Did you have a girl in that car?" Harker roared again, and just for a moment Harker seemed so angry, I thought he was going to throttle a confession out of Jackson.

Lois appeared in the doorway of Harker's office. "What's all the shouting about?"

"It's that shithead over there," Jackson yelled, hooking his thumb in my direction. "He's been filling the guv's head with all kinds of crap."

Then, stepping toe-to-toe with Jackson, Harker breathed into his face and said, "You tell me exactly what went on in that car on Sunday night, or I'm straight on the phone to Complaints and Discipline. This is your last chance, Jackson."

Jackson took a step back from Harker, then throwing me a quick glance, he said, "Okay, so I did have a woman in the car on Sunday night, but it's not what you think. It has nothing to do with the Underhill girl."

"What did you do?" Lois asked, folding her arms across her chest.

"I've been seeing this girl, Michelle, for the last couple of months," he said. "It's nothing serious, just a bit of fun. Anyway, she traveled up from Penzance on Sunday and we spent the day together. I took her for a meal in town. But when I got in the car to give her a lift back to the train station, the bloody thing wouldn't start. It was pouring down buckets of rain, as you know, and there weren't any cabs about. I couldn't let the poor cow walk back to the railway station, could I? I was trying to make a good impression. So I told her to wait in a shop doorway while I ran up the road to the yard. I was in a rush, so I just snatched the first set of keys I came across, signed the book, and went back to fetch her. She got in the car and I drove her to the station."

"What's this woman's full name and address?" Harker asked.

"Oh, come on, boss," Jackson groaned. "I'm telling you the truth."

"Name and address."

"She's married, guv," Jackson said. "It could cause her all sorts of problems. She told her old man that she was visiting her sisters that day."

"Tough," Harker snapped.

"I can make some discreet inquiries," Lois said.

"And what about the perfume?" Harker asked him.

"On the way back to the station, she takes a bottle of the stuff from her bag," Jackson said. "I told her not to use it in the car, but she was worried. You know, we had been together all afternoon and I guess she just wanted to hide the smell of me and . . ."

"You're so gross," Lois sighed.

"Anyway, I dropped her off at the railway station and I was on my way back to work when the call came in for the Underhill girl. I went straight there. That's why I was first on the scene. That's the truth, guv," Jackson said. "That's one of the reasons why I wanted to get the Underhill job wrapped up that night."

"What do you mean?" I asked, stepping from the corner of the room.

"When the guv started asking for the CCTV from the railway station, I knew I would be seen dropping Michelle off," he said. "And then I would've been in the shit for using a job car in job time for my own personal use. But the funny thing is, that CCTV will now save my arse."

"How do you mean?" I asked.

"Well, you seemed to have it all figured out that I'm implicated in the death of Kerry Underhill." He smiled. "But I have an alibi for the time of her death and it's all captured on CCTV."

"You're not out of the woods yet," Harker said. "If you've got nothing else to say, then get out of my sight. I'm sick of looking at you."

Jackson shot me one last look, and then left the office. Once he'd gone, Harker turned to Lois. "Speak to this Michelle—but on the q.t. Then check out the CCTV from the railway station."

"Yes, boss," she said, and left the office.

Harker slumped into his chair. He looked at me. "I should never have listened to you in the first place."

"But . . ." I started.

"No *buts*, Henson," he said. "I just don't know who or what to believe anymore. Now go on, get out."

I shut Harker's office door behind me, and turned to see Jackson sitting at his desk, staring at me.

"Happy now?" he sneered.

"Happy about what?" I asked him, going to my desk.

"That you've got me in the shit?"

"Shut it," Lois snapped at him. "You got yourself in the shit, no one else. Why don't you do something useful and make me a cup of coffee."

"Yes, Sergeant. Anything you say, *Sergeant*," Jackson said, getting up from his desk and striding toward the coffeemaker.

I looked over my shoulder at Lois. She gave me one of her smiles and winked. "He'll get over it," she whispered, but I doubted he would.

CHAPTER 33

D ad, what are you doing here?" I gasped.

"I could ask you the same thing, Charley," he said, stepping in out of the snow. "I locked you in your room for a reason."

"How did you know I was going to be here?" I asked.

"Your taxi driver used to be a mate of mine. Barry recognized you. He was worried, so he called me up and told me where he'd dropped you off. So what's going on? Is this another one of Tom's stupid ideas?"

"It's got nothing to do with Tom," I said. "He doesn't even know I'm here."

"What about that other copper? The one with the eyebrows?" he asked me, sounding bitter.

"No one knows I'm here, apart from you," I told him as the wind began to howl outside.

"So what's going on?" Dad asked, taking a step closer.

"You wouldn't believe me, Dad, even if I told you," I said, half of me resenting the fact he had followed me up here, but another part pleased I wasn't alone.

"It has something to do with the death of that girl, doesn't it?"

I looked at him and nodded.

"Charley, this has got to stop," he said, his voice softer.

"What has?"

"You've got to stop running around the countryside trying to solve these crimes," he said with a long sigh. "It's not your responsibility. And not only that, you could be putting yourself in danger."

"How?" I asked.

"Charley," he said. "You're stuck in the middle of nowhere, late at night, in a blizzard, with no way home!"

"I'm not in any danger," I said, not wanting to admit to myself how dumb I'd been.

"Not in any danger?" Dad sighed again. "What if you'd slipped out here in the snow and broken a leg? What would have happened to you then? No one knows you're out here. You would've had to lie in the snow all night long, and the chances are you would've frozen to death. Did you even consider that?"

"No," I said, shaking my head. "But I had to come out here, Dad. I had to."

"But why?"

"You know why. To prove to you and everyone else that what I see in my flashes is real."

"I do believe you," he said, coming closer.

"Really?" I whispered with surprise. "You're just saying that."

"Let's just go home and talk about it in the warmth, Charley," he said.

"But you don't believe that Mum's death is connected to what has happened to these girls, do you?" I asked him, and with every step he took closer to me, the atmosphere in the shack became more oppressive.

"Your mum committed suicide," he said.

"Where?"

"I've already told you," he said, his voice almost soothing. "On the railway tracks."

"Where exactly?"

"Just at the bottom of this hill."

"And you still don't think that all of this is connected?" I asked, tears standing in my eyes at the realization my mum had died near here, too. "Don't you see, Dad? This man could have been involved in Mum's death as well." Tears trickled down my face. Dad took one of my hands in his and gently squeezed it.

My head jerked backward.

Flash! Flash! Flash!

A small child sitting in a car nearby. The sound of crying. Looking through a window. The run-down chimney just visible through the trees in the distance.

Flash!

The images disappeared as quickly as they had come and my brain felt as if it were spinning inside my skull.

"Charley, are you okay?" Dad asked me, releasing my hand. "You're seeing something, aren't you?"

"I saw the child again," I whispered.

"Child?" he asked, and took my hand again.

Flash! Flash!

I could see the train. It was screaming toward me. No, it was the woman screaming, the woman whose eyes I was seeing through. She was making such a hideous noise. She stood, locked by fear. Rigid. Unmovable.

Flash! Flash! Flash!

"What did you see?" my father asked, sounding concerned. "Did you see him? Did you see his face?"

"No," I whispered, shaking my head. "But I will see it. I know I will."

"How can you be so sure?" he asked.

"Kerry's close by; that's why the flashes are coming," I told him, looking into his eyes.

"What are you talking about?"

"Kerry is close," I whispered, rummaging for my phone. I pulled it out, waiting for her call. "She told me to meet her here. She's going to lead me to her killer."

"What are you talking about?" he snapped.

"I must text her and tell her I'm here, that I'm waiting for her," I said, starting to type.

"Stop that!" Dad tried to snatch the phone.

"No!" I cried, pulling away from him.

The phone started to buzz. Someone was trying to connect with me. Not via text, or phone, but by FaceTime. I hit the CONNECT button. The screen flickered green, black, then blue.

I waved the phone in the air, desperate for a better connection. Then I saw her. Her face was faint, but she was there. It was Kerry staring back at me from the iPhone screen. It was the face I had seen in my flashes. Kerry's eyes were dark and round, her skin pale, translucent. Blackness framed her face as she peered out of the darkness at me. I looked into the phone, my heart racing, feeling sick with fright.

"I'm here, Kerry. I want to know now. Who was it? Who was it who killed you?" I said.

The screen flickered and for a moment she was gone. I shook the phone in frustration and she reappeared.

"Who was it, Kerry?" I urged, fearing I'd lose her again. "Who killed Alice and Natalie?" The taste of decay washed over my tongue and down the back of my throat. I swallowed hard. "Who killed you?" I begged her.

Earth escaped from her mouth and tumbled over her chin, "Look behind you, Charley."

The screen went black.

Very slowly, heart thumping, I turned around and looked at my father.

CHAPTER 34

After making Lois her third cup of coffee of the shift, Jackson grunted, "I'm going for a smoke. If you want another coffee, I'll be in the yard."

Once he'd gone, Lois picked up the telephone and looked meaningfully at me. "Are you phoning his alibi?" I said. She nodded.

"Don't you think it's a bit late to be calling her now?"

"Not my problem." She shrugged, punching the numbers into the phone. "The guv says he wants her checked out, so I'm checking her out."

I turned away and tried to make myself look busy, but I couldn't help but listen to what Lois was saying. Even though I was only privy to a one-sided conversation, I got the feeling that whoever this Michelle was, she was extremely embarrassed by the questions Lois asked her. It was obvious, from what I could hear, that Jackson had been telling the truth.

My heart sank. Not because I wanted it to be Jackson who had taken Kerry and the other girls, but because the real killer was still at large.

Lois finished her phone call, hung up, and, without saying anything, went into Harker's office and closed the door. I sat and drummed my fingers on the desk, then decided to go back to the briefing room and check the rosters pinned on the wall there, to see who else had been on duty that night.

I was just about to leave the office when I heard the fax machine buzz in the corner and a stream of paper began to print. I crossed the office and picked up the printout. It didn't take me more than a moment to realize it was the list of calls and texts sent and received from Kerry Underhill's phone.

With my eyes growing wide, I could see that several messages had been sent to and from the phone since her death. Then, with my heart racing, I realized the messages had been sent to and from the same number. It was a number I knew. It was Charley's number.

"What in hell is going on?" I said aloud, trying to make sense of what I was reading. "How could Kerry be sending texts when she's dead?"

With my head spinning and my knees feeling as if they were going to buckle at any moment, I read the last few messages that had been shared between Charley and Kerry. Whoever had texted Charley had told her to follow the lights. A feeling of dread crept over me; I felt I might just stop breathing at any moment. It couldn't have been the dead girl texting

Charley. Charley must've been communicating with the killer, and now he was waiting up at the derelict house for her.

The sheet of paper slipped from my fingers. With my heart racing, I felt unable to move, as if my shoes had been nailed to the floor. All I could think of was Charley making her way up to the shack in the dark and not knowing the danger she was in or who was waiting for her there.

Think!

Then, pulling my phone from my pocket, I frantically searched through my contacts and dialed Charley. Nothing! The line was dead.

"Bloody phone!" I roared, throwing it across the office.

It bounced off the wall, its plastic shell shattering. But before it had even hit the floor, I was racing from the office.

I barged through the swing doors into the briefing room, snatched a set of keys from the wall, and headed to the yard. The snow was still falling and looked something close to a blizzard. Shielding my eyes with my hands, I cut across the yard to the last remaining marked vehicle. I dived inside and turned on the engine. The windshield was covered with snow, and even though I had switched on the wipers, they were groaning beneath the weight of it.

"For Christ's sake!" I cried, climbing from the car. With my bare hands, I started scraping the windshield. My fingers were soon glowing like raw lumps of meat.

"What's your problem?" I heard someone shout.

I looked up to see Jackson shivering in the smokers' corner. The tip of his cigarette winked on and off in the dark as he puffed.

"Give me a hand over here!" I shouted.

"And why should I help you, exactly?" Jackson called back. I didn't need to look up to know he would have that stupid-looking grin plastered across his arrogant face. "I thought you were top cop around here? I didn't think you needed help from anyone."

"He's got Charley!" I shouted, scooping handfuls of snow from the windshield of the police car.

"Charley who?" he said, sounding uninterested.

I had cleared enough of the snow to be able to see my way, so I climbed back into the car. I looked at Jackson. "Just do one thing for me—tell Harker there is going to be another death on the tracks tonight!"

"How can there be?" He grinned back at me from the gloom. "The prime suspect is standing right here having a smoke."

"Screw you, Jackson," I said under my breath and sped away as fast as the icy ground would allow me.

The wind howled as snow pelted the side of the police car. Several times, I felt the back wheels of the car spin uncontrollably, and then grip the road again.

"Please! C'mon! Please!" I screamed, slamming my hands against the steering wheel. This was all wrong. I had to get to the derelict house, and fast.

CHAPTER 35

The wind screamed around the roof of the house. Over my father's shoulder, I could see the snow falling so heavily that now it was impossible to see any more than just a few inches into the night. It was like the outside world had been smothered—cut off.

"You?" I gasped, unable to catch my breath. My heart felt like a lump of lead in my chest. "Did you kill Kerry . . . Natalie . . . the others?"

"So what if I did? I'm still your father, aren't I?" He shrugged, a smile creeping over his face like a shadow. He looked smug, pleased with himself.

"Please, Dad," I breathed. "What are you saying? You're scaring me."

"There's no reason to be scared." He smiled again. "I'm not a monster. In fact, I'm quite a genius."

"Genius?" I gasped.

"I had it all figured out," he said, his voice eerily calm. "See, Charley, I had to bring Kerry here first. Very important part of the plan. Kerry couldn't have got onto the tracks too soon or the police might have wondered how she got there so quickly. Clever, isn't it? I know how these coppers think, you see. There wouldn't have been enough time for her to have walked from the pub. That would have meant she came up here by car and that would have led to ques—"

"Stop it, Dad," I cried. "You're making this up. Why are you saying this?"

"Oh, Charley," he said, reaching forward and stroking my hair with his fingers. In that instant, I pictured the hand from my flashes reaching out and stroking Kerry's cheek as she lay on the tracks. I flinched backward. I didn't want him to touch me. "It's not so bad," he whispered.

"Not so bad?" I whimpered, my lower lip beginning to tremble. "You killed Kerry . . . You killed Natalie?"

"No, I didn't kill Natalie here." He smiled wistfully. "Two girls' deaths in the same place in just a few weeks? No, no, no." He shook his head and tutted. "That would never do."

I couldn't believe how calculated he had been. It was as if he had planned each of his murders with a callous precision. They hadn't been the random acts of a madman like you see in the movies or on TV. Perhaps that made him worse than mad. Perhaps his cold calmness made him evil . . .

"I took her to that other place. That little outbuilding you stumbled across after dashing away from her funeral," he said, rubbing his hands together in delight. "There was a mattress for her to lie on and everything. It was perfect."

"Why?" I mumbled, numbed by what he was telling me.

"Natalie didn't like me," he said. "I didn't like the way she used to look at me. It was like she didn't trust me. I couldn't have that. Then, that night, she called for a cab . . ."

"And you picked her up," I said, all the parts slowly falling into place. "She would have got into the car because she *did* trust you. But instead of driving Natalie to our house, you killed her."

"No, don't you see the beauty of it, Charley?" he said, hopping from foot to foot with excitement. "I didn't kill her—I didn't kill any of them. It wasn't like I strangled them, beat them, cut them in two . . ."

"Stop it!" I screamed, covering my ears with my hands. I didn't want to hear him. For as long as I could muffle his voice, then he was still my dad, not the killer he wanted to confess to being.

"Listen to me," he whispered, pulling my hands from the sides of my head and holding me close.

"Get off me," I screeched, slapping at him. "You're lying."

He let go of me. "Charley, you know what I'm saying is true. It was only going to be a matter of time before you saw me in those flashes. I couldn't let you find out like that. It's only fair that you heard it from me first. See, I was trying to protect you all along and you got mad at me because I locked you in your room. Tut, tut." He smiled, wagging his finger at me as if I were a naughty little girl.

"Have you lost your mind?" I cried. "Do you think that by not killing them with your own hands, it makes it all right? That it makes it better?" I looked at him through the darkness. "Dad, you're a murderer. However you try and justify it—you killed Natalie, Kerry, and all the others. You laid them on those tracks. None of them would have been on those tracks if it hadn't been for you."

He shrugged his shoulders nonchalantly. "Maybe you're right, Charley. But you don't understand the power."

"Power?" I gasped. "What are you talking about?"

"Ever killed a spider?" he suddenly said.

"What?" I asked, shaking my head in confusion.

"Ever killed an insect?"

"I guess," I mumbled.

"As a kid, I killed hundreds of them." He spoke as if he were giving confession to a priest. "I pulled their legs off and watched them wriggle around on their bellies. Ripped their wings off and laughed as they tried to fly away from me. I had an ant farm as a boy; filled it with boiling water one day from the kettle."

"Why are you telling me this?" I asked, my flesh crawling, as if those insects he had tortured had come back to haunt me.

"Because, you know, when you stamp on that spider, swat that fly, Charley, did you ever feel the slightest bit of guilt?" he asked. "Of course you didn't. Who does? It's an insect, right? But it was still a living thing. And I used to wonder about that a lot as a boy. It kept me awake at night. Then I got to wondering if they knew they were going to die. Did they have thoughts? Did they feel the same fear we would just moments from our death?"

"Dad, please . . ." I begged.

"Then one day, I came across a big fat ginger tomcat lying in the gutter," he said, his voice taking on a dreamy quality. "It had been hit by a car, I think. It was covered in blood and dirt, and its back legs were twitching . . ."

"Please . . ."

"Shhh, Charley, you need to understand," he soothed, placing his forefinger against my lips. "The cat's eyes were open and it was looking at me and I wondered if it knew it was dying. Like those insects, did the cat know it was so close to death? Does a cat have any concept of death— of dying? There was a rock nearby . . ."

"Please stop," I sobbed.

"Shhh," he soothed again, slowly drawing his finger down the length of my cheek.

I shuddered at his touch as he continued, lost in his own madness. "And as I brought that rock down, I looked into its eyes and could see that it understood. To take that creature's life was power. It was a rush. But it wasn't enough. And as time passed, I couldn't forget those feelings of power. I started to wonder what it would be like to kill a person. That would have to be more of a rush, right? Killing insects and animals was one thing, but to kill a human being was something different. That would be murder and that wasn't allowed. To kill someone isn't an easy thing. How do you dispose of the body? I read the newspapers as one killer after another got caught. Very few got away with it. Then one day, I was fourteen, I had gone walking with a friend along the cliffs near Land's End. We were alone. There was no one else around. I coaxed him to come stand next to me on the edge of a steep cliff. As he looked down at the waves smashing and crashing against the rocks way below, I pushed him over the edge. I watched him bounce off the rocks, his body broken and twisted as it floated out to sea. Like any good friend, I raced for help. I raised the alarm. The Coastguard dragged my friend's body from the sea while I sat and cried and was given tea and cookies to help me get over the shock of seeing my friend fall to his death. No one ever suspected a thing. It was perfect. No one knew what I had done. I had got away with murder.

"But then, many years later, what I had done came to light. My secret was discovered."

"Who by?"

"Your mum, Charley." He smiled.

"Mum?" I whispered. "What do you mean?" I felt as if I were going to throw up at any moment.

"Your mum had flashes, too," he said. "And in her flashes she saw what I had done to my friend all those years ago."

Although I could barely see him in the darkness, I knew he was smiling. "Your mum was sick, Charley. Her flashes made her sick. They tormented her, like they torment you. For days, sometimes weeks, she would slip into a deep state of despair. She drank a lot, to try and block them out, those visions of the dead she claimed to see. But the alcohol only made them worse—more intense, she once said. One evening, I came home to find you crying and hungry while she lay on the sofa, a bottle of vodka half-empty beside her. I dragged her to her feet, and it was then she saw what I had done. It was then, in a series of flashes, she saw me push my friend over that cliff to his death. She called me a monster, a murderer. I couldn't have that. Your mother was always drunk and loose-lipped—who else might she tell about what I had done? She was semiconscious, drunk. So I carried her to the car and drove her out here. It wasn't like it was planned or anything . . ."

Fearing what he was going to tell me, I covered my ears with my hands again. "Stop! Please just stop!" I began to sob.

He lunged forward and grabbed my hands.

Flash! Flash! Flash!

In those brief and fleeting flashes, I saw that child again in the car. Tears running down her face as she stared out the window.

Flash! Flash!

Where have Daddy and Mummy gone?

Flash!

"I was that little girl," I gasped, almost choking on my tears. "You brought me out here that evening. You left me in the car while you took her down onto the tracks."

"I couldn't have left you at home," he said indignantly. "What sort of a father do you think I am?"

A large piece of a very difficult jigsaw puzzle suddenly dropped into place. "That's why the flashes I had about Kerry had been so strong—so vivid. They weren't just flashes, they were memories. That's why I was sitting behind you in that car as you waited for the trains to roll over those girls. I was beginning to remember . . ."

"You were just a baby," he said. "Five or six. Even I can't recall, and I hoped you never would. But when you started to tell me what you had seen in your flashes, I knew it would only be a matter of time before you remembered everything."

"You killed Mum, didn't you?"

"Yes, Charley."

"You took her down onto those tracks just like you did with Kerry and those other girls. You left her lying on the tracks." I gripped his hand, and it was his turn to flinch.

Flash! Flash! Flash!

That train was bearing down on me again, as if it was I who was lying in the middle of those tracks. But it wasn't me, it was my mum's eyes I was looking through as the train raced forward. It had been her eyes

I had been looking through the day Tom brought me up to the ruined house. She saw the train coming but was too drunk to move out of its way. My mum snapped her head to the right, hoping that if she didn't see the train, then the pain wouldn't be so bad.

Flash! Flash!

And there was my father, sitting in the darkness of his car. He was younger-looking, just as I remembered him when I was a child. His hair black, yet to be flecked with gray. No tired wrinkles around the corners of his eyes and mouth.

Flash!

I was sitting in the child's seat in the back of the car and crying for my mum.

Flash! Flash! Flash!

I snapped open my eyes and looked at my father standing before me in the derelict house. "You murdered her!" I roared, my head feeling as if it had been split open.

"Yes," he shouted ecstatically. "It was more than those insects, so much more than that fat old tomcat and my friend. To take her life was like standing on the very edge of the universe. I felt like God. I was God. He takes the lives of thousands every day and gets away with it, and so had I. It was perfect. No one questioned what had happened. From the very beginning, her death was treated as a suicide. There was no knife sticking out of her back. She hadn't been gagged and bound. She was drunk, had a history of mental illness—why should anyone suspect anything? The police actually felt sorry for me when they came to tell me that night what had happened."

"You're the one who's sick, not Mum," I sobbed, just wanting him to be away from me, but knowing in my heart he wasn't going to let that happen.

"But can't you see, Charley?" he said, trying to stop the excitement in his voice from brimming over. "I had managed to do what the other killers hadn't. I'd killed again and had got away with it. It was perfect!"

"How many . . . ? How many have you killed like this?" I asked him. In some strange way, I needed to know.

"Seven, I think," he said thoughtfully. Then, with a soft chuckle, he added, "Don't expect me to remember all of their names."

"Alice Cotton?" I asked him, already knowing the truth.

"Ah, Alice," he said. "What a sweet girl. She hadn't been drinking. It was always better if they had. You see, I'd got away with it for years. I was always picking up drunk girls in my taxi. And drunk was good. The police seemed to question it less if they were drunk. It was like they had staggered onto the railway tracks by accident. Perhaps they had missed the last train home and in their drunken state had walked off the end of the platform, deciding they would walk to the next station. Perhaps they had decided to take a shortcut. Who really knew, except me? They always got in my car because I drove a taxi—they trusted me. But there was always a risk to that. Someone might have seen them get in, seen the company name on the side of the car. I could have easily removed the stickers, but then the girls wouldn't have got in with me."

"The police badge," I whispered.

"You saw that, did you? Yes, the perfect solution," he said, his eyes twinkling in the darkness.

I nodded my head; I was too numb to speak.

"I picked up a drunk copper one night," he explained. "As he fumbled to put his ID card and badge back into his pocket after paying me, he dropped it between the seats. He didn't realize. But I did. I saw it. I used it. I took the cabbie stickers from the side of the cab. I didn't need them anymore. The police badge worked like a dream with both Alice and Kerry. One quick flash of the badge, and they were in the car and out of the rain. No questions asked. Alice even asked me if I was a detective. I liked that," he laughed, as if remembering a private joke. Then looking at me, he said, "What else did you see? Come on, tell me how good you really are."

"I saw Kerry scratch your car as you dragged her from it," I told him. My head was beginning to pound as if the flashes were coming again.

"I know," he said. "But I soon got rid of them."

"The dent to the back of your car?" I gasped.

"That's right," he answered, smiling. "See, Charley, you don't have to depend on your flashes to see things. I knew the scratches were there and I knew I had to get rid of them. So I backed the car into a wall. I even fooled your cop friend, Tom." He grinned, and I saw his teeth in the darkness. "He asked me how I'd come by the damage, and I told him a cock-and-bull story about how someone had backed into my car in the supermarket parking lot. See what I mean, Charley? It's all so easy."

"Or maybe not," I spat, my head beginning to hurt really bad now. "Because I've seen what you've done, and I've told Tom and Harker what I've seen. That's why you were pissed off when you found me with them. That's why you locked me in my room. You didn't really care that they might be using me. You were scared I might eventually see you in my flashes, and I would tell them. That's why you sometimes smelled of soap when you came back home. You were washing the scent of the girls off you—the smell of your victims. And the constant cleaning of the inside of your car. You were washing away any evidence that might have been left behind. But why take your wedding ring off?"

"I do have some respect for your mother's memory," he scowled.

"You really are insane," I breathed, no longer able to recognize the man standing before me. He looked like my father, but sounded and acted like someone else.

"Not insane, Charley, a genius. None of the cops saw what I'd done and you didn't see me in your flashes, or you wouldn't be here now," he gloated.

"So what are you going to do? Kill me?" I shouted—almost daring him.

"No, you're going to have a little drink or two and then go to sleep on the tracks," he said, pulling a bottle of dark liquid from his coat pocket.

He saw me glance down at it. With a smile, he quickly added, "Just a special recipe of mine. No more pink lemonade for you, Charley. I've made you a very special Christmas punch this year. It will blow your mind!"

"You won't get away with another murder so soon."

"Believe me, Charley, if there was any other way—but there isn't," he said, slowly scratching his chin with his free hand. "I've thought about what to do with you long and hard. You have to die. It can't be nice for you suffering with those flashes of yours. I see the pain it causes you. I've seen the pain and hurt those comments on Facebook cause you. I know you hurt because you don't have any friends. Well, I'm your father, and all good fathers protect their daughters. So I'm going to take all that pain away, Charley."

"No one will believe I got drunk alone up here and staggered down onto the tracks. Tom will figure it out."

"Tom." My father smiled. "The cop boyfriend who broke the rules by bringing you up here. What a selfish thing that was for him to do."

"What are you talking about?" I screamed.

"A police officer bringing his distraught girlfriend to the place where her mother killed herself." Again, he smiled at me. "A girl who was so mixed up, she became fixated by the death of a girl named Kerry Underhill who died in the same spot as her mother. A girl so screwed up, she believed she witnessed Kerry Underhill's death in a series of paranormal flashes. A girl who, like her mother, had been in and out of hospitals her whole life, claiming to be able to see things."

"You bastard," I cried, tears rolling down my face again. "You don't really believe you'll get away with this?"

"It doesn't matter what I do and don't believe," he said. "What matters is what the police believe. And when they find your dead body on the tracks, they'll believe you killed yourself, just like your mother did."

Then, gripping me by the arm, he dragged me from the old house, down toward that little winding path that led to the railway tracks.

CHAPTER 36

TOM—THURSDAY: 00:23 HOURS

C'mon!" I screamed, pounding the steering wheel with my fist.

The snow was falling so heavily now that everything was obscured by a white blur. The car slipped forward, every few yards the back wheels spinning against the slippery road. I eased my foot down on the accelerator, desperate to keep pushing on as fast as I could in the direction of the derelict house.

I peered frantically out the window to search for any landmarks that might tell me exactly how far I was from the dirt road. But all I could see was a white, swirling haze. My heart raced and my breathing was shallow as I tried desperately not to let my fear for what might have happened to Charley consume me. I had no idea whether she had met up with the man who was sending the texts. But what was worse, I had no idea who this man was.

Charley had not been able to identify him. Had she met with him already? Was she . . . ? No, I refused to think about that. I had to keep believing she was still alive. But however much I focused on that belief, all I could see was the upper torso of Kerry Underhill sticking out from beneath that freight train. One arm twisted grotesquely around her own shoulders, her other arm missing completely and her legs wrapped around the wheels of the bogie six cars farther down the track. When I pictured her, it wasn't Kerry staring back at me, it was Charley.

"C'mon!" I roared again, and pushed my luck by pressing harder on the accelerator. The car lurched forward and seemed to shudder. The back of the car skidded to the right. I felt the vehicle slide, and I yanked at the steering wheel, desperate to keep the car on the road. But the speed of the skid was too great for me to keep control. The car spun almost completely around and then toppled sideways into a ditch.

I was thrown to the right, my head slamming into the window.

A bolt of pain exploded across my face, and I felt the warm gush of blood as it ran across my forehead and into my eye. I wiped the blood away and pressed the flat of my hand against my temple to stop the flow. The seat belt was so tight across my chest, it felt like someone was standing on me.

I gasped, desperate to get air. I fumbled for the clasp, but because of the angle of the car, I was trapped and I had to twist my arm at an agonizing angle to reach it. I cried out in pain, my fingers brushing over the top of it. All the while I knew time was slipping away for me to get to Charley.

With my teeth clenched and eyes shut, I twisted my arm again and pressed down on the seat belt clasp. It sprung free and my chest felt as if it was going to explode. I lay on my side and gasped for breath. I hoisted myself around using the steering wheel as a lever, pushing myself up against the passenger door. It opened and a flurry of snow blew down into the car. I wriggled myself into a standing position, then sticking my head and shoulders through the open doorway, I hauled myself free.

I hit the ground and rolled onto my back. Hot blood streamed down my face. The back wheels of the car were still spinning as it lay on its side. I staggered to my feet. I felt dizzy and disorientated. With legs like putty, I went back to the car. Reaching in, I grabbed the radio handset from the dashboard. It crackled with static as I switched it on.

"X-ray Five-Oh to control, I need urgent assistance." As soon as the words left my mouth, my legs buckled beneath me and I slid down the side of the upturned police car and into the snow. Everything went black.

CHAPTER 37

Even though my dad had hold of me, I slipped and went sprawling onto my back. The base of my spine exploded with pain as I hit the ground. The surrounding bushes, although covered in soft flakes of snow, had sharp thorns and brambles that snagged at my hair and clothes.

"Please!" I cried out.

"It's okay," he hushed, taking hold of my arm again, pulling me to my feet. And as soon as he touched me, the flashes came again.

Flash! Flash! Flash!

My mum. Twilight. The nearby branches snatching at her clothes, as if trying to keep hold of her. Save her. She wasn't struggling. The smell of booze on her breath. She was drunk.

Flash!

Where are you taking me, Frank? she slurred.

He didn't answer her. And I could see his face. Hard. Cold. A close-up of his eyes. Excitement burned in them.

The flashes disappeared.

"Dad, you've got to stop," I said as he pulled me toward the tracks. "Despite what you think, Tom will figure out what you've done to me."

"Do you really believe that?" He smiled, shaking his head.

"That other taxi driver, the one who drove me up here . . ."

"Will say what?" he snapped. Wisps of breath escaped from his mouth and drifted away like dragon smoke. "He'll say he dropped you up here, alone. He'll say you seemed troubled, or why else would a young girl want to be left out here on her own at night and in the snow? He told me he offered to wait for you, but you said no. Sounds like someone who had no intention of ever coming back from here. He was so worried about you, he called me up. Knowing that the last time I had seen you, you had been upset by those two meddling police officers, I came rushing out here in the snow, only to discover I was too late. Poor little Charley, believing she had been communicating with the dead via her so-called flashes, she decided to join them by running out in front of a train."

"But . . ." I started, then slipped again.

"But nothing," he hissed, pulling me up and dragging me back through the undergrowth. "What you've told the police about some man bringing those girls out here means nothing. There is not a scrap of evidence to suggest those girls were murdered. Apart from that idiot, Tom, who else would believe a word you say? You're troubled, Charley, everyone knows that. Christ, there's an army of professionals, doctors and teachers, who know that."

"Please, Dad," I cried.

I heard the sound of a train scream past in the wind and the snow. It was so close the branches of the nearby trees swayed. "Please," I begged him, but just as I had seen in my flashes, his eyes sparkled with excitement. "Don't do this, Dad. I'm your daughter, your little girl."

"I know," he said. "And that's why I want to stop you from hurting, Charley."

Then, from the corner of my eye, I saw a flash of light in the night sky. At first I thought it was the flashes coming again, but I only ever saw them in my head. The night sky lit up again, luminous blue, then white. Over and over again the sky flashed in the distance. Lightning? In a snowstorm? No. I peered over my dad's shoulder, and my heart raced faster and faster in time with those flashes. They were emergency lights, the type you get on top of a police car.

"*Tom!*" I screamed. He was coming for me.

Dad glanced back over his shoulder and saw the blue lights blazing in the distance. Then the lights were joined by the faint *whoop whoop* sound of sirens. He turned back to face me. His look of excitement had faded. Now I could see uncertainty and fear in his eyes.

"Tom believes me," I said to him. Then, at the top of my voice, I screamed, "Tom's coming for me!"

Clamping his hand over my mouth, he dragged me the last few feet through the bushes and to the hole in the fence next to the railway tracks.

CHAPTER 38

TOM—THURSDAY: 00:33 HOURS

I don't know how long I'd been out, but I guessed it hadn't been long, for the back wheels of the police car were still spinning and the side of it was yet to be covered totally in snow. I could hear a faint voice. My head hurt and I felt groggy. Next to me in the snow lay the handset from the car radio.

"X-ray Five-One from control, what is your location?" The control room operator was calling through the handset.

I reached for it and placed it next to my mouth. "I'm not sure of my exact location. But I'm somewhere near Oakgrove Road . . ."

Another voice cut over me. "X-ray Four-Six to control, I'm near that location. Tell him to stick the car lights on to guide me in."

I recognized Jackson's voice. What was he doing out here? I wondered. Deep inside, I was very glad that he was.

"X-ray Five-One to control, my car lights are on," I said, trying to get to my feet.

"Not the headlights, you idiot!" I heard Jackson's voice groan through the radio. "The emergency lights."

I propped myself against the upturned car, reached in, and hit the switch on the dashboard. The night pulsed with the strobes of blue and white lights.

"I've gotcha!" Jackson shouted. "X-ray Four-Six to control, I can see him. I'm making my way to him now."

"C'mon!" I shouted into the night. Then, as if it might make him get to me more quickly, I reached back into the car and flipped on the sirens.

The sound was deafening. I covered my ears. In the distance, I saw two faint beams of light heading toward me. I pushed myself off the side of the car. With the snow driving hard into my face, I waved my arms back and forth above my head. Then, to acknowledge that he had seen me, Jackson switched on his own lights and sirens. To me, in that moment, it was the most beautiful sight I had ever seen.

I waved my arms frantically in the air. "C'mon! C'mon!"

Jackson drew up alongside me and I opened the door.

"What are you playing at?" Jackson shouted as I slammed the car door shut behind me. "And I'll tell you something else for nothing, the guv is going to go ape-shit when he sees what you've done to that car."

"Screw the car," I managed to say, trying to catch my breath.

Jackson saw the blood on my face. "Are you all right?"

"Do I look all right?" I gasped.

"What I mean is, are you injured? Do you need to go to the hospital?" he asked.

"No," I said, shaking my head. "Just get me as close as you can to the railway tracks."

"Why?" he said, moving the car forward again through the snow.

"I haven't got time to explain. Where's the guv? Is he on his way?"

"The old fart was having trouble getting the car out of the yard," he said. "Lois is with him; they're some way behind."

"Did you tell him what I told you?" I pushed.

"I didn't get a chance," Jackson said. "I found him in the office holding a fax printout. He looked like he was going to have a heart attack or something. Then he starts shouting that we've got to get out here. He nearly knocked me flying as he went racing out the office and—"

"There!" I shouted, spotting the opening to the dirt road. "Stop the car!"

"Whose car is that?" Jackson asked, pointing through the window. There was a car parked on the opposite side of the road. It was white and the roof was covered with such a thick layer of snow, it was barely visible. I screwed up my eyes and peered through the windshield. Then, seeing the dent in the back of the car, my heart sank.

"I know who that car belongs to. I need to get out," I shouted, yanking on the door handle.

"Hang on, will you?" Jackson shouted back at me, bringing the car to a halt.

I clambered from the car. "Thanks, Jackson."

"For what?" he asked.

"For coming after me."

"That's what coppers do, isn't it?" he said. "We watch each other's backs, because if we don't, no one else will."

"I guess," I said, before running into the dark.

"Where are you going?" Jackson roared. "Should I wait for the guv? What's going on?"

I didn't stop to explain. With my legs still feeling like rubber and with blood in my eyes, I ran as fast and as hard as I could through the snow toward the railway tracks.

CHAPTER 39

He held me so tightly, I was sure I could hear the sound of his pounding heart over the noise of the approaching sirens. With his hand clamped over my mouth, I was finding it difficult to breathe. I felt as if I was suffocating. I wrapped my fingers around his hand and tried to pull it away from my mouth.

"Stop struggling," he whispered. His voice sounded cold, just like it had in my flashes. He didn't sound like my dad—he wasn't my dad anymore. This wasn't the man who I'd listened to Elvis with by the Christmas tree while I sipped pink lemonade. That man had gone now. Perhaps he had never really existed. It had all just been some kind of act.

With my mouth covered by his hand, and his other arm coiled around me like a snake, he hurried me toward the hole in the fence. I could hear the sirens coming nearer. I tried to dig my heels into the ground, but they just slid over the icy surface. When that failed to slow him, I reached out with my hands and grasped at the thornbushes. My gloves were thick, but not thick enough to stop the thorns piercing my flesh. My eyes rolled in their sockets as I stifled a scream behind his hand.

We reached the fence. Pressing my face against the metal mesh, he brushed his cheek next to mine and whispered in my ear, "I'm going to take my hand away now. Don't make a noise, Charley, or struggle. Don't draw this out. This is as painful for me as it is for you. Your suffering will soon be over and so will mine. Be quiet and let's get this over with. Do you understand me?"

I nodded and felt his hand slip from my mouth. He pulled an old plastic bottle from his coat pocket and unscrewed the cap.

"Here, drink some of this," he ordered, thrusting the bottle at me. Some of the black liquid splashed over the neck of the bottle. "It will numb the pain . . ."

I threw my head back and screamed, "Tom! Tom! It's my dad. He's going to—"

Before I'd finished, my head snapped backward. It wasn't because of the flashes; it was the sheer weight and force of my dad's fist smashing into my face. For a second, everything went black and I felt the coppery taste of blood in my mouth as it gushed from my nose. My head rolled forward again, and before my chin had hit my chest, he was pulling my hair.

"I told you to be quiet, didn't I?" he hissed, his breath hot against my face. "I've been nice and reasonable with you up until now. Can't you see I'm just trying to help you?"

I opened my eyes and looked into his. Then, through a throat full of blood, I screamed again. "Tom!" But it came out as a muffled gargle as my father upended the bottle and poured the foul mixture into my mouth.

With his fingers entwined in my hair, he yanked my head backward. "Swallow," he hissed.

Flash! Flash! Flash!

Feet running. Railway tracks. A set of railway points closing.

Flash!

I opened my eyes to find myself being dragged through the hole in the fence. The ground beneath me felt like a bed of hard, broken stone. It made a rattling noise as I was pulled over it. The air smelled of grease and oil. I glanced sideways, and only inches from my face, I saw the gleaming steel of the railway tracks.

"No!" I tried to scream, but with my head rolled backward and my throat clogged with blood and burning with the taste of strong alcohol, it sounded as if I were drowning more than screaming. I could hear the sound of my dad panting as he dragged me over the tracks. Once he had me positioned between them, he pinned my arms down so I couldn't move.

He leaned over me, lowering his face so the tips of our noses were almost touching. My heart was racing so fast in my chest, it seemed to be beating in my ears. "You won't get away with this," I gargled. "They'll know you left me here to die."

"They'll think you tripped and knocked yourself unconscious," he whispered.

"Please," I choked, a bubble of black blood popping on my lips. I thrashed and kicked my legs, raising my pelvis in a last attempt to throw him from me. But he was too heavy—too strong.

He seemed to enjoy the struggle as he stared down into my face and smiled. "Good night, Charley," he whispered. "Have sweet dreams."

The tracks beneath me began to vibrate. A train was coming.

"It would be so much easier for both of us if you'd had just a little more of my brew," he said.

The tracks began to rattle. I knew he couldn't risk being seen by the driver of the approaching train. I screwed my eyes shut and thought of Tom. I had just formed a picture of his smile in my mind, when my dad lifted my head off the track, then slammed it back down again.

Tom's smile faded as everything went black and I slipped into unconsciousness.

CHAPTER 40

I thought I heard the sound of a scream, but I couldn't be sure. The wind was blowing so hard around me, it drowned out everything, even the sound of my own breathing. I raced down the dirt road. My feet crunched deep into the snow, which now covered my ankles. With my hands shielding my eyes, I peered into the darkness, searching for the gap in the hedge that led to the old house.

"Where is it?" I shouted aloud. Why hadn't I brought a flashlight? Behind me the lights from the police car blazed on and off like streaks of lightning. Then, in one of those sparks of light, I saw the broken-down bushes that led to the path and the house. I stomped through the snow toward it, the blood above my eye congealing in the cold.

With the night sky lit by the distant emergency lights, I could just make out two sets of footprints in the snow. One set looked fresher than the other. I guessed the first set had been Charley's, the newer set, her father's. I couldn't help but wonder what he was doing out here as well. Maybe he had also discovered that Charley was coming to the house. But who had sent her the messages?

Bent forward, I headed up the hill, my face and hands numb with the cold. I followed the footprints to the open doorway of the house and peered inside.

"Charley?" I shouted. "Can you hear me?"

My calls were met only by the sound of the wind that screamed around the building. Then I saw it, the metal shining back at me from the corner of the main room. Charley's flashlight. I picked it up and, heading back to the door, saw that the glass and bulb inside had been smashed. Had Charley been involved in some kind of struggle? Had she dropped her flashlight in fright? If so, what had scared her so much?

I headed back out into the snow and saw footprints leading down toward the railway tracks. Two sets of prints: Charley's and her father's. But why would her dad take her down to the tracks?

In the distance, I heard the sound of a train. But there was something else, another sound. The noise of the driver blowing his horn, as if giving a warning.

"Charley!" I roared. I dropped her flashlight and tore through the undergrowth as I raced down the hill.

CHAPTER 41

The noise roused me. It was loud and very close, and getting closer by the second. It came again; it sounded like a scream. I was cold and my head hurt. It felt swollen and raw. My throat was painful and I found it hard to swallow.

Whatever I was lying on dug into my neck and shoulders—and it was shaking. It was as if my whole body was rattling. Had I had another fit? Had I seen more of those flashes and collapsed?

The sound had a rhythm to it. Like a heartbeat. *Clackerty-Clack! Clackerty-Clack! Clackerty-Clack!* But there was another sound. This one was louder, violent-sounding. Like some kind of warning signal.

I opened my eyes and glanced in the direction of the noise. *Clackerty-Clack! Clackerty-Clack! Clackerty-Clack!* There was a bright light racing toward me out of the darkness. I put my hands over my eyes. Between

my fingers I saw a black shape behind this bright light and it was growing bigger with every passing second. It made that sound again, and it
was so loud now, I flinched. It came again and again and again. And
then, as if seeing those flashes, I remembered my dad dragging me
on the . . .

Tracks!

The driver blew his horn. The train was so close now. I could hear its
wheels squealing against the steel of the tracks. I tried to get up, but collapsed again, as though all of my strength had been sucked from me. I
tried again, but my head felt so heavy, it was pulling me back toward the
ground.

Clackerty-Clack! Clackerty-Clack! Clackerty-Clack!

Nearer and nearer! Louder and louder!

I gripped the rails. Scraping my knees over the sharp chips of stone
between the tracks, I tried to get up. With my back arched and the glare
of the approaching headlights blinding me, I took a step forward, but
collapsed again across the rails.

The driver blew his horn again and the noise was deafening.

Clackerty-Clack! Clackerty-Clack! Clackerty-Clack!

Faster and Faster! The light, brighter and brighter!

I looked up one last time, and the train was so close now, I could see
the driver sitting in his cab, his face a white mask, hovering in a sea of
darkness. The horn sounded again and, wrapping my arms about myself,
I rolled over the tracks and out of the path of the train. I hadn't even

completed my roll when the train screamed past, just inches from me. It traveled at such speed I felt my whole body lift off the ground. For one frantic moment, it seemed I was being sucked beneath the wheels. The sound was like a giant beast, howling and roaring its guts out in anger.

Finally, it was gone, speeding away into the distance, a trail of snow billowing in its wake. I lay and watched the snow settle, gasping in lung-fuls of ice-cold air. As the huge white flakes floated before me, I saw something move on the other side of the tracks. With every one of my survival instincts screaming at me to get up, I peered through the bliz-zard. My dad was crossing the tracks toward me.

Body trembling in shock and fear, I cried out in pain and staggered to my feet. Every inch of me ached and throbbed, and I wondered if I had been hit by that train after all. But the sight of my dad racing across the tracks told me otherwise. I staggered away from him, the loose pieces of stone between the tracks and beneath the snow making me wobble and lose my balance. With my hands outstretched, I lurched forward. I could hear my dad behind me, his feet stomping over the snow.

I glanced back over my shoulder. He appeared like some dark appari-tion. "Get away from me!" I screamed. Then, as if he had punched me in the face again, my head snapped backward.

Flash! Flash! Flash!

Feet running through snow, crunching over stone. A train in the dis-tance. Track points closing. Screaming. I was screaming! Tom! I could see Tom! More screaming.

Flash! Flash!

No, Tom! I screamed. Blood spraying over white snow. *No, Tom!* I screamed again.

Flash!

I opened my eyes to find myself lying on my back. My dad was leaning over me, reaching for me.

"Get off!" I yelled, drawing my knees up to my chest and kicking out at him. My boots landed in his soft belly and he staggered backward. His arms wheeled and he fell onto his back, making a belching sound as the air rushed from his lungs. He clawed at the sky as he tried to get up.

I scrambled to my feet. I didn't know which way to run. Panicked, I followed the tracks into the white wall of snow that fell all around me. In the distance, I could see a light. It grew brighter with every passing second. The rails beneath me started to rattle again, and I knew there was another train approaching. I left the tracks, hoping I was heading toward the hole in the fence.

There was a grinding sound beneath me, and I looked down and blinked. The tracks were moving. How was that possible? Tracks didn't move, did they? Then I realized what was happening. I was standing by a set of track points, and they were closing. I glanced up and saw the train as it raced toward me. It wasn't far away now and was approaching at an incredible rate. I turned away to head back toward the fence, when I was grabbed from behind.

"Charley," Dad whispered in my ear, and then he screamed.

He released his hold on me and looked down. I followed his eye-bulging stare. The points had closed over his foot, trapping it between them. "Help me, Charley," he gasped. "Please."

The train was coming.

Clackerty-Clack! Clackerty-Clack! Clackerty-Clack!

"Please, Charley," he pleaded, the anger in his voice gone. Instead, he just sounded scared and desperate. His voice reminded me of Kerry Underhill's as she had begged for her mother.

The train was just seconds away.

"*Please!*" he screamed.

I looked into his eyes, and I could see his fear. I couldn't watch him die, whatever he had done.

Clackerty-Clack! Clackerty-Clack! Clackerty-Clack!

The driver blew on his horn. I lunged forward and took hold of my dad's hands. I pulled at him, desperate to drag him free. However much I tried to set him free, it was impossible.

Realizing his fate, my father pushed me backward, out of the path of the oncoming train.

"What are you doing?" I screamed. "I'm trying to save you."

"Run, Charley. Save yourself." He smiled. It wasn't a cruel smile; it was like the smiles he'd had the day we decorated the Christmas tree together. It was a kind smile.

"No!" I cried out.

Clackerty-Clack! Clackerty-Clack! Clackerty-Clack!

I tripped backward and was thrown clear of the tracks.

"Stay back," someone roared in my ear. It was Tom. His face was covered in dried blood.

"Tom!" I screamed over the sound of the approaching train. "Tom, we've got to save my dad."

Tom looked at me and shouted, "It's too late, Charley!"

"No!" I started toward the tracks, but Tom held me back. I looked one last time at my dad waving his arms desperately above his head as if trying to attract the driver's attention.

Then he was gone.

CHAPTER 42

CHARLEY—THURSDAY: 01:17 HOURS

Tom folded his arms around me. I buried my face against his chest to drown out the sound of my sobs. I felt as if my heart had been ripped from my chest. I had never known such pain before. The urge to lie down and never get up again was unbearable. I didn't know how I would ever move past this place. Everything I had seen and learned about my mum and dad was agonizing.

"It was your dad who killed those girls, wasn't it?" Tom whispered.

"Yes," I replied through my sobs. "Please don't tell anyone what he did."

"Charley, we can't keep something like this a secret," he said. "Look, we've already got company."

I peered over the crook of his elbow and could see flashlight beams heading in our direction along the tracks. "Please don't tell them," I said, looking up into his eyes. "Please."

295

Tom brushed the tears from my cheeks, then gently kissed me. "Whatever happens, Charley, whatever anyone says about your dad and what he did, I will believe in you. Nothing will ever change that."

"Thank you," I cried.

The sound of feet trampling over the tracks grew closer. I looked up to see Harker and two others coming toward us. "Who's that with Harker?" I asked. I didn't want to say anything about my dad in front of people I didn't know.

"The guy is Jackson, and the woman is my skipper. Her name is Lois," Tom told me.

"What's happened here?" Harker barked, the shoulders of his fluorescent coat covered with snow.

Tom looked at me, then turned to face Harker. "Charley's father has been struck by a train. He's dead."

"Is this true?" Harker asked me, cocking one of his bushy eyebrows.

"Yes," I whispered, holding on to Tom.

Harker clapped his hands together, then looked at Tom's colleagues. "Well, don't just stand there, you two. Let's get the ball rolling. Get some uniforms down here, and, Jackson, you go and speak with the driver."

"Yes, boss," Jackson grunted, and walked away, back up the tracks to where the train had come to a halt. Lois followed him. She hadn't gone far when Harker called out to her. "Sergeant, can you contact the coroner? I think we'll be able to wrap this one up nice and quickly."

"Yes, guv," she said, throwing a quizzical look, then turning and walking away.

"I don't think it will be as easy as that," Tom said.

"Oh, no?" Harker asked, staring at him. "It looks pretty straightforward to me. Death by misadventure, I'd say."

"How do you figure that?" Tom asked. "With all due respect, sir, you've only just arrived on the scene."

Harker produced a beige folder from inside his coat. He briefly flicked through it, and then tucked it away again. "Your mum committed suicide down here eleven years ago, didn't she, Charley?"

"How do you know about that?" I whispered, tears falling against my cheeks.

"I found her file the other day when I was going back over the deaths that have taken place out here over the last ten years or so," he explained.

"Charley, you never said anything to me about . . ." Tom said, sounding shocked.

"I only found out the other day," I told him. "Dad had kept it a secret from me."

"And who could've blamed him?" Harker half smiled. "What a terrible thing to have to tell your child. But the news troubled you, didn't it, Charley? It played on your mind. It ate away at you. Stopped you from sleeping. I can understand that. And what with all the reports lately about the death of poor Kerry Underhill dying up here, and the tragic loss of your friend, it made the news about your mother all the more painful to deal with. So you decided to come here, didn't you, Charley?" he asked, fixing me with his stare.

"You wanted to be close to where your mother died. You wanted to be able to grieve properly for the first time. Then your father comes home to find you gone. He worked out where you had come to and raced out here. Wanting to be left to grieve in private, you ran through that hole in the fence back there. Realizing the danger you were in, he came after you. But in the snow and the dark, he got disoriented and staggered out onto the tracks, where sadly . . . Well, you know the rest."

"You don't really believe that, do you?" Tom gasped, staring at Harker.

Ignoring Tom, Harker looked at me and said, "Unless Charley has anything different to add?"

I didn't say anything.

With a smile of satisfaction, he looked at Tom. "Case closed."

"You know as well as I do that Charley's father killed those girls," Tom snapped, releasing me from his hold.

"Yes." Harker nodded.

"Then we need to investigate it," Tom said.

"Investigate what, constable?" Harker asked. "There is not one shred of physical evidence to say that Charley's father was involved in the deaths of those girls. We have no witnesses. No CCTV. Nothing."

"We have Charley," Tom said.

"Do you seriously think I'm going to file a report stating I believe the deaths out here are the work of a serial killer on the say-so of your seventeen-year-old *friend*, who claims to have seen it all in a series of flashes? Jesus, Tom, use your brain. I'd be laughed out of the force."

"But it's the truth," Tom insisted. "And it's the truth that matters. I didn't become a police officer to cover things up. I didn't . . ."

Before I even knew what was happening, Harker had closed the gap between him and Tom. With his face just an inch from Tom's, Harker hissed, "Why don't you go around to Mr. and Mrs. Underhill's right now and tell them their beautiful daughter was dragged through the filth and the mud by some nutter. Then terrorized, forced to drink until she was unconscious, then laid across a set of railway tracks. And when Mrs. Underhill collapses brokenhearted to the floor, tell her how you know all this. Tell her about Charley and her flashes. Go on, Henson. Go and tell her."

"But it's the truth," Tom whispered.

"That woman couldn't handle the truth!" Harker said. "Jackson was right. Kerry Underhill left the pub drunk, decided against getting a cab, and walked home. It started to rain and she took a shortcut home across the tracks. Not easy for the Underhills to deal with, but easier than knowing that their daughter's last moments on this Earth were a nightmare. Do you understand what I'm saying, constable?"

Tom looked away.

"Do you understand?"

"Yes, I understand," Tom whispered.

Then, turning to face me, Harker held out his hand and said, "Give me your phone."

"Why?" I asked, taking it from my pocket.

"I read the list of messages on the fax that came through to the office," Harker explained, taking the phone from me. He looked at it, and then dropped it onto the ground. He crushed it under his heel and kicked the smashed pieces of plastic into the undergrowth.

"I don't believe I just saw you destroy a piece of evidence," Tom said.

"Believe what you want, Henson," Harker said, turning away.

"And what do you believe?" I called after him. "Do you believe me?"

Harker turned slowly to face me, and said, "Yes, Charley, I do believe you. I do believe you see things in your flashes—things that no one else can see."

"So what now?" I asked.

"I'll be in touch." He smiled. "I'm sure you will be of great help to me in the future."

"What's that supposed to mean?" Tom asked, taking my hand in his.

"Let's just say that, with Charley's gift, she may be able to point us in the right direction should we ever . . . well, you know . . . need an extra clue or two in the future." And he smiled once more.

"But I thought you said no one would believe her," Tom said.

"I'm not planning on going public about getting Charley to help us," he said. "It will be a secret shared only by us three. I'll keep your secret,

Charley, about what really happened up here tonight. I'm sure you can keep one or two for me."

"But—" Tom started.

Before he'd had a chance to get his words out, Harker looked at him. "That invitation for Christmas dinner is still open, you know. To the both of you."

Tom wrapped his arm around my shoulder and said, "No, thanks, sir. I think Charley and I will just spend Christmas Day together."

"You do realize McDonald's will be closed on Christmas Day, don't you?" he said, and winked. Then he was gone, disappearing into the snow.

Tom stood and held my hand. "What happens now, Charley?"

"Take me home, stay with me tonight," I whispered. "I don't want to be alone."

He wrapped his arm around my waist and together we left behind those railway tracks, the dilapidated house, and what happened there.

ACKNOWLEDGMENTS

I would like to give special thanks to my wife, Lynda, and three sons, Joseph, Thomas, and Zachary, for putting up with me. I would also like to thank Barry Cunningham for being the first publisher to take a chance on me, and Imogen Cooper for all her advice and help. Both of you have brought out the very best in *Flashes*. Thank you. Thanks to my agent, Peter Buckman, for signing me on that cold snowy day in March and for telling me to go away and write a gripping mystery for young adults. I hope I've done that with *Flashes*.

Although *Flashes* was the first of my books to be signed by a publisher, I had been self-publishing my stories on the Internet since 2011. During that time, I have sold 300,000 books and none of it would have been possible without the army of loyal fans who follow my stories and tell all their friends and family about them. So I am truly grateful to the following fans who have encouraged me:

Lisa Ammari, Jennifer Martin-Green, Carles Barrios, Shanna Benedict, Carolyn Johnson Pinard, Caroline Barker, Amanda Golder, Sarah Lane, Rose Lennart, Spandana Nallamilli, Louise Chapman, James Hodson, Marsha Meadows, Rose Freeman, Toni Francis, Lindy Roberts, Zoey Burns, Roz Hilditch, Kara Cheney, Erica Paddock, Stacey Szita, Gemma Dahren, Michelle Wilton, Paul Collins Bullet, Shereen Baldwin, Courtney Jackson, Noreen McCartan-Doran, Trish Diehm, Cassie Sansom, Michelle Brearley, Conny CH, Shelley Mckelvey, Cathy Douglas, Tina Altman, Shelbey Proudfoot, Teresa Walsh, Jackie McLeish, Heidi Madgwick, Claire White, Kellie Micallef, Maureen Harn, Rachel Micallef, Nereid Gwilliams, Tricia McDaniel, Jen Rosenkrans Montgomery, Wendy Wiegert, Robbie Parker, Joanne Lonsdale, Michelle Hayman, Sue McGarvie, Lieann Stonebank, Abbey Pearson, Jessica Claire, Jennifer Goehl, Maria Vargas, Stacey Tucker, Michelle Thornton, Kathy Howrey Brand, Holly Harper, Sarah Isherwood-Smith, Kiera Hayles, Savannah Harrop, Amber Mundwiller, Kathleen Guardado, MaryAnn Brittingham, Laura Wootton, Lois Li, Tara Taggart, Andreia Lopes, Kimberly Mayberry, Helen Louise Ellis, Ruth Morgan, Tina Langford, Melissa Wright, Rebecca Holloway, Cally Munn, Rachel Roddy, Sabrina Christine Quarantillo, Tina Altman, Amanda Duke Ne Carlin, Krystale Willis, Etta Mellett, Julie Garner Shaw, Lindy Roberts, Shellie Hedge, Sam

McMullen, Jen Clachrie, Amanda Anderson, Jaime-Leigh Wilton, Jordan Wilton, Jemma Wood, Barbara Grubb, April Harvey, Lisa Kresco-Churchey, Samantha O'Rourke, Jade Sutherland, Stephen Gibson, Kay Donley, Beata Janik, Warren Bixby, Helen Websdale, Fiona Nelson, Gemma Rushton, Kristen Heyl, Nikki Espiritu, Jenn Waterman, Nikki Ayres, Gayle Morell, Nichola Dickson, Lee Creed, Wayne Millard, Jenna N. Waller, Jolene Saunders, Patricia Lavery, Ally Esmonde, Julie-Anne Hope, Hannah Landsburgh, Kayleigh Morgan Griffiths, Clare O'Neil, Bernice Thomas, Abbie Robertson, and Marilyn Waters.

Thank you all so much.

Hugs,

Tim xx

ABOUT THE AUTHOR

Tim O'Rourke was a serving police officer for fifteen years, but now writes full time. *Flashes* is his debut young adult novel. Tim lives in England with his wife and three sons. You can visit him at www.kierahudson.com.

BONUS!

FROM MICHAEL L. PRINTZ HONOR
AUTHOR LUCY CHRISTOPHER

Ashlee Parker is dead, and Emily Shepherd's dad is accused of the crime. A former soldier suffering from PTSD, he emerges from the woods carrying the girl's broken body.

What really happened that wild night? Emily knows in her bones that her father is innocent, but she's got to find out the truth before he's convicted. Does Damon Hilary, Ashlee's charismatic boyfriend, have the answers? Or is he only playing games with her—the kinds of games that can kill?

FRIDAY NIGHT

1. EMILY

Something was draped across Dad's outstretched arms. A deer? A fawn that was injured? It was sprawled and long-legged, something that had been caught in a poacher's trap maybe. A mistake. So this is where Dad had been all this time: in the woods and cutting this creature free. I breathed out slowly, squinted at the mist that hovered around Dad like a ghost. I took my hand from my bedroom window, leaving the memory of my skin on the glass. Then I raced down the stairs, through the hall, and into the kitchen out back. Throwing open the door to the garden, I waited for him there.

It was ages since Dad had brought back something injured, and he'd never brought back a deer, though I could remember helping him free a roe deer from a snare in the woods once. Back then his hands had moved quickly and gently, darting from the wire on the doe's leg and then to her neck for a pulse, stroking her constantly. This was something like that again. Saving another deer could be a good thing for

Dad, something to take his mind off everything else, to help bring him out of his dark place.

I heard Dad's feet scuff on the cobbles in the lane, saw his movement. I tried to pick out the shape of the deer's body, but it was all wrong. The legs weren't long enough, neither was its neck. I took a step toward them. And that's when it made sense: the shape.

It wasn't a deer Dad was carrying. It was a girl.

Her neck was tilted back, her bare arms glowing in the moonlight. Her clothes were soaking. The garden gate creaked as Dad maneuvered through, struggling. How long had he been carrying her? From where? I moved backward into the kitchen. Dad had saved people when he'd been a soldier — carried them to safety — maybe he was being a hero again now.

Then I saw that this girl's skin was gray, blue around the lips like smudged lipstick. Her long hair was plastered across her face, dark from the rain. I saw her green short-sleeved shirt and the silver bangle on her arm. I wanted to sweep the wet hair from her face, but my hand was half raised when I stopped myself. I recognized her. I knew this girl.

"What happened?" I said.

Dad didn't answer. His face was red and damp; he wheezed as he pushed past me. The girl's fingers trailed over my arm, and they were cold — dead cold — like a stone found in a cave. Dad laid her carefully on the kitchen table, as if he were putting her to bed. He turned her head to the side and stretched out one of her arms so she was in the recovery position. He touched her neck gently, just like he'd touched the neck of the trapped roe deer so long ago. But this deer didn't move, didn't struggle or try to stop him.

Her name was Ashlee Parker.

I made myself bring my fingers to her wrist, waited long enough to be sure. I knew I should be panicking, should be calling an ambulance . . . but Ashlee Parker's eyes were staring at me, fixed in position, brown and big.

"She's got model's eyes," Kirsty had said once. "She's beautiful. It's no wonder Damon Hilary follows her everywhere."

Damon Hilary. Something twisted inside me when I thought about him — of how he'd react to this.

I rested the tip of my finger on Ashlee's cheek. I wanted to help her struggle and leap free, disappear into the trees. I could only hope that everything screaming through my head was wrong.

"Is she . . . ?" I hesitated. "Is she . . . OK?"

Dad didn't answer. I don't know what he thought, whether he hoped she would wake up. But I'd seen the small red marks on her neck, the blue speckles of bruises spreading out like flowers. I could see she wasn't breathing at all.

What had she been doing in the woods?

How had she got like this?

I can't remember how long we stood there, with the moon and stars shining through the kitchen window like spotlights. It felt like forever. Eventually there was a creak upstairs: Mum was up.

"Everything all right down there?" she called.

Maybe she'd been waiting for Dad to return too, pretending to sleep like I'd been earlier, listening to the summer storm. I heard her slippers treading in the hall, then the kitchen door swung inward and immediately Mum was complaining about Dad keeping us up, lecturing him about staying out during thunder.

"You know how you get when the weather's like this . . ." she was saying. "You shouldn't . . ."

Then she saw Ashlee.

She made a tight gasping sound as if she'd sucked up all the oxygen in the room at once. She looked at Dad, then back to Ashlee. She stepped across and felt for a pulse.

"Who is she?" she said, her voice low. When he kept quiet, she strode across the room and grabbed Dad by the shoulders. "What's happened?"

She moved toward the telephone on the windowsill, her eyes running over Dad's muddy face and wet clothes, then over Ashlee again. The wheezing sound from Dad's chest got louder.

"Was she in the woods?" Mum's voice rose. "With you?" Her fingers were shaking as she pressed the numbers on the phone. "We need an ambulance . . . police."

I wanted to tell Mum that this was Ashlee Parker from school. I wanted to say that I didn't know what had happened, and neither did Dad, and that he was trying to save her . . . but the words stayed lodged in my throat like something half-swallowed. Mum gave our address, hung up, went back to Dad. Her nails dug into his shoulders. Dad gulped air like a fish, one of his panic attacks starting. I knew I should go get his inhaler, or start talking softly to him — reminding him of where he was and who we were — but I couldn't move. I couldn't stop looking at Mum's frightened eyes.

"Tell me what happened, Jon!" she demanded.

I edged toward the open door to the garden. *Give Dad time*, I wanted to say. *Let him explain.* But Mum wanted answers, and that made me panic too . . . made me want to get away.

"Dad found her," I whispered, saying what I wanted to be true. "She was in the woods, walking . . . lost."

Mum looked at me: the first time either of my parents seemed to notice me that night. "She's dead, Emily."

Her words sent me feeling for the door handle, for something to hold on to. Then Dad's sudden shout made me jump.

"She wasn't supposed to be there!"

He'd said this before when he'd come out of a flashback. The same words. Maybe he was in a flashback again. Mum was right. It must have started from hearing the thunder, from being out in that storm when he shouldn't have been anywhere near it.

Mum brushed the hair from Ashlee Parker's face. "Did you do something, Jon?" she asked quietly.

I stepped forward, wanting to stop Mum's words, stop all of this. "How could he?"

Mum held out her palm, wanting Dad to answer for himself.

"He's just in a . . ." I said. "He's just . . ."

Dad's hands were trembling. He was panicking badly, losing it, like I'd seen him lose it so many times before. Only this time was worse: His eyes were wilder somehow, still glazed in a nightmare. Did he even know where he was? Who we were?

Mum kept looking at Dad. "If you know something, Jon — anything! — they'll take you away, the police will ask you, over and over . . ."

"Away?" Dad's arms shook too. "Away, away . . ." He repeated the word like it was snagged in his mind.

"Away from us. The woods. You'll be gone in a police car . . . Do you understand?"

"Gone," Dad repeated. "Gone."

He looked from Mum to Ashlee Parker and then through the window to the woods, like he was searching for something. Trying to remember. Trying to pull something back. He crashed to the floor like all his bones had snapped, his body juddering as he grasped at the tabletop. I went toward him, but he held an arm across his face as if he thought I'd hit him.

"Sorry," he said, his eyes watery. "Sorry, sorry, sorry . . ." He looked at Mum desperately. "But they were shouting . . . the soldier told me I'd done it." He shook his head and murmured, "Me, me, me . . ."

These were the same words: the same story about the soldier who'd yelled at him during that firefight and told him he'd killed a civilian. Dad was remembering being in combat, flashing back.

Mum realized it too. "This isn't the same night," she told him firmly. "You haven't killed anyone."

"The same!" Dad wailed. "The same."

He lashed his fist into the kitchen unit; blood ran down the cupboard. When Dad got like this Mum usually told me to go to my room, and sometimes she joined me. We'd listen to him shouting into the night, wrecking things as he raged. Outside the rain started again, heavy and persistent, but there was no more thunder. Dad gasped and gasped.

"I was in the compound . . . and she was . . . she was there and I . . ." Dad tripped on his words, stopped, and tried again. "I didn't mean to . . . but the enemy, they were hiding . . . out there in the dark . . . all around."

"You're not in combat now, Jon! There's no firefight! You haven't shot anyone!" Mum was almost pleading with him. "You're in your kitchen. You're with your wife and daughter. You're an ex-soldier in a flashback, that's all!"

Dad blinked. Maybe Mum thought she had him back with us because she added, "But you have brought home a girl, Jon, and she's dead."

"I didn't mean . . ." Dad turned toward the rain coming in sideways at the window. Was he waking up?

"But the soldier . . . he told me. He said it was . . ." He shook his head again, kept murmuring, ". . . me, me, me . . ."